FALLING FROM THE
FLOATING WORLD

FALLING FROM THE FLOATING WORLD

Nick Hurst

Unbound

Unbound

6th Floor Mutual House, 70 Conduit Street, London W1S 2GF

www.unbound.com

© Nick Hurst, 2019

Text design by Ellipsis, Glasgow

A CIP record for this book is available from the British Library

ISBN 978-1-78352-631-4 (trade pbk)
ISBN 978-1-78352-633-8 (ebook)
ISBN 978-1-78352-632-1 (limited edition)

Printed in Great Britain by CPI Group (UK)

For my family – old, new and extended

With special thanks to Michael Gladstone, Takashi Hirata
and The Great Britain Sasakawa Foundation
for their generous support of this book

A QUICK NOTE ON JAPANESE PRONUNCIATION

There are a number of Japanese names and words scattered throughout this book. They are created from a base of five vowels:

> a as in cup
> i – we
> u – food
> e – egg
> o – off

These are then partnered with consonants to make up an alphabet.

Unlike in English, all syllables are pronounced distinctly and equally. Almost none are merged or made silent and there are no specified tones.

So the name Tomoe would be pronounced:

> To as in tomato
> mo – mop
> e – egg

Pronunciation is quite staccato. The exception is for long vowels which have almost the same pronunciation but are twice the length. They are denoted with a line above the vowel.

So the name Chōshi would be pronounced:

> Chō as in hon<u>cho</u>
> Shi – she

KEY CHARACTERS

Please note that Japanese names are read surname first

Tokyo

Ray Clarence

Chōshi Tomoe – Ray's girlfriend

Takata Eiji – leader of the Takata-gumi gang

Kurotaki – a senior member of Takata's gang

Sumida – a member of Takata's gang

The Beast – a strongman in the rival Ginzo-kai gang

Knifeman – a strongman in the rival Ginzo-kai gang

Yabu – head of the Tokyo branch of the Ginzo-kai

Kōda – the intermediary between the yakuza heads and Onishi

Onishi – the Education Minister

Sakura – a soapland employee

Horitoku – a traditional tattooist

Ernesto Aerts – an ex-MMA star fallen on hard times

Tatsuzan – a sumo-wrestling star

Fujiwara Daisuke – an actor

Johnny – Ray's friend

Ishikawa Manabu – a scientist

Edo

Katsuyama

Michiko – Katsuyama's apprentice

Obasan – the overseer of Katsuyama's house

Lord Ezoe – a regular client of Katsuyama

Lord Genpachi – a rival to Lord Ezoe

Mizuno – an ex-samurai merchant ally of Lord Genpachi

Yamaryū – a sumo-wrestling star

Chitairō – an actor

Kaoru – a courtesan rival to Katsuyama

Namiji – Kaoru's apprentice and a friend of Michiko

JAPANESE WORDS

ageya – a grand house where courtesans would meet their clients

bakufu – shogunate officials

daimyō – a lord from the Edo period

fūzoku – the sex industry in Japan

gaijin – literally 'outside person' – foreigner

gaikokujin – 'outside country person' – a polite way of referring to foreigners

horimono – a traditional Japanese tattoo (also known as *irezumi*)

horishi – a traditional Japanese tattooist

kumichō – the term of address used by yakuza to their boss

mizu shōbai – literally 'the water business' – a term used to represent night-time entertainment establishments in Japan who operate on the edge of the law

oyabun – a term of reference for a yakuza boss (this derives from the gang structure with a 'father' at the head of a family)

sōkaiya – yakuza-linked groups who infiltrate legitimate businesses

tayū – the highest rank of courtesan in the early Edo period

ukiyo – the floating world

ukiyo-e – pictures of the floating world

Living only for the moment, savouring the pleasures of the moon, the snow, the cherry blossoms and the maple leaves; singing songs, drinking sake, and diverting ourselves just in floating, floating; unconcerned by imminent poverty, buoyant and carefree, like a gourd carried along with the river current: this is what we call *ukiyo*, the floating world.

From *Tales of the Floating World*, Asai Ryōi, *c.*1665

Fall: Move from a higher to a lower level, typically rapidly and without control.

Oxford English Dictionary

PART ONE

ONE

I was woken by someone pounding at my front door. I fumbled for my alarm clock. It read 3.15. I struggled up.

It was Tomoe. Beautiful, immaculate Tomoe – now dishevelled, her hair tumbling down, mascara streaming down her face.

'Tomoe, what's wrong?'

She collapsed in my arms. I led her to the sofa.

'What's the matter? Are you hurt?'

'Just hold me.'

I held her. After an hour she cried herself to sleep. It must have been another before I dropped off as I remember the birds starting to sing at first light. I woke with a start, sprawled across the sofa, alone. Anxiety started to rise in me but then the bathroom door opened and Tomoe glided out, swathed in the luxury white towels she insisted I kept. She greeted me with a sweet smile and a cheery '*ohayō gozaimasu*'.

I've never been much of a morning person but there was more to this than being confused by slow wits.

'Morning.'

I waited for an explanation that didn't come. Tomoe glanced over as she readied herself instead.

3

'You can use the bathroom now, Ray-kun. I'll put on my make-up out here.'

I decided to dispense with the subtle approach.

'Tomoe, what's going on? You turned up in the middle of the night crying your eyes out. You can't just act like nothing happened.'

She paused and turned towards me.

'I'm sorry, Rei-kun,' she said, managing to lend Japanese pronunciation to a one-syllable word, as she did when playful or trying to win me round. 'I didn't mean to worry you. I just had a horrible day – I needed to be with you.'

She unfolded her legs, leaned over and gave me the most tender of kisses. The matter apparently settled, she returned to her lipstick.

'But I am worried. What made you so upset?'

'It was nothing, really,' she said, looking back up. 'But I can't talk while I'm doing my make-up. Have a shower and we can speak over breakfast when I'm done.'

When I came out of the shower she was gone.

'Sorry, late, had to go. Will be away a few days. Reception bad so can't call. Talk when back. Don't worry! xoxo'

I re-read the text. There was nothing I could do but wait.

She reappeared a few days later, planting a huge kiss on my lips as she kicked off her shoes. 'I missed you, babe!'

Thirty immensely enjoyable minutes later she lay curled around me, her head snuggled into my chest.

'Rei-kun, I need to ask you a favour.'

'Anything,' I murmured. 'What is it?'

'I need you to go to soapland.'

*

Japanese 'soaplands' are home to a specific type of bathhouse, popular since Edo times, where bathing was only a precursor to the main event. Their more stimulating services are made possible by exploiting a convenient loophole in Japan's prostitution laws.

Historically, the provision of sexual services was accepted in much the same way other leisure activities were. But in the aftermath of American occupation post-war, a more puritanical approach was half-heartedly adopted. Perhaps intentionally vague, work-arounds were quickly found for all forms of sexual activity other than intercourse.

Soaplands managed to find a way around even this. They offered stimulating baths followed by exotic massages, but critically the establishment's services ended there. Just as crucially, any of the inevitable activities then agreed by employee and customer were considered private arrangements between individuals and therefore not bound by the prostitution laws.

I knew of men in relationships who had indulged in a soapland's offerings. I'd never heard of any who had visited at their partner's request.

'What?'

I turned to Tomoe trying to work out if this was a test.

'I need you to go to soapland,' she repeated.

'Why would you want me to go to soapland? Girls normally *don't* want their boyfriends to go there.'

'This is different. I need you to go to a place called Matsubaya and see a girl called Sakura.'

I was utterly confused.

5

'But why? I've never even been to a pink salon when I was single.'

She narrowed her eyes. 'I don't believe you.'

'It's true,' I insisted. 'There are some places back home but it's not like here. Maybe we're a bit more prudish about these things.'

She seemed unable to comprehend this. 'Not even a blow-job bar?'

'Not even a massage with a happy ending.'

She shook her head briefly, as though to clear the unfathomable concept from clouding her thoughts.

'Well, this is your chance to start.' She gave me a broad smile followed by a kiss. 'It's a chance to enjoy a new Japanese experience, *ne*?'

I was now convinced this wasn't a test.

'Tomoe, what's this all about?'

She nestled her head back in my chest. When she looked up there were tears rolling down her face.

'They killed my father.'

TWO

That I was in Japan wasn't the result of a long-term life or career plan. The seeds of the move had been sown during what I thought was just another working day in London.

'Ray, thanks for making the time,' said Dave as he ushered me in. 'Please, sit down.'

I closed the glass door to his office and sat at the acrylic table. Opposite, a lap-top and iPhone gleamed from his desk in front of floor-to-ceiling windows. Advertising offices are as ubiquitous in their soulless chic as they are in the unique differentiators claimed on their identikit websites.

'Is everything all right?' I asked. 'You seemed a bit stressed when I saw you earlier.'

'Yes, yes, it's all fine,' he said. 'Well, it is and it isn't. We're turning a corner with our finances but revenues are still a bit ropey and there are some tough decisions to be made before we're out of the woods.'

'That sounds ominous.'

'Well, yes. I mean no. I mean . . . well . . . look, we've just had a board meeting and we have to do some restructuring. And . . .'

His eyes roved the office beyond the glass wall, seeking escape from the task he was faced with. Failing to fit it, they settled back on me. '... and your team's got the lowest profitability. And, well, it means we have to lose headcount.'

My heart sank. Headcount. I'd never considered it an adequate way to describe the foundation on which a person's hopes, dreams and dependencies are based. Especially now that person seemed to be me. As Dave went on it became clear this was a limited restructuring effort, one that was particularly 'precise'.

'Am I the only one being let go?' I asked, too crestfallen to be angry.

'Well, right at the moment, yes. Unfortunately, profitability on your account is the weakest in the group and we've had to make some tough decisions.' Dave was prone to management-speak when under pressure.

'But it's only one decision, isn't it? There aren't any other changes being made?' A thought flashed in my mind. 'You're not getting someone in to replace me are you?'

'Ray, we can't be sure what's going to happen long-term on your part of the business ...' He shifted uncomfortably. 'Look, from an HR and management point of view, I can assure you this is a restructure. You're on three months' notice. You're going to get that plus another three, assuming you agree. But you can leave as soon as you've done your handover. That's a pretty good settlement for a redundancy caused by the adverse economic climate.'

He paused.

'And, of course, that's the truth. But if we were to meet as friends over a drink, I might tell you that you're an extremely smart guy whose intelligence seems incompatible with advertising. You can beat me hands-down in a debate but you can't land a campaign when everything's been handed to you and I've got no idea why. But, assuming we were in that non-working environment talking as friends, I'd say you're getting a great opportunity to sit back for six months and work out how to make the best use of your brain.'

I slumped in the Charles Eames chair.

'Didn't you do Japanese Studies at uni? And you lived there too?' Dave asked. 'You always seemed fond of the place – you even speak the language, don't you? Why not head back for a while?'

It had seemed as good an idea as any as I tried to pick up the pieces.

I met Tomoe in a bar which, if I was to believe my friend Johnny, meant the relationship should only have been good for a one-night stand. But it wasn't that kind of bar and Tomoe wasn't that kind of girl. In fact, she was the kind of girl I'd never have thought I stood a chance with. But our eyes had met and there had been enough in the look for me to summon the courage to talk to her. And somehow, out of all the men in Tokyo, she'd seemed to find something appealing in me.

I should point out she wasn't getting a dud – I'd entered my thirties in good enough shape to allow my mother some pride not solely based on maternal love. But Tomoe was special.

She had these brown-black almond eyes that sparkled mischief and a smile that brightened your day. Her dress sense was faultless, accentuating the curves of her body in a way that was immaculate yet effortlessly cool. Then there was her lustrous, jet-black hair, which she tied with a white ribbon in an endless array of styles.

But her looks were the least of her. She was a force of nature, with a devil-may-care attitude that left you helpless to resist her desires. It was balanced by the sweetest disposition that she subverted with a sense of humour that was boisterous yet feminine.

She was almost too good to be true.

We spent our first date tucked away in a restaurant gem in Nakameguro I would never have found for myself. Just as when we first met, I found Tomoe so gorgeous I got butterflies. And just as when we first met, she offset the effect by being completely unaware of it. I was lured in by the melt of her eyes and had to hold myself back from touching the unblemished skin on a forearm or where her neck met the top of her chest. Watching her as she spoke, I lost lines of conversation to the thought of kissing her daydream-inducing lips.

The date went well enough for us to have another, then another, and a flurry after that. There was no fixed pattern – we might meet in a high-end, high-rise restaurant in Ebisu one evening, before going to a rowdy izakaya bar in Ameyoko the next.

Her sparkle and spark remained constants but they were the only things I could predict. Soft and caring when I turned up with a sprained ankle, she was equally spiky when a doorman questioned my suitability for a show – she only relented when he convinced her he'd been concerned I wouldn't understand, his hurried apologies for not letting me demonstrate my Japanese slowly bringing her back from the boil. On other occasions she simply dazzled, whether sending currents of electricity sizzling through staid dance floors or bringing a sedate bar to life.

I could never be sure which Tomoe I'd meet and whenever I thought I'd pinpointed her character she'd surprise me by revealing another side. The constant sense of discovery intrigued and excited me. And it made me thirst to find out more.

It was on a trip to Ishigaki Island when we really clicked. Having spent time only on short dates so far, the long weekend let us get to know each other through relaxed conversation and the frenetic physicality that a new relationship charged by warm weather and skimpy clothing permits.

It had been Tomoe's suggestion to go and it had taken me by surprise – a sleepy island hadn't seemed a fit for her big-city style. It was only we got there, both of us slopping around in T-shirts and shorts, that I realised the easy-going environment suited her best. With me a fair way from the suave sophisticate I'd thought she'd admire, the idea of us as a couple suddenly made more sense.

The thought had struck me as we lay on miles of deserted golden sand at Yonehara beach. As we made our way back to our rental car, passing eyes drawn uncontrollably to Tomoe's curves, the sense it made had seemed limited again.

Despite being a bachelor without ties or commitments, it had been surprisingly hard setting off to Japan. Having spent time away before, I knew I'd come back to friends doing much the same as when I left. But saying goodbye to my parents, who insisted on seeing me off, brought a lump to my throat and the sense of enormity that comes with major change.

Tokyo also disorientated me subtly – so similar to when I'd

been there ten years before that its differences felt like optical illusions, like seeing something familiar through warped glass. There were new buildings and some areas had changed but it no longer had the 'blink and you'll miss it' feeling of rapid advance.

There was still enough to throw me off guard – in an increasingly homogeneous planet it had remained one of the few places able to provide the jolt of a culture shock. Even normal things felt that little bit different, whether being bamboozled by the functions of a high-tech toilet or seen out of a barber's by five bowing staff. Just as when I'd first arrived, it left me wondering if I hadn't flown to another country but been transported to a parallel world.

My response was to seek familiar ground, finding a flat in Takadanobaba in the centre of Tokyo, just around the corner from where I'd previously lived. The students from nearby Waseda University continued to give the area its lively buzz, whether thronging the streets in daytime or drunkenly revelling through the night. They helped keep it pleasingly rough at the edges and ensured it retained a welcome affordability for such a central spot.

I quickly found work that wasn't outside my comfort zone either. I contacted the high school I'd taught at after my degree and had a stroke of luck. Their English teacher had just left and they were delighted to take me back on a generous wage that saved them on agency fees. With days that ended at three o'clock, I had time to take on private students and still work fewer hours than I had in my office job. I might not have found the way to maximise my intellectual potential, but I was earning well with minimal stress.

With home and employment providing the reassurance of the old, I had the freedom to enjoy the excitement of Tomoe's new. Add to that six months' redundancy pay sitting in my bank account and life felt pretty good.

My financial comfort paled beside Tomoe's resources, though, not that she seemed to care. She was certainly willing to spend her money, as her impressive wardrobe, perfectly coiffed hair and readiness to pay any bill could attest. But she never gave the impression she needed it. For her, being in possession of money seemed to be an unpleasant necessity that spending it could relieve.

The best description I could get for the job that allowed her this lifestyle was 'cultural curator'. Rather than work for any specific museum or gallery, she was employed by a specialist agency that contracted her out.

She was certainly impressive. A visit to her apartment would introduce you to the greatest *ukiyo-e* woodblock prints – a framed Hokusai leaned against a cupboard, a Kuniyoshi on her desk, a Yoshitoshi on the living-room wall. She could provide histories for all of them, accompanied by explanations of technique, artistic innovation and symbolism within the designs.

She might receive a text asking her opinion from a novelist one day, then have her view sought by a musician the next. Such was her span of contacts I learned to curb my tongue after offending her with an ill-informed opinion on a dancer who turned out to be a friend.

'Why can't I find you online?' I asked her once.

'What do you mean?'

'I've googled your name but I can't find a thing.'

'Why are you trying to find me online?' she said suspiciously.

'There's no need to be defensive. You're my girlfriend. I just wanted to find out about the things you've done.'

'You won't find anything,' she said, turning back to the *kabuki* theatre catalogue whose introduction she was writing. 'Japanese artists and performers go by inherited names. It's the same for me – even then I'm normally not announced. People in the industry know me, but there's no reason the public should.'

Before we could discuss it further she was off, her whirr of energy taking her to an exhibition in Hokkaido this time.

Before I first went out, people talked about Japan as a losers' paradise for *gaijin* foreigners, especially males. But I never found it was really the case. Admittedly, there were men with girlfriends they wouldn't have stood a chance with at home. But the real catches tended to be on the arms of suave Japanese men. There was also the prospect of creeping into a higher social stratum, or getting a better package on an ex-pat deal with work. But I'd seen a bit of both and neither seemed the epitome of Eden to me.

Yet here I was, coming straight from the sack into an untaxing job that left me free of financial concerns. I had friends and a place to live that was convenient, even if it was a little compact. And if my girlfriend could be more elusive than the floating world in which she worked, it was more than compensated by a personality that matched her looks. In fact, her sense of mystery only attracted me more.

For all my doubts I might have been the mythical gaijin, the one winning in a losers' paradise. It certainly felt like everything had come good. Unfortunately, when you're at the top there's only one way to go.

THREE

'Who killed him?' I asked, shocked. I couldn't say our relationship wasn't complicated but this was a disturbing new turn. 'What happened? Have you called the police?

'Yakuza,' she spat. 'It happened two weeks ago but I just found out. I couldn't even go to his funeral.'

The words were cold and hard where normally her voice was sweet and soft.

'But what happened? What are the police doing?

'Nothing!' Her lip curled. '"Our investigation concluded this was an unfortunate event, a suicide. Please accept our condolences for your sad loss,"' she mimicked bitterly.

It was a branch of normality. I grasped at it. 'So it was a suicide? He wasn't murdered?'

Now she aimed her contemptuous look at me. 'Chōshi is a samurai name. We're descendants of a high-ranking family. If there was a serious matter of honour my father *might* have taken his life. But to jump from a bridge with a note saying he was unhappy?'

Her disdain prevented her from continuing. I wasn't going to contest her. I didn't know her father. As for the samurai thing – a ruling class of warriors who lived by a code of honour formed by art and war that reached its zenith in death? It had seemed best to back away when she pulled out that card.

But if I'm honest, the real reason I held back was the look on her face. It scared me.

'But why are you so sure it was the yakuza?' I asked tentatively, stroking her shoulder. 'If you've got information maybe you could go to the police and get them to reopen the case?'

'The police?' she snapped. 'The police are part of it. Why else would they conclude the investigation before it could even start? Why would they pretend they could find no relatives, not contact me, and have him cremated within a week?'

I was hoping it was a case of incompetence but I didn't venture the thought.

'But what makes you think it was the yakuza?' I asked again as gently as I could. 'Was he, uh, did he come across them in the course of his work?'

She stopped as she was about to answer and a half-smile brought a glimpse of the old Tomoe.

'Ray-kun, I appreciate you trying to be sensitive, but no, he wasn't a yakuza. And while you can never know what they're into, there was no reason for them to be involved in his work. He'd had some debts but they were paid off. He was just a regular businessman. He had no connection to crime.'

'So there shouldn't be any reason for them to kill him should there?' I asked softly, not wanting the other Tomoe to return. 'Why are you so sure it was them?'

Her face became a mask again. 'I know someone who knows that world. He's the one who told me about my father's death.'

We were back on the murder track rather than the sad but reassuring suicide. I had a bad feeling about where it would go.

'Could you not put him in touch with the police?' I asked, trying to lead her away.

'I told you the police are involved,' she said, scary Tomoe once more. 'He'd be in danger if he went to them.'

'So what are you going to do?'

'I'm going to find out what happened. That's why I need you to go to soapland.'

It wasn't what I wanted to hear.

'Then I'm going to make them pay.'

Tomoe had a complicated family dynamic. I didn't fully understand it, which wasn't surprising given my lack of understanding about much of her life. But whereas the rest was an intriguing enigma, I knew some difficult facts lay behind this particular door. She'd allowed me a glance in once and I hadn't been anxious to open it again.

We'd gone away for the weekend to Hakone, a town in the mountains south-west of Tokyo, famous for its *onsen* hot springs. We'd spent the afternoon strolling the hills of the open-air art museum, then soaked out our exertions in an onsen before heading back to our traditional *ryokan* inn.

When we had finished the feast brought to our room, the table was cleared and thick futons with puffy duvets rolled out on the *tatami* mats. Another eye-opening experience later and we were spent; minds and bodies entwined around a perfect day.

'Ray-kun,' Tomoe said, her limbs draped around mine. 'Doesn't

21

your family worry about you living so far away? Don't they mind you changing your career?'

'I don't think they were delighted by the latest change, but that was more because it wasn't exactly my choice to leave. And I'm sure they'd prefer it if I was in England, or at least somewhere closer than here. But I'm not a kid any more and they accept that. Once you leave the nest there's no knowing where you're going to end up.'

I thought for a moment.

'I suppose they just want me to be happy. And if being out here makes me happy, then, for the most part, they're happy too.'

'Mm, that sounds nice . . .' she drifted off.

'It's not like that with you?' I ventured cautiously.

'It's different.' She was silent a short while. 'My mum died when I was a baby. I've seen pictures and my dad told me about her – apparently she was a lot like me. But I don't have any memories of my own.'

She sighed and stared out at the stars that twinkled through a gap in the sliding door. A chorus of frogs serenaded us with lusty song from the garden below.

'And your dad?' I prompted.

She stayed as she was, as though she hadn't heard me, but two rapid blinks – to prevent a tear or clarify a thought? – made me leave the subject alone.

'We had a falling out,' she said softly, just as I was starting to drop off. 'He's very traditional. He never showed his emotions even when I was a kid, but he doted on me in his own way. I think he saw my mother in me and that made him love me even more.'

She paused.

'But I upset him.' Her voice wavered. 'I did something to let him down and he can't forgive me. We haven't spoken for over two years.'

'But he's your dad,' I said. 'I don't know what you did to upset him but you're his daughter. It's not the kind of love you can switch off.'

'I'm sure he does still love me.' She was now on the verge of tears. 'But what I did, the kind of upbringing he had, the kind of man he is – he can't just pretend everything's fine. He isn't to blame. It's my fault.'

I brushed the tears from her cheeks.

'Even if it is, I'm sure you can do something to put it right, something to show him it was a mistake.'

I said it to soothe her and bring a less melancholy end to the day. But then, before I could stop myself, I asked, 'What did you do that was so bad?'

She buried her face in my neck. 'I'm sorry, I can't talk about it. Not yet.'

I stroked her hair, silently cursing myself.

'No, I'm sorry. You don't owe me an explanation. But I'm here if you do ever want to talk about it.'

With that ineffectual piece of counselling we'd slowly drifted off to the sound of the frogs under the moon and the stars. Drifted off to a place of melancholy, but a place of peace nonetheless. A place it would have been ridiculous to even contemplate murder and revenge.

FOUR

Who really knows another person's mind? While Tomoe was adamant her father wouldn't have killed himself, it seemed that every time a suicide was in the news it was inevitably accompanied by people saying the same, all reflecting on how happy the person had been only the day before. We each have our darker side and some hold it closer. A traditionally minded man in Japanese society would seem likely to do just that.

So I held on to a sense of hope that Tomoe was just distressed and would become more rational as time went on. Trying to second-guess her wasn't wise, so I needed a backup. A way to avoid being drawn into a murder mystery, if that's what it was going to become.

This wasn't a classically heroic response, but I'd seen plenty of films where the lead was forced into action only when he was the last one left. That wasn't the case here. There were 130 million people in the country – their country – a legal system, a police force. I was just a lost gaijin trying to get my life back on track, a visitor in their land.

For all the vicarious heroism you may feel at the cinema, facing a real murder sobers you up. It forces you to examine yourself and your depths of bravery. It provides a blunt assessment of who you really are. This might bruise your self-esteem but it's very helpful in determining your propensity for life-threatening risk.

I loved being with Tomoe. She made me laugh when I was happy and comforted me when I was down. She was intelligent and she was interesting and she made me look at things in different ways. But I'd only known her a year and there was more I didn't know about her than I did. So when talk turned to murder I had to ask questions about her state of mind.

If it hadn't been unsettled by her father's death, helping her would mean seeking out a killer. And by looking for a murderer you give yourself a chance of finding one. I'd spent my life trying to stay out of harm's way. I wasn't keen to put myself in the firing line for a man I didn't know, even if that man was Tomoe's father.

'So, Rei-kun, when can you go to Matsubaya?'

It had been a couple of days since Tomoe had first made the request. We were curled up on her sofa and until that point my focus had been on her tattoo – a small black fox that fascinated me with the way it seemed to leap and dance around her ankle.

'Tomoe, are you sure you want to do this? I know you need to find out what happened to your father, but taking on the yakuza, it's, it's . . .' I struggled to find the right words. 'It's dangerous. I mean, they hurt people – they kill them. I know you said the police are involved but there must be some who aren't corrupt. We could speak to them, let them know something's wrong.'

'It doesn't work like that,' she replied. 'Of course there are policemen who aren't corrupt, but what am I going to say to them? "I think my father was killed by yakuza because it wasn't in his nature to kill himself? Your colleagues are involved so you'll need to take over their investigation – oh, but I don't have any proof." Even you don't believe me and you're my boyfriend.'

I started to protest but she silenced me with a kiss.

'I'm not blaming you. I know it must sound crazy and we haven't known each other long enough for you to have blind faith in me. Maybe I haven't let you know me enough . . .'

She looked distracted for a moment before she snapped back.

'This is my problem. I don't want you involved and I certainly don't want to put you in danger—'

'I'm not afraid for myself,' I cut in as an internal voice tried to scream me down. 'I'm worried about you. I just want to make sure you're safe. I'll do whatever needs to be done.'

It was not what I'd been planning to say. My moment of clarity seemed to have been missed by my pride.

'No. I don't want you involved,' she said again. 'But this time it's impossible for me. It needs a man.'

'I'll pay,' said Tomoe the next day after her inevitable victory in our battle of wills. 'You're doing this for me.'

'Tomoe, you can't pay for me to go to a prostitute. It's weird.'

'You're not going to a prostitute. You're going to soapland to help find out what happened to my dad. It's different.'

I was still struggling to get my head around the idea of a first-time visit to the sex trade at my girlfriend's request. We'd avoided discussion of the lengths I should go to maintain my cover, but I had to assume my fidelity would be in doubt. Her taking the cost didn't seem right.

'I don't care how you put it. I'm paying.'

It was a straightforward plan. I was to visit Matsubaya and ask for Sakura. At an appropriate moment I would subtly elicit what information I could on Takata Eiji, head of the Takata-gumi, Tokyo's largest gang. It was obviously a sensitive subject and the chances of getting detailed information were negligible to none. What I needed to find out, most likely by gauging the reaction to my light-touch prompting, was whether the man himself had been there.

'How's that going to help us find out about your father?' I asked.

'You don't need to worry about that, Ray-kun. I need to know if Takata's connected to the place, that's all. If you can find out it will help.'

Despite my initial reservations, I'd slowly come to terms with my new role. It seemed I might be able to help without imperilling anything but my morals, and on the scale of risks that didn't seem too bad.

FIVE

'You know Takata-san!?'

My outburst surprised me as much as it did her. I could only put it down to the release of tension. The timing was unsettling, coming as it did, just at the point of climax. The lack of subtlety was also unideal. Sakura stopped dead. I was unable to follow up with an explanation for a short while.

'I worked with someone who knew him,' I gasped when I was able to speak again. 'He's the one who recommended you.'

It was weak. Sakura looked unconvinced. I tried to gather my wits.

'I'm sorry, that's not true. I did Japanese Studies at university. I was always fascinated by samurai, then after them I started finding out about the yakuza – watching the films and reading the magazines.'

That wasn't as strange as it might have sounded. You can find a magazine for everything in Japan, including those that cater to yakuza fans.

'I heard this was a Takata-gumi area and thought with your place being the most prestigious, you might have had the chance to meet the senior people, maybe even Takata-san himself.'

It was more plausible. It would have benefited from a smoother lead-in. But it was enough for Sakura to pretend to believe me and return to her ministrations, in this case towelling down the lubricant I was slathered top to toe in as I lay on my back on a blow-up bed.

The experience had been awkward, which perhaps wasn't surprising given my lack of sleuthing experience or brothel know-how. That didn't stop me feeling unhappy my first foray into detective work had not been handled as best it could. Tomoe was relying on me and I'd let her down.

The taxi had turned from the main road at a petrol station fronted by a distinctive weeping willow. The road it turned into cut an unusual S-shape in the surrounding street grid. It was lined with shiny-fronted buildings on straightening, the establishments' names lit in neon above doorways in which rough-hewn men failed to look welcoming.

Power cables criss-crossed the road as they did elsewhere in Tokyo, but here it gave the impression of complicity, as if uniting these havens of sin. They ranged from the gaudy – the lower end of Las Vegas with a Japanese twist – to pristine, marbled-fronted palaces more akin to five-star resorts.

'Senzoku-yon-chōme crossing,' announced my driver.

I got out and made my way toward the shrine Tomoe had told me would be on the right.

'*Asobi*?' a doorman proposed as I passed.

'You want play?' another managed in heavily accented English.

I politely declined and the smile chiselled into his face instantly reverted to a snarl.

When I saw the shrine ahead I turned into an alley on my left, as Tomoe had said. There was an instant transformation, a sense of Tokyo as it used to be. It's not that the buildings were historic. For the most part they were like those in any other side-street. But their layout – the small blocks of houses inter-coursed by alleys – suggested street architecture from centuries gone by.

A few more turns and despite being only fifty metres from the rows of soaplands, it felt like I was in a different Tokyo. A place of the past.

The entrance to Matsubaya was so unassuming it could have been somebody's home. It was housed in a new building, its façade covered with dark matt tiles that rose to latticed balconies finished in a tasteful charcoal grey. It couldn't have been in greater contrast to the flashing lights and intimidating doormen of the nearby world so far away.

I hesitated, confused by the lack of a sign or bell. But it was as Tomoe had described in the place she'd said it would be. So despite its contrary appearance, I had to trust this was it and I wasn't about to barge into a stranger's living room with demands to be sexually pleased.

The heavy wooden door opened at my push, leaving me with no option but to go in. The building's well-maintained minimalist interior was aesthetically aligned with the outside. I made my way down its hallway, up a staircase and toward a matching door at the end of the corridor. Again there was no nameplate, but there was a buzzer this time.

'Konni—'

Her welcome, already quizzical, was cut short when she saw me.

'—chiwa. I'm sorry, may I help you?'

Her diction was as exquisite as her kimono, as fine as the make-up applied to her delicately ageing face.

'Konnichiwa,' I attempted to reply in equally polite, if less beautifully weighted, Japanese. 'I believe this is Matsubaya. I was very much hoping to enjoy the services you provide.'

'I'm so sorry, but we operate on an appointment-only basis,' she said with a perfectly executed bow. 'I do hope you haven't gone too far out of your way. Perhaps I could recommend somewhere nearby?'

Tomoe had debated the best way to get me in. She'd decided an attempt to make an appointment would be useless. I had no introduction and I was a foreigner – neither aspect conducive to entry. She reasoned the best approach was to arrive unannounced in the afternoon, after the lunchtime business but before the evening rush. I could then try to impress them with my best attempts at being impeccably Japanese.

'Please excuse me,' I returned her bow with my own. 'I'm afraid to say I was unaware of the procedure for visiting. Your establishment was recommended by an acquaintance who couldn't compliment it enough. Unfortunately, he declined to inform me of the necessary protocol. There's no excuse but I hope you'll forgive my bad manners.'

'Well, it's always pleasing to be the subject of praise. May I enquire who your kind friend was?'

'I'm so sorry but I have to admit I'm not entirely sure. We were at the British Embassy,' I lied, hoping to portray myself at home mixing with the elite. 'It was towards the end of a function and they'd been quite generous with the drinks . . .'

She smiled. If my etiquette visiting her premises had been flawed, I had at least behaved as one should at a Japanese party.

'I believe he may have been a diplomat, although I was speaking to a company president for a while. Unfortunately by the time I returned home I couldn't remember which business card came from whom.'

It seemed enough to get the benefit of the doubt.

'Well, it isn't normal procedure but we've had a couple of late cancellations. If you'd like to come in, I hope we may have something to meet your taste.'

She opened the door to reveal a scene of Edo-period finery – I could only assume the building was joined with the neighbouring one and perhaps a couple more after that. Lustrous wooden boards extended away from me, glowing under a thick lacquer of varnish. They led to a small stone bridge that straddled a stream flowing in and out of the room filled with brightly coloured carp. There was a tatami resting area across it and to the sides latticed sliding doors mazed away. It was more like a hamlet than what had appeared to be a small residential house.

She led me over the bridge and lowered herself to a kneel when I sat down. A younger doppelganger immediately slid out from behind a screen and bowed at the edge of the tatami mats. She quick-stepped forward to place a leather-bound book on the table before me before apparently disappearing into thin air.

I opened it at the proprietor's gesture to find a menu offering refreshments of a more unusual kind. Even with the mind-expanding possibilities Tomoe had introduced me to, my imagination was inadequate to their gymnastic implications. After leafing through for the sake of form I went for the recommendation of the house.

'Oh, and I'd like to choose Sakura-san if I may. My acquaintance spoke very highly of her.'

'I'm so sorry, but Sakura won't start for another half hour. I can assure you, you'll be just as happy with Kiku.'

'I'm sure she's wonderful, but I'd very much like to meet Sakura-san. If you don't mind, I'll wait.'

'Ray-*sama*?' she asked, using the honorific of san.

I looked up. The flattening effect of Sakura's kimono only made me more excited at the curves that couldn't be contained. Her twinkling eyes and subtle pout intimated there was more to her than the demure sartorial display. I scrambled to my feet.

She led me to a bathing room not dissimilar to the ones you find in a ryokan but with a finery beyond compare. Every flat surface was lined in granite and a sunken bath consumed one side of the sizeable room. To its right were shower fittings that gleamed like freshly polished platinum and I'm sure cost about as much. And in front of them was a beautifully crafted wooden stool.

Sakura stripped me slowly with no acknowledgement of the untoward, her hands brushing gently against me before maddeningly pulling away. When undressed, she took me to the stool, sat me down and started to shower then soap me. At this point

I noticed she was now miraculously naked as well. An arm pressed against me, then a breast, then a smooth-skinned thigh. Then soft, firm hands that teased and caressed before disappearing into a sea of suds.

Once soaped, rinsed and thoroughly aroused I was taken for a bath quite unlike any I'd had before. Then the blow-up mattress, generous applications of lubricant, and a massage that was not only hands-on but involved plenty more as well.

Every moment was a sensorial overload, an explosion of nerve-endings crying out for more. Hence my distraction when the moment for clear thinking came.

'I'm sorry, I don't know anyone by that name,' Sakura said sweetly.

'You don't? I'm sorry, it's probably just me getting things wrong. I'm a bit of a beginner in yakuza studies!'

I pretended to laugh it off. She obliged me by giggling but showed no inclination to say anything more.

I tried again.

'But it is a yakuza area, isn't it? You must hear great stories and meet some real characters?'

'I wish I could say I did but in truth it isn't very exciting. We tend to get wealthy salarymen with a few rich kids thrown in – you're the most interesting client I've had. We don't get many foreigners, especially ones as handsome as you.'

She'd clearly marked me as the sucker for flattery I am.

'I don't know – the yakuza must have some special gangster places for themselves,' she lied through an innocent smile. 'I have a friend whose friend was in a bikers' gang though. I could try to get some stories from her.'

'So, how did it go?' asked Tomoe when I got back.

'I didn't get anything. I'm sorry.'

She looked far less devastated than I felt.

'You weren't expecting me to, were you? You knew I'd screw it up.'

'That's not true, Ray-kun,' she consoled me, a sympathetic crumple in her brow. 'I was hoping, but I knew it would be hard. And that's nothing to do with you. It's a sensitive subject – there was no way she was going to open up. We just had to hope she'd let something slip. It seems she was too smart.'

She grabbed my arm and pulled me to the sofa, a glint in her eyes.

'Now, tell me everything about it.'

I recounted my experience, broad brushstrokes at first, then in increasing detail as she prompted and then made exclamations and offers to replicate what we'd done. This wasn't entirely unwelcome but after a while it started to feel strange.

'Don't get me wrong, Tomo, it's not that I mind telling you about it and I'm more than happy to try some things out. But isn't this conversation a bit odd?'

'What do you mean?'

'I've just spent two hours with a prostitute.'

She looked at me blankly.

'You're my girlfriend. You're not supposed to be happy about something like that. Do you really want to know everything we did?'

'Of course I do, I'm a girl!' she said, as though it explained everything. 'We don't get to go to these places. This is my chance to find out what they're like.'

Admittedly, it was an unusual thing to say, but it had sounded so plausible at the time.

SIX

Two raps – a polite but firm way to let someone know you're waiting at their door. I opened it to find a tall, well-built gaijin man on the other side. I recognised him instantly – champion martial artists didn't make a habit of turning up at my flat. I looked behind me, as though the person he actually wanted might have miraculously appeared. Finding my flat still empty I turned back.

'Are you Ray?'

'Er, yeah.'

I continued to stand there, unsure of what else to say.

'Do you mind if I come in?' he said.

I ushered him into a flat that was too small for me and certainly not spacious enough to comfortably afford a martial arts fighter as well. I threw a pile of clothes from the sofa into a corner and offered him a drink.

'A cup of tea would be nice.'

'I've got English breakfast or *genmai*, whichever you'd prefer.'

'Oh, if it's from an Englishman I surely have to take the breakfast,' he said politely.

I put the kettle on.

*

Ernesto Aerts was a fight-game legend in Japan. After winning the hugely popular K-1 championship three years in a row (think boxing with the addition of elbows and kicks), he'd decided no challenges remained and moved on to Pride, whose rules allowed fighting to continue on the mat. While it may not sound so different, it required a new set of pugilistic skills. Ernesto had much impressed the Japanese with his dedication to learning them, immersing himself in an intensive regime with a jujitsu sensei and an Olympic wrestler. A year after his last fight he stepped back into the ring and proceeded to destroy fifteen of the world's best fighters before retiring without loss.

This wasn't specialist knowledge on my behalf. Martial arts competitions were massive in Japan at the time and everyone knew Ernesto Aerts. What he was doing in my flat a couple of years into retirement was far less clear.

'I'm sorry, I should really tell you what this is all about.'

'I was wondering,' I said, still star-struck.

'Well, ah, it's a bit awkward actually,' he continued in his sing-song Netherlands lilt. 'There are some associates of mine who feel you've been paying them more attention than they'd like.'

He may as well have been speaking Dutch. I knew no one in the fight game and if I had come across any of its characters, my instinct would have been to back away. I gave him his tea and sat on the floor, the coffee table between us.

'I'm sorry, I don't understand.'

He shifted uneasily.

'I've been asked to come here by a Japanese organisation – I think they assumed it would be more comfortable for a fellow gaijin to talk to you,' he said, looking anything but. 'Apparently you've been asking questions about them. They asked me to request you stop.'

My jaw dropped.

'You work for—'

'I don't work for anyone,' he interrupted, some of the steel he was famous for in the ring edging out the warmth he was better known for outside. 'I don't know how much you know about me, but I suffered a couple of disappointments after I retired. There was a business venture that didn't work out and I went through an expensive divorce.'

He paused for a second but kept me fixed in his stare.

'I'm telling you this because it has some bearing on your situation, you understand?'

I nodded.

'I had to find some money quickly at one point. The problem with quick money is it doesn't come cheap and the people who lend it are linked to people you don't want to borrow from. Before you know it, you're in debt to them and they ask favours in return.'

He rolled his shoulders. It appeared to be habitual but it served as a reminder of his power and size.

'Now, you seem like a nice guy, but if I don't do the favours asked of me, all of a sudden I'm in your position.'

I didn't like the sound of that.

'What's my position?'

'They've allowed me discretion in what I do. If I think you're taking me seriously, I just need your word you'll back off. If I don't, they suggested I give a taste of what they'll do if they have to come knocking at your door.'

I didn't let the roll of his R finish.

'You have my word.'

He'd had to face down hard men in his career, fighters practised at masking their fear in the ring. He could spot a coward soiling himself in his own home.

'And I'm confident you'll keep it,' he said, his eyes friendly once more. 'So, what are you doing in Japan?'

Apparently seeing the unpleasant business as over, he relaxed on the sofa with his tea. We proceeded to have a charming conversation during which he regaled me with tales from his fighting days and stories of life as a megastar in Japan. He was every bit as likeable as his persona.

'Well, I must be going,' he said, getting up from the sofa.

'Yes, of course.' I stopped, unsure of the correct platitude. 'Um, it was a pleasure meeting you.'

'You too,' he said, turning at the door and shaking my hand.

He squeezed it a little tighter.

'Now, just to confirm, you won't let me down?'

'No, no, of course not,' I shook my head. 'We're shaking on it, aren't we?'

'You're a nice guy. I wouldn't want to have to . . .'

He let the sentence drift and any bravado a braver man might have had died with it. I hadn't been affected in the first place.

'No,' I insisted. 'It was a one-off thing. I've got no interest in your acquaintances.'

'I'm pleased to hear it,' he said, brightening again.

We shuffled awkwardly.

'Well, perhaps we could grab a beer sometime when this is all over.'

It felt ridiculous even as I said it.

'That would be great.'

He seemed to mean it and even gave me his number. He took a step back.

'Well, I'd better be going – things to do.'

I shuddered at the thought and closed the door.

'That's fantastic!'

Tomoe was delighted. She'd rushed to my place as soon as I texted, insisting I give her the details in person. She arrived, face flushed, eyes wide. Even the curls of her hair were buoyant as they cascaded from the white ribbon wrapped south-east of her crown.

'He threatened you? He told you to back off?'

'Yes he did,' I said, put out. 'He's a good guy, but he can be scary. It wasn't very nice.'

'Of course not. I'm sorry,' she said, putting on a sad face but failing to pull it off. 'But it's good news – it's what we were trying to find out. They wouldn't be threatening you if we hadn't been right. You did it!'

She successfully played on my pride.

'I suppose so,' I said, my chest a little fuller. 'But he was very careful not to mention anyone's name. We can't be sure.'

'Oh, come on,' she said, dismissing my doubts. 'Who has the power to use Ernesto Aerts as muscle? And why would anyone who isn't Takata threaten you for trying to find out about him?'

'I see what you mean. But at the same time it's not that great. It means we have to stop.'

'Why would we do that?'

'I told you what he said. If we keep on we're going to get hurt.'

'Oh, that. Don't worry, I'll be careful,' she said absently, her mind already on the next stage of her grand, unexplained plan.

'Come on, Tomo, these are serious people. We've got to do as they say.'

'You worry too much,' she said, ending the argument in a way that me feel stupid, despite the fact I could think of no way I wasn't right.

'But what about Ernesto? I gave him my word.'

She didn't hear me. She had her head in the fridge looking for something to rustle up for dinner. She'd already moved on. Despite her confidence I had the feeling further probing wouldn't end well.

SEVEN

Dreaming of the Floating World 1

She woke with a start. Something wasn't right. She looked around her, trying to work out what it was and groaned. She'd rolled off her takamakura, *the hard, raised pillow that kept her head elevated and preserved her elaborate hair. Or at least it did when she didn't roll off it.*

She turned towards the paper shutters that allowed far more light through than she liked, the beams dancing off pristine tatami mats to sting her eyes and offend her aching head.

'Michiko!' she called out.

Almost immediately the shōji *door slid open and her apprentice appeared with a tray. Fish, rice and pickles peeped from the top of exquisite plates and steam twisted and wrestled from tea and miso soup.*

'Ohayō gozaimasu!' Michiko greeted her cheerfully as she set down the tray.

'Mm. Ohayō.'

She was less favourably inclined to the new day. Assuming it was new.

'What time is it?'

'It's still early – just after midday.'

In their line of work that wasn't late.

'It was a wonderful evening Onēsan, *Elder Sister, but I'm not sure how you managed to keep drinking throughout.'*

As an apprentice, Michiko was expected to bring youthful vitality to such affairs but she wasn't expected to lead them and could therefore exercise restraint. Yet there were those who didn't drink at all and, if she were honest, she had to admit she did so partly for pleasure. It was just never as pleasant the following day.

But it had been a good night. There were clients who sought culture and refinement and she had had enriching engagements with such men. But it was with customers who sought entertainment for its own sake that most fun was to be had. Of these, Lord Ezoe was a favourite, and with his friends, more courtesans and other hangers on, they had continued past dawn.

Blurred memories of the night slowly took shape. She had been on fine form. Stealing to the entrance she had snuck a pair of swords inside, despite the ban on weapons in the quarter's buildings. With a man's kimono slung around her she had swaggered through the tea-house, ridiculing the samurai. But instead of drawing anger, it had created a scene of hilarity and not a little lust.

'Is my hair all right?'

Michiko giggled in reply. 'Almost. Let me.'

It was patted into more respectable shape.

'There – that will do until someone comes to fix it properly. After all this time I don't know how you fall off. Even I can sleep through the night.'

'Fetch me more tea,' she ordered, her anger too affected to have effect. 'The standards nowadays – the trouble I'd have been in for such cheek.'

As she rose unsteadily she remembered something else of the night, something that had disturbed her. Lord Ezoe's retainer had pulled him aside at the height of festivities. It would have earned him censure had there not been good cause. But instead of rebuking him, Ezoe had held a pose of contemplation the alcohol consumed should not have allowed. He had broken from it to detail orders in the ear of his retainer, then returned to the revelry, his spirit apparently intact. Yet at the end of the entertainment he had excused himself rather than sleeping there as planned and paid for.

'Michiko.' She called again more sharply. 'Michiko! Why must I wait so long?'

The door slid open and her apprentice reappeared.

'I'm sorry, Onēsan,' Michiko bowed. 'What is it I can do?'

'I need you to go about the quarter. I have the feeling something may have happened last night. Find out what it was and report back to me please.'

She reached for her thin cotton yukata *kimono.*

'And make sure a bath is readied,' she told the departing apprentice, who relayed the message in urgent calls that echoed among the servants as she departed the house.

She didn't have to wait long for the news. She had made her way to the bathhouse, crossing stones set like summer clouds reflected in the waves of white gravel that washed across the lawn. Shortly after entering, the supervisor of the house's courtesans had come in.

'Have you heard?' Obasan, Auntie, asked by way of a greeting.

She turned quickly, disturbing the two assistants soaping her down. 'Heard what?'

As her looks had faded and then softened, the retired courtesan's character had grown hard. Eager to be first with gossip, the more scandalous it was the more it seemed to placate the demons that resided within.

'One of Genpachi's retainers was defeated in a duel by the great gate at dawn,' she began. 'But instead of being slain, his nose and ears were cut off and his swords taken. He couldn't commit seppuku. *He had to walk back to town in shame.'*

The retainer had slandered her family, and her in particular, less than two weeks before. He wasn't someone for whom she had sympathy, but the timing of the incident and Obasan's manner put her ill at ease.

'It isn't a pleasant thing,' she replied. 'But I can think of many I would shed tears for before that man.'

She turned to face Obasan as water was poured over her to wash away the suds and allow her the hot bath she craved.

'But you have something to add.'

Obasan appeared to be caught in a dilemma, the thrill of the gossip tempered by the harm it could bring to the house. When she spoke her voice was laced with concern.

'They say it was your father.'

She looked up from her calligraphy, which was for once failing to bring her calm.

'I've already been told,' she said to Michiko, who was struggling to catch her breath. 'But Obasan didn't know anything of my father. Do you have any news of him?'

'I'm sorry, there's very little,' the apprentice gasped. 'They say when

the duel ended he departed in the direction of your village. But when the bakufu *shōgunate officials came to arrest him, he was nowhere to be found.'*

'That's impossible. My father would have known the repercussions for defending our family name. If it was him, he would have returned home. He would have committed seppuku and brought an honourable end to the affair. Are you certain?'

'Yes, Onēsan, I heard it from an apprentice of the Corner Tamaya House. She was told by the gateman and he witnessed the whole affair.'

'In that case my father would have taken his life.'

She said it with certainty but without a body there had to be doubt. Michiko shifted uncomfortably as her mistress's forehead knotted in a frown.

'We need to get word to Lord Ezoe,' she said finally. 'He knows what happened. I can find out what's become of my father from him.'

'And what is it you really wish to discuss?' Ezoe asked after the formalities that civilised discourse required were complete. 'I believe you value my company beyond the normal platitudes but it hasn't been a full day since we last met. What service can I be to the most distinguished courtesan in the land?'

'You're too kind,' she replied, bowing her head slightly. 'It's true I'm lucky enough to hold some respect within the quarter and perhaps with some of its clientele. But beyond its closed walls . . .'

'You wish to know if I have heard news of your father?'

'I was hoping you might have. You have a way of knowing what politics are being played, what power struggles fought.' She looked at him keenly. 'Sometimes I get the sense you hear of such things before they even occur.'

He looked up quickly and then smiled.

'I shouldn't have underestimated you. Despite having out-drunk an entire room, I should have known your senses would not have been dulled.'

She said nothing.

'You're right, a message was conveyed to me – although just after the events of which you infer occurred. I had two men sent to the village, for you know I care for the family as I do the daughter. But they were too late. He had already been intercepted by rōnin *and taken away.'*

'Rōnin?' she exclaimed. 'What would masterless samurai want with my father?

'It's a good question. And it begs another. Why would they be in such readiness that they could abduct him immediately after an unanticipated event?'

She admired his guile.

'But you usually have the answers to such questions. And I believe when the occasion demands, you're capable of gathering that kind of man.' She searched his face for clues. 'So little happens without some detail coming to your eyes and ears – do you really not know who acted before the bakufu could?'

'I'm touched by your faith but I'm afraid I can't yet repay it. All I can tell you is he was taken by rōnin and there are rumours they were disposed of when their work was done.'

'Disposed of?'

'On this I'm less certain, but this morning the body of a rōnin was found snagged on the banks of the Kanda River. I have a suspicion that before its discovery others may have floated past.'

'But none of this makes sense. It was a straightforward matter of

honour. Who would want to abduct my father and why would they go to such extremes?'

'That's exactly what I intend to find out,' he said, and at that moment she saw the steel he withheld in the quarter but was feared for outside. 'But I'm afraid that's for another day. For now, you know as much as I.'

'In which case we must move to lighter matters,' she said, lifting her voice from its hushed tones. 'You've been tending to me so I'm bound to repay the debt. Michiko, bring me the shamisen so I may entertain Lord Ezoe while he is helped into his sleeping robes.'

The screen door slid open and Michiko and an assistant came in. Two further servants entered after them to assist Ezoe into his night-time attire. Once eased into his yukata he reclined on three layers of futon that had been laid out, each stuffed thick with cotton and clad in the finest red silk. He closed his eyes and allowed the haunting music to spirit him away to a place man's excesses couldn't trouble his spirit, a world where tumult was replaced by stillness and calm.

So taken was he, he didn't notice when the sounds of the shamisen stopped, or hear the servants help the courtesan into her robes. He was only brought from his reverie when a body sidled up to his and he felt a soft breeze across his neck. A hand reached over and stroked the curves of his chest. Its teasing fingers glided downward, dancing on the muscles of his stomach, then the top of his pubis, before they paused. Just as their curtailed promise threatened to overwhelm him, they returned to life and began to feather a tantalising path down.

'Mm,' he murmured, now captured in a real paradise. 'Yoshi—'

EIGHT

'Yoshi!'

I woke sitting bolt upright. I looked beside me to see Tomoe staring up.

'Who's Yoshi?'

'Ah, no one,' I said, settling back.

'You seem very excited about no one,' she said, thrusting a hip into the evidence.

'It isn't anyone. I don't think. I was just dreaming—'

'I know you were dreaming. I'm wondering who you were dreaming about.'

'I don't— It was just a stupid dream about—'

But she had already turned away. I was too drowsy to protest any further and drifted back to sleep. When I woke up she was gone.

I called her that evening.

'Hi,' she said, her voice devoid of warmth.

'Hi.'

There was a pause.

'You're not really pissed off at me for dreaming about a geisha, are you?'

'How do I know it's a geisha? How do I know you haven't met another girl?'

'For god's sake, Tomoe,' I said, exasperated. 'Go and get a picture of us. Then tell me if you really think you're the one who needs to worry about being two-timed.'

Something in my voice must have sounded genuine because she giggled.

'Geisha turn you on, do they?' she asked. 'Is it the heavy white make-up? You know they used to blacken their teeth? Do you want me to blacken mine – would that turn you on?

'She wasn't like that in the dream and I'm happy with your teeth the way they are. Although, fix me up with a nice geisha girl and you never know . . . Maybe I'd get a thing for the kimono and *tabi* socks and trade you in.'

'Oh yeah, we could send you back in time to when they'd never seen a *gaikokujin* before, you'd like that,' she teased, using the polite form for foreigner. 'Oh, Rei, Rei! Big gaikokujin man.' She dropped an octave. 'Oh, you like my loving, geisha girl? Call me Raging Rei!'

'So, are you going to stop being moody with me then?' I asked when I'd stopped laughing.

'I'll stop being moody with you. Come round, I was about to watch a film.'

Things seemed to go back to normal for a week. But they didn't stay that way long. When Tomoe appeared as a stranger at my door again, it wasn't a flood of tears that disturbed me but the lack of any emotion at all. Getting an explanation was no less challenging than it had been when she'd arrived upset before.

'Please, just hold me,' she said in a small voice borrowed from someone else. 'I need you to hold me.'

'Tomoe,' I coaxed as I held her tight. 'Tell me what's wrong. I can't do anything to help you if I don't know.'

'I went to the yakuza offices,' she said flatly.

'You did what?'

I thought a moment.

'They have offices?'

'Yes.'

It was the kind of conversation that needs one side to drive.

'But you think these people killed your father. Why did you visit them? They could just as easily have hurt you.'

I stopped and lifted her head from my chest so I could look in her face.

'They didn't do anything to you did they?'

'No. I'm OK.'

'Sweetheart, you say you're OK but you don't look it at all. You keep turning up like this and I sit here like an idiot because I've got no idea of what's happened or what I can do. Please, let me help you.'

She looked at me and I could see a hint of the Tomoe I knew behind her eyes.

'I'm sorry. Nothing happened, I promise. You don't have to worry about me like that. But I heard things about my father, things that were really difficult to hear.'

Her voice caught.

'They're going to take years to come to terms with. I want to talk to you about them, I really do, but I can't, not now, I just can't—'

A lone tear struggled from her eye and wound a melancholy trail down the contours of her face.

'Please, hold me like you love me. Don't let go.'

It was the last I was to see of her for nearly three weeks, weeks in which she was apparently occupied by work – a poetry convention in Kobe followed by an ukiyo-e exhibition in Osaka – but I suspected were spent tracking her father's killers. Seemingly indestructible, she was the Tomoe I knew again, but she wasn't inclined to talk about work or investigations when we spoke on the phone.

'Oh, Ray-kun, please – I'm either working my fingers to the bone or being bored to death by earnest academics. Just talk to me about nothing. Please?'

One part of me, admittedly the larger part, was happy to oblige as it meant I could keep my promise to Ernesto and avoid any follow-up calls. But I had to fight a sense of shame. She was my girlfriend. I surely should have been doing more.

'New addition to the list!' announced Johnny.

'What's that?'

He tutted in disappointment. 'Come on, work with me, show some creativity. At least have a guess.'

I'd met Johnny on the plane. He'd interviewed with an English language school in London and flown over with twenty other teachers who happened to be on my flight. He was the same age as me but his decision to leave his job in IT had been out of boredom and solely his. Fifteen months in, he remained fascinated with the *fūzoku*, the sex industry in Japan, in particular the innumerable ways it catered to every fetish and whim.

'OK, so it's not the role-reversal club where the schoolgirls touch *you* up on the train?'

'Old news. This is better.'

'The peep room with the hole in the one-way glass where the manga character tugs you off after she's stripped down?'

'No, but come to think of it I haven't been there for a while . . .'

'Something to do with the places you get AV and *ebicon* girls?' I asked, referring to the Adult Video stars and 'event concierge' girls who work the stands at motor, technology and other fairs. Both had major fan bases and, for those who could be persuaded to capitalise on their popularity, fees to match.

'You're getting warmer, but it's better than that.'

'Better?'

Johnny had referred to them as the epitome of an advanced capitalist society when he first heard of their existence. He'd been half-heartedly looking for a job that would enable him to appreciate this pinnacle of marketplace evolution ever since.

'Better. They're just prostitutes—'

'That kind of comes with the territory with paid sex.'

'Not necessarily. They're at the luxury end of the market but that's still all they are. I've found something different.'

'So you've said. Do you want to just tell me what it is?'

His face lit up. 'These are like the ultimate untouchables – in the good sense of the word – a super-select group, like Japanese super-models. Except they're more than just models, they're the cultural elite, I don't know, the biggest artists, writers or musicians, that sort of thing. Obviously, they've got to be fit as well.'

He warmed to the theme.

'They're so exclusive there are only a handful in the country and it's impossible to know who they are. But the next time you're watching TV and you see a particularly hot actress or singer, she could be one. And if you have the money and know the right people . . .'

'And I suppose you do?'

'I might not have the money – yet,' he said. 'But I'm getting close on the people front.'

I gave him a suspicious look. I was pretty sure he knew no one of significance in Japan, England or anywhere else.

'You know Tom?' he asked rhetorically of a friend we'd met in a bar. He was reasonably senior in an electronics firm and had been transferred from the States.

'Well, the son of some politician or other – it might even be the home secretary – he started working for Tom's firm last month. I went out with them at the weekend and this guy got completely wasted and told us about it. The thing is, they're so exclusive that even though he's the stinking rich son of some big-shot, he still can't get a look-in. That's how special these girls are.'

'It's a great idea but I don't believe a word. He's just a drunken rich kid taking the piss or trying to impress you.'

'No, he was for real, I promise. He swiped a business card from his dad and tried to book a girl but he got totally stonewalled. Then they got on to his dad who gave him an almighty bollocking for even knowing they exist. Don't look at me like that.'

'Don't blame me. Just because you fell for it doesn't mean I have to.'

'I swear, it's completely legit. He even showed us the card. Thick cream paper, super understated with just the name and phone number embossed.'

He looked away dreamily, imagining the paradise just beyond his reach.

'Tanzen,' he murmured.

'What?'

'Tanzen. That's what it was called. I just wish I'd been able to memorise the number.'

But I'd stopped listening. Having my blood turn cold seemed to have affected my ears. The name may have been new to Johnny but it was very familiar to me. What's more, I already had the number. I just had to hope it was for a different Tanzen, because the one I knew was where Tomoe worked.

NINE

'*Moshi moshi*, Tanzen.'

'Moshi moshi,' I replied. 'Is this Tanzen Cultural Consultancy?'

'Yes it is,' she answered in polite Japanese. 'How may I help?'

At this point I hesitated. Confronted with the kind of voice that would greet you at a five-star hotel, I wasn't sure of the note to strike when enquiring whether my girlfriend was an elite prostitute and, by extension, the owner of the voice a facilitator of paid sex. Who might, in fact, be the very person responsible for making arrangements for my girlfriend to sexually service men other than me.

'Um, may I speak to Chōshi Tomoe-san please?'

'Chōshi Tomoe-san?'

She wasn't willing to give up even the name.

'Yes, Tomoe-san,' I said. 'This is her boyfriend, Ray.'

'Oh, hello Ray-san. It's great to speak to you after hearing so much. I'm afraid Chōshi-san isn't here at the moment but I'll be sure to let her know that you called.'

In normal times, I'd have taken her friendly tone in the spirit it appeared to be offered. In the circumstances I took offence.

I'd ummed and ahhed before calling. I knew there was no chance of them opening up to me, but in the end I couldn't think of what else to do. I could have asked a Japanese friend to try but that would have meant explaining a situation I didn't want to think about and would have succeeded only in trashing Tomoe's name. All in search of something too outlandish to be true. Something I desperately didn't want to believe.

But I couldn't sit around doing nothing so I made the call. After getting nowhere I waited and as I waited my mind ran through different permutations of what could be the truth. It dwelled just briefly on the innocuous before settling on the unsavoury. And with each new thought my stomach turned as I contemplated the sweetness of the last year abruptly going sour.

'So why did you call my company?' Tomoe asked while unpacking her bags. 'What's up?'

'Oh, they warned you, did they?'

I'd been on edge since she opened the door and my mood hadn't been helped by her failing to notice. She'd seemed distracted by something else.

'What do you mean "warned me"? I spoke to the secretary and she told me you called, that's all.' She looked up from her bag. 'Is everything all right?'

'I think that depends on what you mean by all right,' I said, building to the confrontation that had been repeatedly playing in my head. 'Someone told me the place you work for is a front for high-end escorts. I thought it might be something we should discuss.'

This helped her get a sense of my mood. 'What are you talking about? Who said that? Is it that pervert friend of yours again?'

She'd never been a fan of Johnny.

'What does it matter who told me? I need to know who I'm going out with. Is it Tomoe the cultural curator? The person who's made such a difference to my life? Or are you in an alternative line of work?'

I heard the desperation in my voice. While my fears had been dragging me towards anger, this was only to protect myself from the pain that would be released if the heart-wrenching falsehoods turned out to be true.

Tomoe had stopped unpacking and turned to face me. She looked unsure of what to say.

'Ray, why are you talking like this?' she managed finally, her voice quiet and pained.

'Are you a prostitute?' I said, also quietly, partly in an attempt to remain calm and rational. Partly to hide the waver in my voice.

'Don't say that!' she cried out, her fire flaming again. 'Take it back!'

But I wasn't prepared to submit to her this time.

'Help me take it back,' I said, the jealousy and pain now clear in my voice. 'All I want is to have to apologise for being wrong. Just tell me you don't take money for sex.'

'It's not like that.'

'What do you mean "it's not like that"?' I demanded, her failure to dismiss the lie as damning to my frazzled mind as an admission. 'You either do or you don't.'

She made to reply but I interrupted before she could. 'I don't believe it. I'm going out with a call girl.'

Her fleeting blossom had withered.

'Ray-kun, don't say that. You're hurting me.'

'I'm hurting you?' I said, my pain revealing itself in sarcasm rather than the tenderness from where it came. 'Here's me thinking I'd finally found something good after one of the shittiest years of my life, that I'd found someone I could be happy with. Then I find out your job's a front and you get paid to sleep with other men. But I'm hurting you? How insensitive – I'm sorry.'

'It's not like that,' she repeated.

'So you keep saying. Why don't you tell me what it is like?'

'My job isn't a front. I've never wanted to be boastful but I have a certain level of expertise. I'm sought worldwide for my knowledge of ukiyo-e, my haiku have been published internationally and I advise theatres throughout Japan. None of these things is a "front". I'm proud to have achieved what I have.'

She paused. Unfortunately, it gave me a chance to cut in.

'That's fascinating. I knew you were good at what you do but I never realised you were that highly regarded. It's great, really. But to be perfectly honest, right now I'm a lot more interested in the other things I didn't know, like how often you get paid to have sex with other men.'

She continued as though I hadn't spoken.

'But I come from a tradition where social entertainment has often been intertwined with the arts. You know geisha are at the pinnacle of culture but they keep their clients entertained in other ways too. They serve drinks, they tell jokes—'

'Oh, so you're like a geisha then?' I interrupted, the chaos of emotions leading me to a harsher tone. 'I didn't realise they got paid to be fucked.'

'Do you want to hear what I have to say, or are you just here to abuse me?' she asked softly. 'I thought what we have is worth more than that.'

I didn't reply.

'Geisha are a more recent incarnation of cultural entertainers, and if you must know, historically some of them did. But this is about their predecessors, the courtesans of Kyoto, Osaka and Edo. They appeared after the shōgun unified Japan. There'd been endless wars until then so when the fighting stopped people suddenly had time on their hands. Cities became packed with warriors and the people serving them, and without battles to wage they needed other things to do. So the shōgunate licensed entertainment quarters. It was in or around these that many of the arts you know began.

'Before you ask, yes, physical entertainment was provided – the arts evolved as a consequence of the quarters, they didn't form their foundations. And yes, there were women who worked as prostitutes and had nothing to do with art.

'But the best places, the ones that defined the quarters, were grand houses owned by writers and artists, sometimes even samurai too. They were built by the best craftsmen, housed incredible art and had beautiful gardens. They were treasures in themselves. Their courtesans weren't prostitutes. They were the intellectual and artistic elite.

'The highest ranked were called *tayū* and they were the stars of their time. They couldn't focus solely on culture – they were courtesans – but in many ways the balance of power lay with them. They picked and chose their clients, not the other way around. Theoretically, they could decline even the shōgun. If a man wanted to spend time with them he couldn't just make an appointment and

69

be good for the fee. He had to raise himself to their level, by proving his good character or gaining refinement in an art.

'It would have been a waste to hire them just to satisfy physical desires and you'd have been declined if you tried. They didn't sell their bodies because they had nothing else to offer. They were exceptional women who made the best of where they were.'

She looked exhausted by the explanation.

'That's the heritage I've been caught up in. I wish I could have remained on one side of the line but it wasn't to be.' Her chin jutted in an act of defiance the rest of her looked unable to match. 'Of course I have regrets but I'm not ashamed. I've done the best I could in the situation I was thrown into.'

I tried to absorb everything she'd said. The journey from dream girlfriend to escort had addled my brain – and that was without trying to fit in courtesans from the past. The fine thread that had been holding rational thought together snapped and anger surged through in its place.

'That's very poetic, but we're not in Olde Worlde Japan now. I don't know why these women ended up where they were but I'm assuming they had no choice. You do. If the cultural side of things doesn't pay for the bags, clothes and whatever else you so clearly need, you could live without them. You decided not to. You chose to become a whore.'

'I'm not a whore,' she said emphatically, but the fight was fading from her. 'You don't understand.'

'You're fucking right I don't understand,' I snapped back, voice rising. 'One minute I'm going out with a dream girl, the next I find out I'm getting leftovers when she's done for the day.'

'It's not like that at all,' she responded. 'I'm sorry it has to be like this and I'm sorry you found out the way that you did. But you've never been second to anyone. I've never been as happy as I am with you.'

She stopped.

'Please don't abandon me too.'

It seemed a strange thing to say.

'I love you,' she said.

She looked so deeply into my eyes with a look so genuine and at the same time so sad, that for a moment she cut through my anger. But it was just a moment. The flames were raging too fiercely to douse.

'It doesn't "have to be like this". You're not in poverty fighting for your life.'

I searched for an insult that would wound her even if it hurt me, the kind you say in the heat of the moment and regret at length.

'You're just a whore happy to get fucked for the latest bag or purse.'

'Get out,' she said. 'I will explain but not when you're like this.'

She was like a beautiful flower crushed, an affront to nature that hurt me as it did her. Yet something inside hankered for more insults, as though they would somehow help put matters right.

'Get out before you say something you'll regret.'

She stopped me before I could abuse her further. I channelled all I would have said into a look instead and stormed out.

TEN

'Tomoe, give me a call. I want you to explain.'

It hadn't been a good week. In fact it was about the worst I could remember. My anger had remained undiminished at first. I'd played the conversation back endlessly, becoming more cutting in the repeats, with sharper put-downs and more devastating retorts. But then uncertainty had started to creep in, just at the edges at first. Her expression as I called her a whore; her broken voice as she tried to explain. With each memory came a doubt, and with each doubt my stomach twisted a little more. But I fought them. Because I was certain I was in the right.

Yet as the week continued the sickening feeling got worse. I'd wanted her to rail at my unfairness, to shout at me, to have been so outraged she'd given me a slap. But she'd wilted. And the thought made me feel as good as if I'd kicked a new-born kitten.

My mind increasingly went to her replies and the denials that weren't denials but intimations of a bigger picture I couldn't see. A place I wasn't right.

'It's not like that.'
'You don't understand.'
'I will explain.'

I still felt angry; angry at who she'd turned out to be, angry that despite the revelation I was having to struggle with guilt. But in the end it didn't come down to rights and wrongs. It was something else she said.

'I thought what we have was worth more than that.'

That I was going through this mental torture meant she had to be right. I needed to hear her explanation. Where we would go then I had no idea – my world view was quite liberal but it didn't extend to sharing my girlfriend with paying clientele. But I had to understand.

Having held out an olive branch I was less than delighted when it wasn't grasped.

I texted a few days later.

'Did you get my message? I think we should talk.'

Again, there was no response. It started to needle. I'd said some unpleasant things, but in the context I didn't think they warranted having my explanation taken away. After another ignored voicemail, my voice now curt rather than hurt, I went to her flat.

There was no answer. It started to feel strange. I peered in the top of her foyer mailbox. It was full with what looked like a week's worth of post. Something definitely wasn't right.

I tried to approach the situation rationally. She might have gone away to get some space after our argument. But having just got back it would have been an odd thing to do. My mind went to the unanswered calls and messages. Running away from a problem was unlike Tomoe. She usually tackled things head on.

Unwelcome scenarios started to force their way into my head. If she hadn't gone away, if she wasn't ignoring my calls, what was going on? My unconscious came up with an answer I immediately tried to reject. Not Tomoe. Not over an argument with me. But there was the situation with her father to be considered and whatever had happened with the yakuza too. Then there was the fact you should never second-guess samurai types when it comes to taking their life. Perhaps it was a grand gesture of rebuke to her father's killers. Or possibly to me.

I searched the ground floor and found the sixty-something caretaker pottering around. Despite his friendly demeanour. he had clear misgivings in allowing unknown gaijins access to his building's flats. My increasing distress seemed to convince him I was genuine, but it was only at this point he revealed he didn't have the keys.

'But that whole floor is owned by one company and their offices are just around the corner from here.'

We hurried off, the caretaker now almost as anxious as me. This meant I was left to take a backseat when we reached the agent's, leaving me little to do but fidget and try to avoid thinking of what I might find in Tomoe's flat. The caretaker, meanwhile, tried to inject some urgency into the floppy-haired jobsworth who appeared reluctant to do anything that would take him from his daily routine.

'That's highly irregular,' he said, sitting straight-backed behind his desk.

'Yes it is,' cajoled the caretaker. 'But you know me. When do I come around making strange requests? Please, as a favour. She's such a nice girl. We've got to make sure nothing's wrong.'

When he realised the caretaker wasn't going to take no for an answer, the agent grudgingly agreed to help. Even then the release of tension was short-lived – the caretaker wasn't the fastest on his feet and pigeon-stepping in time with him ratcheted my anxiety back up.

We finally reached Tomoe's building. But the wait for the lift was painfully long and I fought to contain myself on the way up to her floor. Then we arrived at her apartment. I was suddenly less sure it was where I wanted to be.

The agent opened the door and took a sharp intake of breath.

'What the heck?'

I weaved behind him trying to look around his shoulders and into the flat. But having teased with his initial response he now tortured me further, taking an age to slip off his shoes, tutting and exclaiming as he did.

Finally he moved inside and I saw what had shocked him. It looked like the Tasmanian Devil had raged through in a vortex-spinning fit. Side-tables were overturned, lamps smashed, even the TV, firmly mounted on the wall last time I saw it, was hanging off on its wires.

Moving from the living room, I looked in at her bedroom and then picked my way through the dining room into the kitchen. Furniture and belongings lay smashed and scattered throughout the apartment. But Tomoe was nowhere to be seen.

It didn't make sense. When I left her she'd been a butterfly with crumpled wings. It would have taken someone possessed to have done this kind of damage to their own flat.

Then I realised I hadn't checked it all. The bathroom. The door had been closed when I walked past. I retraced my steps, slowing as I neared the door until it felt like I was fighting through viscous air. I managed to force my hand to the handle, but when it reached the cold metal it stopped. Only when the weight of my arm did what my brain couldn't command did the handle start to inch down. After a pause at the bottom I pushed.

My bathroom was a pokey thing referred to as a 'unit bathroom' in small Japanese flats – estate agents' lingo for inadequate and ridiculously cramped. Tomoe's was much bigger and equipped with mod-cons like underfloor heating and an element behind the mirror to stop it steaming up.

It was the place of inspiration for her ever-changing hairstyles and I loved watching as she swooshed the sumptuous folds this way and that. She'd sometimes ask my preference and I'd glow inside, as though I was a co-creator of the work of art the length of white ribbon completed, a kind of *ikebana* for hair.

I felt entirely different now.

The door swung back against the wall. The room was empty – if you discounted the soaps, shampoos and potions strewn all over the floor. I felt like a valve had been opened and the terror holding me taut expelled.

I became aware of the others again. The caretaker was staring at me intently, having followed the direction of my thoughts before returning with me from their horrific trail. Released from the morbid curiosity that had held him, the agent returned to the complaints that had been an annoying buzz when I was lost in my death trance.

'. . . then the marks on the walls – they're going to have to be filled and re-papered, and that's saying nothing about the floor. Those are deep scratches, they're going to have to be worked on and that sort of thing doesn't come cheap—'

'SHUT THE FUCK UP!'

It was a break from decorum, the polite verbal code that gets you further in Japan than losing your cool. In fairness, this time it proved effective.

'I don't give a flying fuck about the marks on the floor or anything else. You worry about what the place looks like at the end of the tenancy. My girlfriend's missing and at the moment I'm a lot more concerned about that.'

For some Japanese, even the thought of a gaijin in an explosive, screaming fury holds the same fear our ancestors had of wild and mythical beasts. Faced with the reality the agent went rigid. He tried to speak a couple of times but his voice box was less willing than his silently stuttering mouth.

The caretaker stepped in.

'You must be incredibly busy,' he said in a soothing voice. 'Why don't you head back to the office and let me help Ray-san clear up. I can drop the keys back when we're done.'

Released from the spell the agent nodded sharply and bolted for the door.

The caretaker turned back to me.

'You thought she was dead?'

'Yes.'

'But now you think someone's taken Tomoe-chan?'

'Yes – there's no way she would have done this herself.'

I turned to him, surprised he was familiar enough to refer to her in the affectionate form of 'san'.

'She's been very good to me,' he explained. 'She helped me when my family had some problems. She's like another daughter to me.'

Tomoe had that about her. Those who didn't want or couldn't have her as a lover saw her as a surrogate daughter or sister, or the dearest of friends. Everyone wanted to be close.

'Why would anyone want to abduct her?' he asked

'It's complicated.'

'You're a foreigner here, let me help. I know people and I know how things work.'

I thought about it. I had no idea what to do and it would at least be a start.

'I don't know,' I said. 'It's beyond me. The whole thing's crazy. I think we need the police.'

'So let's get the police.' He pulled an old feature phone from his pocket and punched in some numbers. 'I know the guys at the local *kōban* police box.'

He turned to talk into the phone and I zoned out, only picking up on the conversation as it neared the end.

'Yes, but— OK, we'll come to you.'

He hung up.

'Useless. *Manual ningen*,' he said, using a phrase for people only able to do things by the book. 'My generation weren't like that. He says he's on his own today so he can't come to help us as he might be needed to help somebody there. The irony's lost on him.' His eyes crinkled into an encouraging smile. 'Never mind. We'll go to him.'

We left the building and headed into a typical maze of neighbour-hood side streets, their quiet calm so incongruous with the hustle of Tokyo's main roads. Too narrow for pavements and reluctant to allow cars to squeeze through, they left our escort to a murder of raven-sized crows, the city's thuggish alternative to pigeons. We arrived at the kōban to find its resident policeman pottering around, consumed by Tokyo's lack of crime.

'So your girlfriend's gone missing?'

'That's right,' I replied. 'She's been taken. And her apartment's been smashed up.'

'OK, let's take things from the top. When was the last time you saw her?'

'About a week ago.'

'And what was her mood like then?'

'She was a bit upset – we'd had an argument. But it's not—'

'Please, let me ask the questions and try to answer clearly. We have a lot of experience in these matters. When you proceed in a tried and tested manner you'd be surprised at how effective it can be.'

I bit my tongue.

'So, you last saw her a week ago when she was upset at an argument you'd had. Have you had any contact with her since?'

'No. Her phone hasn't been on, but it's not—'

'OK, so she hasn't been taking your calls since the argument,' he scribbled in his notebook as he spoke.

'No, it's not like that. She's been abducted – her phone's not on.'

'What is it that makes you think she's been abducted?' he asked, looking up. 'Surely it's more likely she got in a bit of a strop, stormed off somewhere and will make her way back when she's calmed down?'

'If you'd managed to get yourself all the way to her apartment—'

The caretaker nudged me and I began again.

'If you saw her apartment you'd understand. It's been totally destroyed. There was clearly a struggle.'

'It's true,' the caretaker chipped in. 'It's in a terrible state.'

'Well, you know what a woman scorned can be like. You should see my wife. Plates go flying like Frisbees; anything not nailed down is liable to get swiped. The number of times I wish she'd gone missing . . .'

His mind wandered to the unfortunate women who had to endure him.

'So what does her work say?'

'Her what?'

'Her work,' he repeated. 'You've checked in with them?'

I bit my lip in frustration.

'Just a minute.'

I stepped outside the small police box and dialled her 'office'. The receptionist answered and after some unpleasant pleasantries we got to the point.

'I haven't been able to get through to Tomoe for the last week. You've not had any contact with her have you?'

'I'm sorry, no, not for the last week,' she replied.

I gave the policeman a knowing look from just outside the doorway. She interrupted it.

'She had to go to a small island in Okinawa quite suddenly. I know from previous experience getting a mobile signal and even the internet is virtually impossible there.'

That threw me.

'You sent her there for work?' I asked, inwardly cursing as I saw the policeman make the face to the caretaker I'd been about to make to him. 'You've got no reason to think she isn't there?'

'Well, no,' she said, sounding surprised. 'Chōshi-san's extremely dependable so I don't check in on her everywhere she goes. But I'm sure if she hadn't turned up the organisers would have communicated it to me one way or another. She's very important to their success. Is there a problem?'

'No. Well, yes. No.' I tried to gather my wits. 'I hadn't heard from her. I was worried.'

'I'm certain you have absolutely no need,' she cooed, her voice riling rather than soothing me. 'I'll be sure to get her to call you as soon as we speak. But it may be a while yet – there was quite a lot to do.'

I may have been new to the investigations industry but none of this sounded very likely.

'Could I have the name of the organisation?' I asked. 'You know, just to put my mind at rest.'

'I'm so sorry, Ray-san,' she said, sounding entirely unapologetic. 'I'm afraid our clients work with us under strict conditions of confidentiality. But I'll follow up and try to get confirmation of her arrival so you don't have to fret.'

I ended the call and turned back to the policeman.

'Don't worry,' he said, accepting my unoffered apology. 'We love them, we hate them and we get ourselves worked up when they flounce out. I've seen it hundreds of times, experienced it a few too. If we investigated all of them we'd have half the female population on missing persons' lists. But you see, follow the process and it comes out all right.'

I had an urge to punch him in the mouth but instead I thanked him through gritted teeth and waited for the caretaker to say his goodbyes.

'You don't believe it, do you?' he asked as we made our way off.

I didn't. And it was then it struck me why – aside from the unreturned calls, the smashed up flat and the receptionist's deceit. The bathroom flashed in front of my eyes. All of her stuff was in it – her make-up, her cleansers, her contact lenses and glasses. It doesn't matter how much of a hurry you're in – and let's face it, there can't be many emergency art exhibitions – you take the essentials.

'No. She's been taken. Without a doubt.'

ELEVEN

I'd done the right thing. The police are there to investigate and solve crime and I'd given them their lead. But I'd been shooed away. So now I tried to think of what the best of the wrong things would be.

I had to assume the police would eventually take Tomoe's disappearance seriously – someone can only leave all their worldly goods and take off on a lovers' tiff/work event for so long. But with the line her company was taking this was likely to be weeks away. And the thought of what could happen to her in that time made my stomach turn. She'd hurt me but that wasn't the kind of hurt I wanted her to feel back.

But I was no detective and I was struggling even for bad ideas. I decided to work my way back from the end. It seemed certain the yakuza lay there, and they had to be left to the police. I tried to think of who could have led Tomoe to them. Well-connected clients perhaps, but I had no idea who they were. The only way I could think of finding out was through her company, but they'd already shut the door on me and seemed to be in on whatever this was.

Which meant the only logical option was the police, except I'd exhausted that possibility as well. It was hopeless.

Unless . . .

'No,' he said flatly. '*If* he was killed by them it probably means he was mixed up in their business. And *if* your girlfriend has been taken, it means by looking into it she got caught up too. So if I was to speak to them, all of a sudden I'd be in the middle of things. You seem a nice enough guy but that's not a favour – that's a suicide pact.'

He went silent for a moment, as though belatedly assessing the implications of associating with gangsters.

'You see, even if I'm the one who does your bidding, *you'll* be a part of it too. And you don't want to be a part of the yakuza. They're like a big, bad octopus. Dip a toe in the water and they'll slip and slither their way up your legs and drag the rest of you in too. And once you're in there's no way out – try pulling a tentacle away and even if you succeed, you'll see another seven have taken its place.

'You want my advice? Stay away from them. And while you're at it, stay away from me. I'm going to do you a final favour and pretend this conversation didn't happen. That way I don't have to report it and put us both in the shit.'

He hung up.

It seemed a safe bet Ernesto wasn't going to be the answer after all.

I gave up looking for another before I fell asleep that night. My unconscious, however, was more diligent. It worked while I slept and gave me its unwelcome conclusion in the morning.

There was certainly logic to it. If I really did want to track Tomoe down – and despite our recent issues, perhaps even partly because of them, I desperately did – realistically it was the only way left. The challenge lay in my inverse samurai spirit. I found my honour in life and I was very keen to preserve it.

My instincts had always worked in harmony with this outlook, pulling me from trouble rather than thrusting me towards it. That I was now being so dramatically betrayed gave me pause for thought. Unfortunately, that thought came up with nothing else. That was why, despite it being the idea first and most firmly rejected, despite every sinew straining against it, I decided to visit the yakuza.

The beaming smile I was greeted with didn't disguise the slightly squashed features of a face that had seen its fair share of life. His words came back to me: *'I know people. I know how things work.'*

It was as good a bet as any.

Once we'd said our hellos, the caretaker was concern personified again.

'Have you heard any news of Tomo-chan?' he asked, truncating her name in affection.

'No, nothing. That's why I'm here. I need to ask a favour.'

'Anything, I told you. Just tell me what.'

'Well . . .' I started. 'If I needed to visit a yakuza office, how would I go about finding one?'

This warranted a curious look. I wasn't sure whether it was because of the involvement of the yakuza, my desire to meet them, or that Tomoe might have contacts in the underworld.

'Tomo-chan was caught up with the yakuza?' he asked.

'No,' I said. 'Well, in the end yes, but only because of her father.'

'But he passed away. It was suicide wasn't it?' he said pointedly.

'Yes,' I replied. 'But Tomoe thought it more of an assisted suicide her father may not have willingly participated in. I think she went missing because she was trying to find out who provided the help.'

'And now you want to follow the same path?' he asked. 'Who's going to come after you when you go missing? I'm getting a bit old for that kind of thing.'

'No,' I said, more firmly than I felt. 'I'm not going to tread on anyone's toes, or do anything to make them feel it would be better I wasn't around. But it's got to be the yakuza. And if they've taken her because she annoyed them, I can explain her probing's all done. We know it was a misunderstanding. Her dad had been unhappy for a long time – in the end work and family pressure got too much. Tomoe got carried away in her grief but everyone's come to their senses now.'

'And you think it will be as easy as that?'

'I don't know,' I said, desperate he shouldn't undermine the line I'd been pitching to myself. 'If you want to know the truth, I didn't want to get involved in the business with her father and I don't know if I should feel guilty about that or not. But now Tomoe's gone missing I can't do nothing. And right now this seems to be the only thing left.'

He looked at me a moment longer and then gave a faint nod.

'Which yakuza is it?'

'The Takata-gumi.'

He nodded again, this time in a resigned sort of way.

'I was a bit wilder in my youth and I ran across them once or twice, although they were known as the Dewaya-gumi then. I think they've moved their headquarters to Ginza but back then their main office was in Kabukichō, just around the corner from where the Koma Theater used to be. We could start there.'

I looked at him. The crow's feet, usually so eager to dance into smile, stood still. There was something reassuring about him and I wanted to take up his offer, but Ernesto's voice played in my ears.

'I appreciate it, I really do. But either my plan comes good and everything's OK, or it doesn't and there'll be more trouble. Either way, I don't see how it will help to put another person in the firing line.'

He opened his mouth to protest but I stopped him.

'Like you said, your wild days are behind you. Leave them there and enjoy your family. Maybe I've got my adventures up ahead.'

I said it just to placate him. I'd come to Tokyo to get my life back on track. Showdowns in the Wild East were not in my plans.

TWELVE

'Fuck off, you big-nosed, foreign, cock-sucking prick. Go cry to someone else about your whore bitch of a girlfriend.'

It was an aggressive response, made worse by the fact he looked like his bite was worse than his bark; a menacing hulk formed when an unstoppable force met an immoveable object. My normal reaction would have been to do exactly as he said, but recent events appeared to have unhinged a part of my brain. Unfortunately that part now took control.

'I'm sorry,' I replied in my most polite Japanese. 'I'll try again. I came here because I was hoping I could meet someone from your organisation with whom I could speak intelligently. I don't suppose you could help me find them – perhaps someone who isn't an utter cunt?'

A misplaced look is enough to start a yakuza swinging. The most impolite word in Japanese is enough to incite a priest. The man-mountain didn't look like he engaged in frequent spiritual discourse, so it was unsurprising he responded with a missile of a right-hand fired straight at my head.

*

Deciding there was no time like the present, I'd headed out on foot from Tomoe's place. I cut through Shinjuku Southern Terrace, crossed the East Deck Bridge to Takashimaya Times Square and descended the long escalators from the department store's walkway into East Shinjuku.

The piped tones of Frank Sinatra were immediately shattered. Restaurant vendors bellowed offers, schoolgirls shrieked at friends and the din of games machines blasted from arcades. The wall of neon was no less jarring, an eye-blistering array of colour wrapped around disorderly buildings squeezed into whatever space they could get.

I wove through ant-like hordes to Shinjuku *Dōri* Road where massive screens mounted high up buildings projected discordant cries. From there, it was only a short block's walk to Yasukuni Dōri but there was a rising agitation in the throng and the atmosphere began to change. I reached the road just as the lights turned and was swept over with the tide of the crowd and deposited on the opposite bank. On the border of Kabukichō.

Kabukichō. A corner of Shinjuku a few hundred metres squared with possibly the highest concentration of bars and restaurants in the world. Burrowed deep among them were the fūzoku. Massage parlours, 'health' clubs, hand-job joints, blow-job bars and whatever else the mind could conceive.

It had an energy all of its own, throbbing with extra power even amid Shinjuku's high-wattage glow. And beneath its pulse an undercurrent, the spark of danger that comes from being a gangster land, Tokyo's yakuza heart.

The gangsters were in thrall to its grey money, made on the borders of legality, where a payoff is preferable to trouble and the chance of the boundaries being unfavourably confirmed by the police. The industry that dealt in this shade of currency was referred to as the *mizu shōbai* – the water business – possibly another echo from the bathhouses of Tokyo's Edo past.

Despite its mention arousing concern in many Japanese, I'd never found Kabukichō that intimidating. This could have been due to Tokyo's general levels of safety. Or because for yakuza, dealing with gaijin was more trouble than it was worth.

It may also have been because I'd never sought them at their offices before, accusing them of kidnap and demanding the return of my girlfriend.

It was in one of the small side streets that I saw the Takata-gumi crest – an *uzumaki* spiral that looked like the whirlpools or wind Tomoe was so fond of in woodblock prints. It sat above a small doorway between a cramped broom cupboard of an estate agent and a moneylender's corridor shop. As an entrance to the office of one of Japan's biggest gangs, it seemed particularly unassuming. I presumed they thought a low-key presence was preferable even for legitimate organised crime.

I hesitated as I looked at the dingy stairway a few feet back from the door. It was enough in itself to make me want to turn around. But I'd decided before I set out I wouldn't submit to my instincts, that I was going to go through with this whatever my fears. I took some deep breaths to build myself up, sharply exhaling on each. Finally I forced myself forward.

I was about five steps up when the gloominess darkened and I started to wish I'd stayed where I was. The light had either been blocked by the figure at the top of the stairs or repelled by his sheer menace.

It was a narrow staircase and he had to pull in his shoulders to fit. If he hadn't he probably would have carved into the walls on either side like a glacier ripping through its rocky banks. He was a few steps down before he saw me.

'You're in the wrong place,' he growled from his stone-carving of a head. 'Fuck off.'

It seemed good advice and I was sorely tempted to take it.

'I'm sorry,' I stuttered. 'I was hoping to speak to someone about my girlfriend. I think she came here a few weeks ago and there may have been a misunderstanding. I thought I might be able to talk to whoever she spoke to and iron things out.'

It was at that point he insulted Tomoe and my rational mind lost control.

He moved astonishingly fast for a man his size. Fortunately, he couldn't match my incoordination. I'd stopped and taken half a step back when he entered the stairwell. With stairs made for smaller feet than mine, that had already put me off-balance. My flinch at his first sign of movement did the rest. I toppled backwards, staggering frantically to stay on my feet.

His punch whistled close enough to my nose for me to feel the air break before it. But it was my stumble from the stairs that saw me fly out of the doorway and land flat on my back in the street. Passers-by rippled out around me. They fanned back even further when the man-monster exploded from the door.

I tried to push myself up before he could reach me. It was that movement that took my head from the point of maximum impact and made the difference between decapitation and blinding pain.

The force of his punch was still enough to catapult me backwards. I rolled with its momentum into a crawl, desperate to put distance between him and me. But before I made any discernible progress I felt a huge paw reach under me. It grabbed me at the chest and spun me around for the knockout blow.

But the punch never landed.

As I flailed out in desperation a hand reached around his recoiled arm.

'Not here,' rumbled a voice so deep I wasn't sure if I heard or felt it. 'The boss says not out front. Bring him inside.' It rose aggressively. 'What are you looking at? Get on with your business. There's nothing for you to see here.'

I can only imagine any sane passers-by did as he commanded, because by this point I was being dragged by the chest, into the building and up the stairs.

THIRTEEN

'So what makes you think we know anything about your girl-friend? I believe we move in different worlds, do we not?'

I'd been dumped face down on the floor in the middle of a small, smoky office. There was a low coffee table just beyond my head and a compact sofa to the right. It took a moment before I realised I'd curled into a ball. I reluctantly uncoiled and lifted my head. A man sat at the other end of the table with one leg crossed over the other in a way that seemed more European than Japanese.

'Are those fingers?'

It wasn't the answer I'd intended to make, but an instant reaction to the contents of the jars on display behind him. A huge paw-swipe knocked me flat and set my right ear ringing.

'Answer when the boss asks you a question,' a voice thundered from behind me.

'That's OK.' I looked up to see 'the boss' hold out a restraining palm. 'Let's hold off beating him senseless for the moment. I'd like to hear what he has to say.'

I guessed he was in his early sixties but he could have passed for younger. He was as smooth as Nat King Cole's voice; his high cheekbones and taut skin set off by a suit so beautifully tailored it could have been an extension of him.

'May I speak?'

I was terrified of doing anything that might be considered a transgression.

'I wouldn't have asked the question if I didn't want you to answer,' the boss said. 'Why don't you sit on the sofa though – the conversation feels somewhat awkward with you on the floor.'

Before I could move I was hoisted by the scruff of the neck and dumped on the sofa. I rubbed the side of my face as I tried to summon the courage to speak.

'So, why would we know anything about your girlfriend?' he asked again.

'I think she came to see you a few weeks ago,' I said in a meek voice. 'At least it may have been you. It was a Takata-gumi office.'

His expression didn't change.

'Her name's Chōshi Tomoe.'

He still didn't react. I was too scared to say anything else.

'You're Chōshi Tomoe's boyfriend?'

In the circumstances it seemed even more implausible than normal.

'Yes.'

He deliberated a moment.

'Come into my office – no, it's OK,' he turned to the others. 'Just . . . ?'

'Ray *desu.*'

'Just Ray-san. I don't think he poses a great danger, do you?'

I followed him through a door on his right into a far more luxurious room. He made his way towards a polished hardwood desk with plush leather chairs at its front and back. The shelving to the side was made of the same wood and filled with books, a decanter and cognac glasses, and a statuette that looked like an award. My feet sank into deep pile.

'I hope you'll excuse the squalor,' he gestured at the exquisite room. 'Our head office is in Ginza but I spent my formative years here. I have a soft spot for the place, hence the satellite study. Please, sit down.'

While his courtesy was preferable to his henchman's aggression, it didn't put me at ease. I didn't know much about the yakuza but I couldn't see why a local boss would refer to his own office as a satellite. And if he wasn't a local boss that implied he was someone very senior. His air and the way he was talking made me wonder if he might even be Takata himself.

He reached for the decanter.

'Would you care to join me? Hine Antique – it's excellent but quite difficult to find in Japan.'

I'd have nailed a shot of paint-stripper. I nodded.

'As for the fingers, I can only apologise. It's another of these ridiculous traditions I'm trying to ease out. The idea we can no longer proclaim criminality and sever body parts hasn't been easy for everyone to grasp. Of course, it's important we retain an ability to use force, but we're no longer just the rogues of the past. We're bankers, art dealers, businessmen – missing digits don't sit well with these roles.'

He was too suave to be exasperated but a hint of frustration edged through in his voice.

'The grasp of tradition holds strong though. Yakuza all want to see themselves as chivalrous outlaws, men of honour who help the weak and bring down the strong. I appreciate one needs a business identity and on many levels ours works well, but the Robin Hood-isms and counter-productive customs can be tiresome.'

He looked over as though waiting for me to play a part. I wasn't in a state for enlightened contribution.

'But you're a yakuza. Isn't that what it's all about?'

His face was a mixture of bemusement and disdain.

'It's about business. It's about money and power.'

'But I thought you kept crime among yourselves? That's why you're accepted – you help local communities and so on?'

'You believe so? Maybe in the pre-war years, I don't know; that was before my time. Now? We go where the money is and we make it from whomever we can. We're accepted because we pay off or scare the people we need to. Those who don't accept us are dealt with in other ways.'

His look became curious.

'Do you know anything about the yakuza?'

'Not really. They came up in my studies but it wasn't quite the focus of my degree.'

'Well, you'll hear about righteous outlaws and Edo-period codes of honour, but in truth we come from gamblers and street peddlers. No great heroes, just people looking to make a living who weren't afraid to bend a few laws.

'Their trades and that mindset created opportunities and when they took them their interests expanded and their cash piles grew. Before long people began approaching them for loans.

'But there were others who looked to appropriate their assets more directly. This meant they had to develop their security as well. Lo and behold, they found this was a service that could be monetised too. They continued to diversify and their small enterprises became empires.

'Then Japan opened up in the Meiji era. But the internationalist spirit wasn't just about letting others in – we'd seen what the Europeans, Americans and Russians had achieved by venturing overseas. Their pillage of Asia gave ideas to people here. And when their views were opposed, who do you think was unleashed? In return for silencing the doubters the yakuza shared the spoils of war.'

I couldn't see what this had to do with Tomoe but I reasoned that any rapport I could establish would lessen my chances of being fed to the monster next door.

'But the, er, the result of the war must have changed things?'

'It did. The nationalists were hammered but the occupation proved hugely beneficial to us. Rationing meant anyone able to get hold of goods had the means to a fortune and the American army had a wealth of supplies. We teamed up with them and the money flowed in.

'As time went on and the region's politics became more compli-cated, the US decided they liked communists even less than those they'd deemed guilty of war crimes. So they released the latter and helped them create the LDP party which, as you know, has remained in power almost ever since.

'So yes, the war did change things. It enriched the yakuza and put our political partners in charge.'

It didn't seem a very healthy foundation for democracy. It was possible we thought differently on the matter so I kept my mouth shut.

'It was a glorious time. Japan was an empty page and there were exceptional leaders to write its next chapters. But despite expanding the organisation on a massive scale, our interests for the most part remained the same. It wasn't until later that they really evolved. Scandals in the sixties led to laws that restricted us in our traditional fields. Fresh pastures were sought in response. Finance, trade and business manipulation were added to a base of labour, moneylending and vice. The eighties bubble was like an injection of steroids – that's when we peaked.'

He glanced over his cognac.

'There's no need to look so worried. These aren't dangerous secrets – you could easily find them online.'

I was more concerned about sitting before the head of Tokyo's yakuza. After that, I was fretting about how to get past his henchman in the next room. I made an effort to look less anxious all the same.

'So the yakuza, the nationalists and the government – they're actually one and the same?'

'No, we're not the same. We have our own specialities and we operate in different spheres. We sometimes have our difficulties too. But you could say we're fingers of the same hand.'

'Surely Japan isn't that corrupt?'

My stomach knotted even as I said it. It wasn't the affinity-building prompt that I'd meant.

'As opposed to whom?' he said sharply. 'The Americans? Their government was a partner throughout. It put the people in place and funded them for decades.'

He raised his eyebrows.

'And you, you're English?'

Despite the past and repeated efforts of my university teachers my pronunciation clearly wasn't as good as I thought.

'You think there isn't the same complicity in your country? What about your companies, your politicians? We found HSBC an excellent place to do business, so this isn't a criticism. But when they were caught laundering money for Mexican cartels, their chairman was made a minister in your government – he wasn't hauled into court.

'We're all the same; you just have different ways. You're the fingers on the other hand.'

He held me in his stare. I felt like a pheasant eye-to-eye with a debonair snake.

'But I've strayed from the point. I was trying to explain my situation. You see, the generations before me were blessed with opportunities, chances to do things differently, ways to leave their mark. I've contributed to the industry but I haven't fundamentally changed it. I'd like to redefine it for the generation to come.'

His eyes sparkled. He looked less gangster boss, more CEO working on a final master strategy prior to his succession plan.

'You see the crackdowns in the sixties – they helped the *oyabuns*, the bosses; they forced them to explore and expand. But the recent laws have been far more restrictive and we've already reached into every corner we can. So now, we face decline – our numbers are down and revenues are going the same way. I want to turn that around. And while doing so, make sure the Takata-gumi comes out on top.'

He stopped. I let him ruminate lest he be in the middle of his big idea. I was starting to wonder at what point comfortable silence becomes awkward when he spoke again.

'I'd like to thank you. This isn't a conversation I can have with others in the organisation and my wife is bored of hearing the same song. You're very easy to talk to – I'm pleased you could come around.'

He made it sound as though I'd popped along for a cup of tea instead of being bludgeoned around the head and dragged in. It seemed an opportunity to depart in a manner similarly suited to social norms.

'Oh, it was my pleasure. It's been fascinating – thank you so much for your time. But I'm sure I must have taken too much of it already. I should really get out of your way.'

He ignored the hint.

'So now we must turn to your girlfriend.'

I have to admit, my focus had moved from the quest for Tomoe to saving my own life. I wasn't sure how to react now Takata brought it back.

'I take it from your visit you no longer know where she is?' he asked.

104

I nodded.

'And you think that I might?'

I shook my head.

'I'm sure you don't,' I said, desperate not to offend him. 'I just thought, perhaps, you might have an idea of someone who would know or you could possibly ask questions to find out. She was very upset by her father's passing and may have had some outlandish ideas. I'm sure she's calmed down now though. She'll have realised how ridiculous they were.'

I managed to say my piece but it was a battle. A large part of me just wanted him to dismiss me so I could escape.

'We had nothing to do with the disappearance of your girlfriend. You're right, she did come to talk to me, although she was more conventional – she made an appointment to see me in Ginza and received a more cordial welcome as a result. Your girlfriend is a lady of culture, an artist, someone deserving of respect. We spoke, she said some things – things I was willing to accept from someone of her stature – and there were areas in which I could enlighten her as well. But that's all there was. If she's missing that saddens me and I truly hope she returns safe and well. But I have no further connection to her. It isn't my affair.'

'But—' I said, my mouth prompted by the memory of her when she returned, the distress his 'enlightenment' had caused.

'That's all there is,' he interrupted, the finality in his voice putting it at the scarier end of suave. 'I had no compulsion to tell you that much. It was out of respect to your girlfriend and because I enjoyed our talk. But there's nothing else. It's time for you to end your investigations. It's time for you to leave.'

It was both exactly what I wanted to hear and precisely not. I started to get up.

'You need to leave Japan. There's nothing for you here.'

That stopped me. It's an unusual experience being thrown out of a country, even more so when it's at the hands of a gangland boss. But there was something else. His choice of words seemed to imply something had happened to Tomoe.

'What do you m—'

'I would suggest you make a fulsome apology to Kurotaki as you go out. You must realise that face is everything for a yakuza. To be insulted by another yakuza is bad enough; to be insulted by a non-yakuza is even worse. For the person to be non-Japanese – and I hope you realise this is a mentality I'm describing and not my own view of the world – it's completely unacceptable.'

'But—'

'Thank you once again for coming by.'

It was said with finality. My time was up. Trying to extend it would only anger a man whose whims could mortally affect my life. I bowed, thanked him and, stomach churning, made for the door.

Kurotaki and the other yakuza turned when I stepped out. I bowed to a right angle before they could react further, apologising profusely and showing the total submission I assumed was necessary to have any chance of walking out. When I righted myself, Kurotaki was looking over my shoulder. I sensed Takata's presence and realised it was only his say-so that would save me. He must have given it silently because it was Kurotaki who spoke.

'Get the fuck out of here now.'

This time I took his advice.

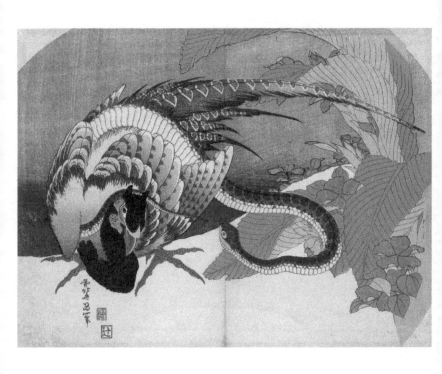

FOURTEEN

Takata's 'nothing' played in my head when I got home. Its implications disturbed me. Now I was being kicked out of the country I wouldn't be able to find out what they were. I wouldn't be able to look for Tomoe. I might never see her again.

The thought wouldn't leave me and I tossed and turned as I lay in bed, working myself into ever greater levels of distress. But beneath it another emotion was lurking, one that in some ways upset me just as much.

I felt relieved.

Relieved to be alive. Relieved I was being sent back to England where I had an excellent chance of staying that way. It felt cowardly despite the circumstances but I couldn't shake the sentiment off.

I woke the next morning feeling like I'd been beaten around the head with a bat. I struggled to the mirror and saw the left side of my face was puffy and red. Yet instead of being cowed by my reflection I felt strangely emboldened, as though I'd developed some kind of inner strength as I slept. It felt like it was driving me on, telling me I couldn't give up, that I was all that Tomoe had.

But it was false bravado. A boldness afforded by the distance from my oppressors and the fact there was nothing I could do. Even if I had been the brave, fearless type, I'd just used my last card. The police weren't going to help me, I didn't know Tomoe's contacts and her company was actively involved. The yakuza had been all there was left.

The following week was painful. I told people I'd suffered a family bereavement, hoping they'd leave it at that. I was lucky with my school – we'd just broken up for half-term and that gave them the chance to scramble together a replacement. Even with friends I stuck to the line. The truth still seemed implausible. Even if it hadn't, I wasn't keen to recount it and drag more people into my mess.

In some ways, I was being truthful; I was grieving. It just wasn't for a family member but for my girlfriend. The girlfriend who'd betrayed me but I couldn't disown. The girlfriend I might never see again.

Even with Johnny it felt too raw to fully explain, but when I mentioned the yakuza he was quickly convinced that going home was the best thing to do.

There wasn't much to pack up in my flat and I was finished a couple of days before my flight. That left a final piece of business – Tomoe's place. I had to hope she would be back there at some point and I didn't want her returning to the scene of destruction I'd witnessed earlier in the week.

I've always been slow when it comes to cleaning, taking as much time on breaks as the actual work. At Tomoe's there were even more distractions than normal. My mind wandered as I held a scarf to my nose and I became sentimental as I packed away her favourite things. Hardest were the pictures: Polaroids of her as a child beaming up at an austere father; photobooth shots of her clowning around with friends.

A photo of the two of us caught my eye. A blurred picture brightened by smiles – the blurring a result of her jumping on my back as I held out the camera, the smiles a carefree couple's happy glow.

'Come on, you lazy barbarian,' she'd berated me after bursting into my apartment at dawn – it was a time before surprise visits equated to murder or the yakuza. 'We're going skiing in Kusatsu for the weekend. Hurry up and get dressed – you're wasting valuable holiday time.'

I'd known nothing about this unplanned trip. She was meant to be away on work – what kind of work, I wondered now – and I'd been out the night before. But her infectious energy had driven me from my hangover into the day and we'd had a wonderful weekend in the snow-dusted, picture-postcard town.

I pulled out the photo. If – no, when – she came back, I'd scan it and send it to her if she didn't have the original file. I slid the tin box back in the shelf. Everything was neat and tidy again, better than I kept my own flat.

Except for an envelope that had slid forward as I jiggled the box back in place. I tucked it in and started to get up but something drew me back down. I pulled it out and opened it. Her work contract was inside. I looked through it, curious to know what the job description for a tayū is like. But it was all legalese, even more baffling for not being in my native tongue.

And an address.

It was like being poked with a cattle prod. I'd been racking my brain for leads, the lack of which had nearly got me killed. But I hadn't thought to check Tomoe's flat. Everything I needed was probably there.

I devoured the apartment, this time seeking clues rather than trips down memory lane.

But there was nothing. Nothing except the address.

'Ray-san?' she said. 'What a surprise.'

Which was as I'd intended. I'd already had the last throw of the dice. This was a bonus roll, a lucky dip, perhaps not even that. But if nothing else it would give me the chance to face down this sweetly spoken devil. I'd had no intention of forewarning her and getting fobbed off.

She made an attempt all the same.

'I'm so sorry, Ray-san, we're incredibly busy. There's an exhibition starting tomorrow and we're in a state of controlled panic. You know how these things are.'

She paused as though trying to gauge the effect. This was complicated by the conversation taking place through an entry system voice box. I said nothing, forcing the onus back onto her.

'I'm so sorry to have wasted your time, but would it be at all possible to come back when it's over?'

'I'm sorry, I'm going away for a while and there were one or two things I was hoping to leave for Tomoe with you. I'll be in and out before you know it.'

I felt a thrill of satisfaction at finding her effortless lying such an easy trait to pick up.

There was a moment of silence as she struggled to find an excuse to refuse me. The sound of the buzzer acknowledged her defeat.

*

I'd come out of Akasaka Mitsuke Station and turned into a small grid of roads that looked like Kabukichō's better-bred cousin. For what it lacked in its relative's current of energy, Akasaka compensated in cash. Road-hugging limos disgorged reams of silk kimono, made-to-measure suits and carefully crafted hair. Even the girls were more refined when propositioning, and the thugs and touts better dressed.

I'd gone down the road and then cut into a yesteryear alley, walking until I came to a small restaurant with a miniature maple tree at its front. Beside it, a four-floor building exemplified the flipside to Tokyo's utilitarian structures in a futuristic construction of wood, steel and glass.

An unembellished metal nameplate greeted me at the doorway.

TANZEN.

As one might expect, the offices of Japan's leading cultural curators were impeccable – lustrous and modern yet finished with traditional hints. The receptionist was as superficially perfect as her surroundings, their rich lacquers concealing something rotten that lay underneath. She stood, bowed and smiled sweetly, looking as calm as one might expect of someone caught in a crisis that didn't exist.

'Ray-san, I'm so pleased we could finally meet,' she lied. 'I've heard so much about you, all of it good.'

I detested her person as much as I had her voice.

'That's very kind of you to say. Tomoe speaks of you in glowing terms too. Oh, she hasn't been in touch since we last spoke?'

She showed no acknowledgement the game was now overtly covert.

'I'm sorry, Ray-san, but I haven't been able to speak to her. However, the organisers have told us the event's been extended, so we'll have to wait a while longer before we have the pleasure of her company again.'

She let her smile fade to allow a look of inquisitiveness play on her unblemished features instead.

'But I'm being rude. You told me you were in a hurry to drop something off and get going, and here I am holding you up.'

I realised I hadn't worked my plan through to its conclusion. I patted my pockets.

'Um, I seem to have misplaced it. Oh, damn! I know – I left it in my other coat.'

'Oh dear, I do hope it wasn't anything important?'

'Er, no, I'm not sure. I think it was a letter, or possibly some files. It was sealed so I don't know. But it was with some other stuff that had Tanzen's name and address on it – that's how I knew where to come.'

It made a kind of sense, but less to me than it seemed to her.

'Oh, that does sound like it may have been important. Why don't I get someone to drop you home and they can pick it up?'

She started tapping at her iPad before she finished speaking.

'No. I mean, that's OK – I'll send it in. I still have one or two things to do in town.'

She kept tapping.

'But as I said,' I continued. 'I'm going away for a while and I really need to contact Tomoe before I go. I know you said the name of the organiser is confidential but it's essential we speak.'

She stopped typing, looked up and smiled.

'I'm afraid that's impossible – we're contractually obliged. Chōshi-san understands this perfectly. It's just a part of the business we're in.'

She was using her veneer of friendly politeness to scrape at my nerves.

'But surely you have contingency plans for emergencies? What happens then?'

'Is there an emergency?'

'Yes.'

'May I ask what it is?' she asked when I said nothing else.

'I'm afraid I'm unable to tell you – it's private. But Tomoe would want it. I'm sure you understand.'

Our icy-smiled face-off was broken by the ping of the lift doors. I looked behind me to see two men: a massive, ugly, mean-looking monster, the equal of Kurotaki, the Takata-gumi thug I'd insulted before. This one's sidekick was smaller, the kind of man you wouldn't notice until he had a knife hilt-deep in your ribs.

'Oh,' she said brightly. 'Here's your driver.'

I had no reason to doubt his ability behind the wheel but I didn't believe for a second that was the extent of his job.

She turned to them. 'Thank you for coming so quickly. What a stroke of luck you were nearby.'

The big one grunted, although it was more the sound of a pride lion than a man, a sonic boom that would have carried miles had we not been in an enclosed space.

'Yes, thank you,' I faltered. 'But I'm terribly sorry – we'd just agreed that you didn't need to collect me. I've got a few things to do and we decided it would be best for me to bring in Tomoe's stuff when they're done.'

The monster gave no indication he heard me.

'Get up,' he ordered.

'No really, thank you for the kind offer but I have an appointment I really must make.'

'Well, thank you for coming, Ray-san. It was such a pleasure to meet you,' the receptionist said warmly, adding to the number of people who seemed incapable of hearing anything I said. 'These good gentlemen will take care of you now.'

Again, her mode of reference was a misnomer, a tacit acknowledgement she had game, set and match. I sat where I was, unable to move beyond a slight trembling and the preventative tightening of my sphincter.

'Let's go!' the Beast barked as he wrenched me to my feet.

The devil incarnated in a blankly pretty receptionist smiled after me as I was manhandled towards the lift. Her expression would have had you assume a pleasant meeting had been concluded rather than the last rites recited before an execution walk.

The new beast guided me out of the building in a vice-like grip and tossed me into the back of a Toyota. I wondered what the blacked-out windows had prevented being seen in the past. What they were about to hide now.

'Where to?' he demanded, as he and the knifeman got in the front seats.

'Takadanobaba,' I stammered. 'Near the station. I'll direct you from there.'

My brain raced as we set off. To subdue my rising panic, I forced myself to think rationally and break the situation down. First I needed to be clear who my captors were. No one looked or behaved like that other than yakuza so there wasn't much puzzling to do there. The next step was to work out what they wanted. They'd already killed one person, possibly more. I'd been told to stop meddling and get out of the country. I hadn't. The logical answer was they wanted to kill me too.

I decided I'd done enough clear thinking. I pulled the door handle and shunted myself to the side.

'Oomphh.'

I grunted in pain as my shoulder slammed against the child-locked door. The yakuza broke from their conversation in front.

'Sort him out,' the Beast ordered gruffly.

Knifeman turned and swung in a single movement, my eyes catching up just as my field of vision was swallowed by his fist. A bright light blazed at the dull splat of his punch and my head snapped back and then lolled on my neck.

'Try anything else and I'll pull you out of the car and run over your fucking legs.'

He turned back. My head continued to roll like the nodding dog missing from the back shelf. I directed it against the window which I lowered slightly to let in some recuperative air.

A thought hit me with the cold blast. The receptionist had only called them when I told her I had something. They were after a letter or documents they thought I had. There must have been ends left untied from the disappearances, things they needed back. Things important enough for me to be kept alive. Things that might set Tomoe free.

Things I didn't have.

It was essential they didn't find out I didn't have them. As I had about half an hour before they did, there was only course of action to take.

I groaned, leaned to the side and wound the window down further, as though to get more air to my throbbing head. It reached the bottom just after we took off from some traffic lights. As it did I launched myself out.

WWWWWAAAAAHHHHHhhhhhh ... A car horn exploded near my head and then faded as it swerved to avoid me and continued the other way. I shook myself and looked up. The Toyota was screeching to a halt a hundred metres or so ahead. It must have had more time to accelerate than I had thought, which was lucky as I might have bottled it if I'd known we were going that fast. It was also fortunate because it gave me a head-start.

I scrambled to my feet but almost fell straight away as my right side screamed out in pain. Ahead, Knifeman leapt out of the car and started running towards me as the Beast handbrake-turned into the opposite lane. The sight proved an excellent anaesthetic.

I bolted through cars backing up at lights on the other side of the road. I was running blindly towards a station, which in Tokyo can only ever be minutes away. If Knifeman was like the other men of his generation, he likely smoked as though in fear of a tobacco drought. And I had terror on my side. I was running from the grim reaper and even if Usain Bolt was under the robes there was no way I was going to be caught.

I saw Yotsuya Station ahead. My mind raced through a mental train map. I could get on the Sobu Line, change to the Yamanote at Shinjuku, and be back at Takadanobaba in a trice. I bounded down the taxi ramp to the entrance, piled through the ticket barriers, and shoved my way down the stairs and onto a train just as it was about to depart.

I sat and my heart started to pound with a little less violence, giving me a chance to think. In the traffic, they'd take thirty minutes at least. I could be back at my flat in fifteen, grab my passport and bag, and be in a taxi heading towards a nice, safe airport hotel in twenty minutes' flat. Then all I had to do was keep myself shut away, get the room service going and I'd be on my flight this time the next day. My breathing eased. I was on the home straight.

My own situation resolved, my mind went to Tomoe. It felt like Knifeman had plunged his weapon of choice into my heart. But I'd done everything I could, more than I thought possible. You only had to look at me to know I'd given my all. I'd go to the Foreign Office as soon as I was back, the Japanese Embassy, wherever I could go to bring the situation to the eyes of authorities who cared. Who knew, doing it from England might take the situation beyond the yakuza's reach and give her a better chance. I just had to get through the next twenty minutes. Be calm but fast.

I darted out of Takadanobaba station into Sakae Dōri, then turned quickly off it to the right. I went over the bridge, down an alley and in a couple of minutes was back at my flat. I looked at my watch. Fifteen minutes. Bang on plan.

I took the stairs three at a time, turned right at the top of the stairwell and soon had my key in the door. I was in. More importantly, a minute's turnaround and I'd be out. Four more and I'd be in one of the cabs at the station and on my way. On my way to safety and normality again.

A massive hand grabbed my throat. It lifted me a foot in the air and slammed me against the wall.

'Why the fuck didn't you do as you were told?'

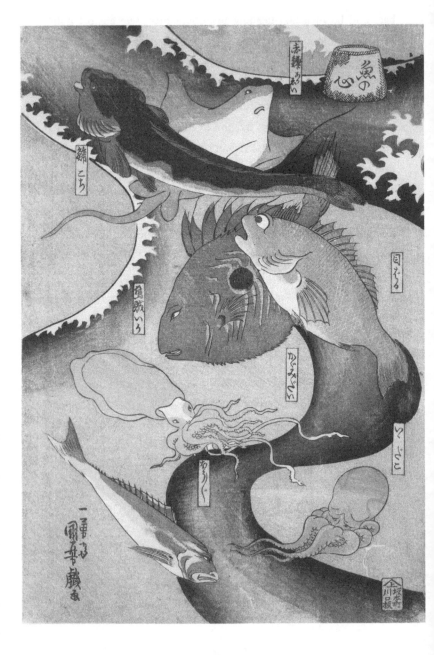

FIFTEEN

Kurotaki was singing along cheerily to *Eloise* as he drove, the whole thing surreal even before he broke up an octave for the chorus. I was slumped in the back seat, my head propped up by the window. My aches and pains were crying out for attention but I wasn't responding. And I wasn't thinking of ways to escape.

I'd run out of bright ideas. I'd pushed myself to my limit and failed. I was now resigned to my fate.

Takata looked up as I entered his office and ushered me to my seat.

'I thought we agreed you were going home.'

'We did,' I answered, too drained for an apology. 'I've got my ticket. I was ready to go.'

'But you didn't. You went looking for your girlfriend instead.'

'I found something with her work address on it. I couldn't help it; I had to try.'

'And what did you find out?'

I wondered what his point was. I couldn't see why he would want me to tell him what he must already know.

'Not very much. I know they were involved in Tomoe's disappearance but that's about it.'

'And what were they so keen to get from you?'

'They wanted documents they think Tomoe left behind.'

'And what documents are these?'

He was looking at me keenly. I knew the answer would decide my fate but I could think of nothing to tell him but the truth.

'There are no documents. I had to pretend I had something so they'd let me in. Documents were the first thing that came to my mind.' I rubbed my eyes. I was exhausted. My mind and body had had enough. 'I don't have anything.'

He turned and stared into space. I wondered what would happen next. Probably a call out to his underlings so they could come in, take me and do whatever they were going to do. At any other time, I would have been terrified and it would be wrong to say I wasn't scared. But it felt as though the sensors in my brain had been disconnected and I was looking in on someone else's fear.

'You had an opportunity to get out,' he said. 'There was no need for you to be involved. I gave you that chance.'

'You did.'

'But you didn't take it. You dived in and unfortunately for you that changed things. There's no longer an escape. You're either going to sink or swim.'

I had no idea what he was talking about.

'I'm sorry, I don't understand. I know I wasn't supposed to do anything but I didn't think there would be any harm in going to her office. I didn't find out anything and there's nothing anyone can find out from me.'

I felt a flash of pain from where Knifeman had hit me and put my hand to my cheek.

'I still have my plane ticket for tomorrow. If you don't want me around it would be easier to let me use it than do anything else.'

As pleas for one's life go it wasn't exactly impassioned, but in the circumstances it wasn't such a bad attempt. But Takata just looked at me, a hint of a smile playing at the corners of his mouth.

'You think we're planning to kill you?'

'Aren't you? Isn't that what this is about?'

'No, it isn't,' he said. 'You're not here to die.'

My brain slowly absorbed his words, my joy at them as detached as my earlier fear.

'You're here to join us. You're going to become a yakuza.'

When I'd been at the office the week before, I feared being killed but had been hopeful of coming away with my life. I'd left the building in a short-term state of euphoria, a feeling unlike any I'd experienced before. This time I'd been certain of death. The release from its jaws left me bewildered. This twist confused me even more.

'Now of course you'll play a different role to someone like Kurotaki – you don't have quite the same skills. But that's not something to worry about. Kurotaki and his like are the visible face of what we do and, aside from the fact that we need men of that ilk, that's no bad thing. They reassure the public and help maintain the impression of gamblers and peddlers; rough men who ultimately live by an honourable code.

'But as we discussed, we need to be able to move in the circles where real power is exercised. For that we need specialists. In this case, it means people like you.'

If he was hoping to clarify the situation, he failed.

'English teachers?'

'No, not English teachers. We'll talk about the details another time. Right now, you need to rest. You thought you were going to die and now you know you're going to live. It's something I've experienced and it's not to be taken lightly. You need some space to yourself.'

I did feel light-headed. But while time on my own sounded welcome, I was confident I still wouldn't want to be a yakuza when it was up.

'Thank you for your understanding – I do feel a little drained.'

I paused to consider how to continue but I wasn't capable of gauging nuance at that point so I dived straight in.

'Of course, it's nothing against your organisation, but what would happen if I thought I wasn't entirely well suited to being a yakuza? I'm not sure I have any skills that can help.'

'It wouldn't really matter because I'm telling you that you do. You know I said you had the chance to sink or swim? Well, this is the swim. Don't choose to sink – it would be an unnecessary waste.'

He said it in the same even tone he always spoke in, but the implication was clear, even in my state.

'You need to stop overthinking. Accept where your actions have brought you and make the most of it. There's no need to look so concerned. We're a diverse, dynamic organisation – you'll find us far less one-dimensional than perhaps you expect.

'So perhaps you weren't anticipating your career path would lead you this way. You're not alone – there are plenty of others who needed a little encouragement at first. But if you approach it with an open mind and give it your all, you'll have an interesting and rewarding career. I mean, this teaching thing, you can't do it for ever.'

Career advice upon being forcibly enrolled in the yakuza. It anything marked the death knell of normality, it was surely this.

'But I'm a gaijin.'

'You have no argument from me on that.'

'Don't I have to be Japanese?'

'Not at all – we're the equal opportunities employer of Japan. We take in Koreans, Chinese, the *burakumin* underclass; we've even got a scattering of westerners too.'

He backtracked a little.

'They tend to be associates rather than full members though, so you could find yourself in the minority on that front. But quite frankly, it doesn't matter. This is my organisation and I decide who joins.'

The stimulus being thrown its way was slowly bringing my brain back to life. Unfortunately, its functioning was unpredictable as it worked its way up the gears.

'But you killed my girlfriend's father and abducted her.'

His face clouded. 'I thought I told you that wasn't us?'

'But your men turned up at Tomoe's work the minute they were called.'

'Those men weren't Takata-gumi.'

'What do you mean? Who were they?'

'Clarence-san,' I wasn't sure where he'd found out my surname but I suppose it wasn't surprising considering they'd discovered my address. 'You haven't just been trampling over my territory; you've been making yourself an irritant to other people as well. You announced yourself with a bang. You've shaken things up.'

'But, but who, wh-what have I done?'

'The company your girlfriend worked for isn't in my portfolio – other parties have an interest in them. The reason you're here now, probably the reason you're still in one piece, is because I have a network that provides us with information on occasion, as it did in this case. We've been keeping an eye on you. Once we knew you'd escaped, we assumed you'd head back to your flat. As that is in my territory, we were able to get there first.'

I'd gone from being a nobody teacher no one knew, to a prospective yakuza with God knows how many gangsters after my life.

'But what's to stop them hurting me now?' My voice quivered. I couldn't face a Groundhog Day version of the last week. 'I'm not a gangster. I can't live like this.'

'Well, strictly speaking you will be a gangster soon,' said Takata. 'And actually, that's what's going to stop them. Anyone who comes after a Takata-gumi member faces repercussions.'

He gave a phlegmatic shrug.

'Although if they can get you without it being obvious they'll probably try.'

If he was attempting to reassure me he wasn't going about it in the best way.

'Fortunately, we operate a buddy system for our new joiners so you'll have the protection of a Takata-gumi member as well as its name.'

A gangster bodyguard. That did make me feel better.

'Anyway, I think that's all for now. Under the circumstances, I think it will be better to bring you on board sooner rather than later so we'll do the ceremony in the next couple of days. The boys will take care of you now.'

I was at the door before I realised I had one last question.

'Who's my buddy?'

SIXTEEN

'You know about *honne* and *tatamae*?'

'Yes, I do.'

He ignored me.

'We,' he began, using the word exclusively to separate Japanese from gaijin like me, 'we use honne to describe true feelings that we keep to ourselves – for example, if we hate the fact an arsehole is going to join an organisation we love. But we use tatamae as a front to the world, where we can pretend this person doesn't disgust us and everything's OK. And if we get drunk and tell the little faggot what a cocksucker he is, we can use it again the next day to pretend that we didn't.'

It was a different explanation to the one my Japanese teacher had given me. I smiled weakly and hoped he didn't get bored and decide to crush my skull to fill the time.

I was sat in a karaoke booth with Kurotaki who, it had turned out, was my 'buddy', although it seemed safe to assume this was only in a tatamae sense. I had tried to probe the wisdom of the pairing as gently as I could with Takata.

'You don't have to like him, and I'm afraid I have my doubts he's going to like you. But if you want to stay alive, he's the best man to keep you that way.'

It had been a culturally enlightening day. It's probably safe to say that very few Westerners have witnessed a yakuza joining ceremony and far fewer been part of one. The day had started with an early morning summons to the office by Kurotaki.

'Make sure you're dressed up nice.'

'I will do.'

'And make sure you do exactly as I told you.'

'I will.'

'You refer to him as Kumichō – boss – in the ceremony and whenever you speak to him, but you might hear him referred to as Oyabun – it's like father of the group – as well.'

'Understood. I promise, you don't need to worry. I'll do everything just the way you said.'

Kurotaki's face contorted, making him even uglier.

'Don't tell me what I do or don't need to worry about, you gaijin prick,' he exploded. 'I've been stuck with you, the most useless motherfucker ever, and from now on anything you do comes back to me. That means if you fuck up, it's like I've fucked up, and seeing as you're a useless fuck the chances of that are high. So I am going to worry and if I'm worried you should be too. That way you might fuck up less.'

I wasn't just worried I was terrified, even more so for what he'd just said. I didn't see how it was going to help.

'You do what I tell you when I tell you and show me respect. I might have to keep you alive but don't think I won't give you a beating.'

Life as a gangster. From what I remembered of *Goodfellas*, Henry Hill had joined the mafia for power and respect. I couldn't help thinking I'd been forced into the wrong mob.

'Why are we doing it at Kumichō's house? And why's he leading things? It's all wrong,' Kurotaki fretted to himself. He turned to me. 'You know it's never like this?'

'No, I don't. I've never done anything like it before.'

'Shut up. A new yakuza doesn't do the ceremony with Kumichō – they do it with the boss of a subgroup. And it doesn't happen at Kumichō's place.'

The whole thing was clearly unsettling him. It seemed a consolation of sorts to release his misgivings on me.

'Listen, you know-nothing prick, Kumichō is the boss of everything, he heads up the whole organisation – thousands of people. Nobodies like you, they don't talk to him. You'd need to move way up the ranks before you even get the chance to see him in the flesh. For someone at your level, speaking to him is like a cockroach getting an audience with God.'

I was getting the picture. I should be even more nervous and uncomfortable than I already was.

'Why he wants some dickhead gaijin . . .' he said, scanning me with a disgusted look. 'The shit we're going to get from the other gangs. You know they're already calling us the gaijin-gumi? And for what? What are you going to bring?'

He snorted in contempt.

'He must know what he's doing, there must be something he's got worked out for all of this.'

He looked me up and down again and sneered.

'But the shit we're going to take. Look at you. You're a fucking disgrace.'

I had no idea how to respond to this torrent of abuse from someone who scared me so completely. I stayed as I was.

'What the fuck are you standing around for? I told you how important this is. Get your shit together. Go on, fuck off.'

If I had to describe the polar opposite of Kurotaki it would have been someone like Takata's wife.

'Look at him,' she said, coming to greet me in the wood-lined entrance of their beautiful home. 'So handsome – like a Hollywood star.'

It was impossible not to warm to her. I thanked her as graciously as I could.

'What wonderful Japanese too.'

She turned to Takata.

'With gaikokujin like Clarence-san around, why have you only chosen to employ one now?'

Fussing over me, and I imagined quite contrary to decorum, she led me through the house and into a room with a long table laid for a meal. Cushions were set around it on the tatami floor, one for each guest. Just beyond its head sat a small shrine generously endowed with whole fish, vegetables and rice. Alongside them was a sake decanter and two unglazed cups.

'You sit here, *ne*,' she said, directing me to a spot near the top. 'You can get a view of the garden, for all its faults.'

Despite the invitation, I couldn't help thinking her dismissal of etiquette was a privilege accorded only to her. Instead of acting on it I waited for Takata and the other attendees to file in. I was given an almost imperceptible nod by Kurotaki in return.

Takata sat and waved everyone down, a collection of dark-suited, crew-cut, mean-looking men. And me: completely out of place and totally out of my depth.

There was no need to clink a glass. When Takata shifted the gruff murmurs immediately died down.

'I want to thank you all for coming at such short notice,' he began. 'I know it has been an inconvenience for some of you and I want you to know your efforts are greatly appreciated.'

The faces around the table gave nothing away.

'The next thing to say is I know this is unusual. Clarence-san arrived with us quite suddenly. He hasn't served an apprentice-ship and he hasn't gone through the normal rites. I understand you may have reservations about his lack of experience and quite rightly so. I'd like to explain and put your minds at rest, but unfortunately, I can't. There are things happening I can't expound upon yet.'

He looked around the table.

'So instead I must ask you to trust me, to hold on to whatever faith I've built with you over the years, and to believe me when I tell you he's going to be incredibly important to us. In return I give you a guarantee, a promise that you'll have cause to look happily upon this day before the year is out.'

Heads bowed to him as he scanned the table again. I wondered what they were really thinking, if any of this made more sense to them than it did to me. They certainly didn't look convinced.

'We have a slightly unusual situation in that it was me who

proposed Clarence-san. Fortunately, Kurotaki has kindly offered to act as guarantor.'

Kurotaki made an attempt to arrange his features in a way that suggested he'd volunteered.

'So unless there are any objections we'll move on to the ceremony itself.'

No one voiced the numerous objections coursing silently through the room.

I followed Takata to the shrine and we knelt in *seiza* opposite each other, our feet tucked under our legs. When Kurotaki and another brute-faced man were satisfied with the arrangement of dishes, they poured sake into the unglazed cups; Takata's near to the brim, mine much lower. Then they scraped some scales from the fish and sprinkled them in each.

With the preparations complete, Kurotaki handed Takata his cup. The other man held out mine. As prepped by Kurotaki I lifted it with both hands to my mouth after Takata had done the same.

'From now on, you have no other occupation until the day you die. Takata-sama, your oyabun, is your only parent. Follow him through fire and flood.'

I bowed my head and placed my cup in front of Takata. He put his in front of me. We picked up the other's and sipped again.

'Having drunk from the oyabun's cup and he from yours, you now owe loyalty to the *ikka*, your family, and devotion to your oyabun, your father. Even should your wife and children starve, even at the cost of your life, your duty is now to the ikka and your oyabun.'

And that was it. I was now a yakuza. Part of a select group of extortionists, murderers, people-traffickers, fraudsters, thieves, pimps and thugs. Bring a wife into this and then betray her for it? It seemed more likely I'd just signed up as a bachelor for life.

We rose and returned to the table just before the blood was lost permanently to my legs.

'Now, everyone: eat, drink,' said Takata. 'I hope you'll find it satisfactory.'

We got down to eating and drinking and the rising levels of noise and enthusiasm suggested it was up to scratch. This meant everyone was well lubricated by the time it was announced that some of us would be going to karaoke.

'Mm, my darling tell me when!'

You earn respect in Japanese karaoke from a good voice or enthusiastic participation. I was warmly received for the latter by an audience of drunken, boisterous yakuza and skimpily clad hostesses pouring drinks or pawing at their clients' chests.

When I started, Kurotaki had given a happy cry, grabbed the two closest girls and started swinging them like ragdolls in a drunken dance. He now discarded his partners and gave me a nod as I went back to my seat.

'Good choice. Humperdinck let his talent breathe more than Tom Jones.'

The 'breathability' of the singers' talents had had surprisingly little impact on my choice of song, but I sensed an opportunity to bond with my 'buddy', the guardian of my life.

'Er, yeah. You can't beat "Quando Quando Quando" for a party vibe.'

He continued to sway as a hostess sang Utada Hikaru's 'Automatic' surprisingly well. I sat down and tried to deflect the attentions of another as she attempted to clamber on me for a literal interpretation of a lap dance.

I'm not sure what I'd have done in normal circumstances. It's likely temptation would have convinced me that in the scheme of things a lap dance wasn't outrageously wrong. But with Tomoe missing and the memory of our parting still playing through my mind, it felt like betrayal, despite the agonising betrayals I'd discovered came before. So instead of provoking a desire to get even, my thoughts of her ensured any amorous urges were lost to the room's febrile air. I even felt a sense of relief when Kurotaki plonked himself down and swotted the girl away.

'I can train my dog to fetch my newspaper, but he's still a dog and I wouldn't let him fuck my wife.'

Having explained honne and tatamae, Kurotaki had moved on. This was his explanation for why he could enjoy foreign music but still see gaijin as inferior, unworthy and unwelcome in Japan.

'Fetching a newspaper and writing songs you like, inventing things you use – they're different. The argument doesn't hold.'

Retrospect showed this to be an unwise line of conversation but after twelve hours of drinking it had made sense at the time. I have a vague memory of thinking I might get through to him.

'All right then, what about you and the blacks?'

'What do you mean "me and the blacks"?'

'You like their music and you rip it off, sometimes very well. But you think they're at a lower level to you. That's why you discriminate against them.

'No, don't worry,' he said, cutting me off as I was about to erupt. 'I agree. It's just that for us you're one and the same.'

'That's absolute bullshit!' I exploded, the alcohol embolden-ing me. 'I don't see anyone as being on a lower level to me. Obviously, there's still racism in the West but you can't say every-one black is suppressed. Look at the last president of the United States.'

'He's not black.'

'What do you mean he's not black?'

'His mother, what race was she?'

'I'm not sure. I know one of his parents was white.'

'Which means he's as much white as he's black.'

'I suppose you could say that.'

'So why don't you? You don't like someone with negroid features even if he's got as much right to be called white as black? What, you find his hair too curly, is that it, is that what causes you offence? You're just like the Boers in apartheid.'

I stared at him open-mouthed.

'You know what they'd do? They'd stick a pencil through the hair of someone they couldn't classify. If it fell out they were white, if it stayed in they were black.'

He picked up a chopstick.

'Come to think of it, Matsumoto has very dark skin.'

He turned around to a man I assumed was Matsumoto, who at that moment was sitting in a booth with his back to us as a near-naked girl writhed on his lap. Kurotaki stuck the chopstick through the back of his thickly styled hair. It stayed.

'Hey, Africa-san!'

'Africa-san' was still not aware of the conversation or the fact there was a chopstick in the back of his head. He was preoccupied with other concerns on his lap. Not to be defeated, Kurotaki

137

grabbed its mate, leaned around Matsumoto and prodded it in his cheek.

'Hey, Africa-san. We've just given you a race test. It turns out you're black.'

At this point, Matsumoto became very aware of what was going on around him. He roared and sprang to his feet, propelling his dancer across the booth into another doing her dancing with her mouth. There was a scream from her client, higher-pitched than you'd expect from such a burly man. But I didn't see what happened after. My view was blocked by Kurotaki's head as it cracked into my face, presumably the result of a punch.

He struggled up from where I'd cushioned his fall and drove back into the crowd. The room was soon a writhing mass of brawling yakuza, splintered furniture and hostesses fleeing the scene. I felt someone lift me by the arms. I looked up to see the deep-voiced gangster I'd learned was called Sumida ushering me to the door.

'Welcome to the yakuza,' he said.

PART TWO

ONE

'So, you had a good time the other night?' Takata asked. 'It certainly looks like it.'

I assumed he was referring to the colourful array of bruises offered up by the others. My own facial rainbow was mainly the result of prior events.

'Yes, it was very interesting,' I said, bowing. 'Thank you very much.'

He waved my appreciation away.

'You certainly have a knack for making things happen around you,' he said, looking like he was working through the end of a chess game I'd yet to start.

His voice became businesslike again.

'But anyway, I want to talk to you about what you'll be doing for us.'

I'd been dreading the moment. My hungover anxiety only made me feel worse.

'As I mentioned previously, you're not much use to us in our traditional activities. I need you to work on a side project instead. We don't have anyone else on it but if you need support at any time just let Kurotaki know. He'll either help you himself or press the right buttons to ensure someone else does.'

The thought of Kurotaki 'pushing buttons' made my stomach go tight.

'Understood,' I said. 'I'm sorry, but could I ask exactly what it is you want me to do?'

'Energy. We're taking an interest in the energy industry. I need you to head an NGO we've set up.'

I stared at him blankly. I knew nothing about energy.

'Thank you, I'll do my very best. But I should probably point out I'm not vastly experienced in the field. Are you certain you want me to lead it? Perhaps I'd be better providing support?'

'No, you're going to lead it. So if you don't have the requisite knowledge I'd suggest you acquire it quickly. Like I said, we can get you the very best help. You need to be proactive and make use of it.'

At the ceremony, Takata had suggested I was going to be at the centre of a transformational event. I was deeply concerned about how I could conjure it from this. For if I failed – as I had no doubt I would – my prospects seemed dim. The rest of my skillset had already been considered and dismissed.

'I'll do my very best,' I said again with a bow, while every curse I knew ran through my head.

'You're to start with nuclear,' Takata went on. 'I want you to get a good understanding – you'll need to know about its development, its pros and cons, major events, that sort of thing. That's the generic part. I then want you to look at its history in Japan, the when, where, why and so on. Who's been involved, who's still involved, what are the stories, what's behind them, who's been steering them and why. The KanEnCo AGM is in a fortnight's time. I want you prepped and ready by then.'

I kept my face a perfect mask to conceal the panic rising inside me. Two weeks to go from knowing nothing to sticking my oar in at an energy conglomerate's AGM?

'You look concerned, Clarence-san,' he said. 'Don't be – this is an opportunity.'

'Thank you. I'll do everything in my ability to take it.'

'I'm sure you will. Like I said, don't worry. Do as I tell you and do the best that you can. Everything else will fall into place.'

I nodded, trying to look upbeat and proactive.

'You never know. It might even help you find your girlfriend.'

That got my attention.

'Tomoe's disappearance is related to nuclear power?' I asked, failing to see any connection.

'Not directly. But sometimes the players in one game get involved in another. Before you know it, pieces start tumbling all around. When that happens some fall down that should have stayed up.'

I tried to return his look with one that didn't reveal this was too cryptic for me.

'If I look into the energy industry, I'll get close to the people who pushed the first piece?'

'There is that chance.'

A cryptic chance was better than none.

After an afternoon spent trying to develop some expertise, I started to wonder whether death would be preferable to nuclear research – science was never my thing. I decided the AGM wouldn't end up as a debate on physics and changed tack to look at the industry's Japanese history instead.

Initiated just nine years after Hiroshima and Nagasaki, Japan's nuclear power industry had had its share of controversy from the start. The Fukushima disaster meant the entire nuclear sector was facing calls to be shut down. It seemed unlikely Tomoe's abduction was related to these events so I decided to look at others in-between. I was surprised to find a litany of near-catastrophes and cover-ups that combined the corruption and incompetence of a banana republic and the transparency of a Soviet regime. One scandal in particular caught my eye. The Kamigawa reactor.

Commissioned in 2003, it had suffered a scare almost immediately when an earthquake measuring 7.5 on the Richter scale occurred just miles offshore. This was a problem. The reactor had only been designed to withstand shocks of up to 5.5 as it was built in an area that wasn't thought to be on a major fault.

KanEnCo ran the reactor and their readings showed the earthquake had only measured 5.5 in its grounds – something particularly fortuitous given its maximum resistance and the fact all other local readings had it at 7. Their post-shock investigation concluded the plant had withstood the earthquake without ill-effect. The national inspection agency concurred and normal service quickly resumed.

However, the story didn't end there. The first sign of trouble came when reports emerged that two workers had been rushed to hospital on the quiet. This led to the first postscript. It turned out a number of barrels containing radioactive material had been upturned during the quake. The workers had endeavoured to repair the damage but they were poorly trained and didn't take the precautions necessary to safeguard their health. They died within a month.

Then came stories that radioactive water was leaking from the site. These were first denied and then admitted, with the caveat that readings were so low they didn't warrant concern. But offshore tests by an environmental group forced the plant to admit contamination was at multiples of safe levels and far more water had escaped than first thought.

With the situation unravelling, the plant shut suddenly for 'planned maintenance' and remained closed for a year. At this point, the inspection agency, the one that had passed it previously, gave a new, glowing report and activity resumed once more.

Shocking as it was, this was the fifth scandal I'd read that day and it seemed pretty much par for the course: a pattern of negligence, leading to incidents, followed by cover-ups and lies. But at this point the story veered in a different direction.

Within a few years, rates of childhood leukaemia suddenly spiked. Distressed parents wanted to know the cause of their children's plights. They looked to the plant for answers but received an unenthusiastic response. After six months' silence, the plant abruptly changed tack and the president agreed to meet. He presented reams of data that proved the barrel incident's effects were restricted to one room and the water leaks had not affected the local supply. Beyond that there had been no damage and the surrounding area had borne no ill-effects. He expounded on other possible causes – a mobile-phone antenna in the area and a recently banned fertiliser that had been used in local farms.

The parents remained suspicious but they were compelled to look into the alternatives. At least until a leaked report blew the president's story apart. It revealed there had been damage to two reactor buildings. This had resulted in significant radioactive emissions in the weeks after the quake – the weeks the company had declared the plant safe and resumed operations.

Predictably, the parents were livid but they responded in a most unpredictable way. On the premise of delivering a letter of protest they were granted entry to the plant. They proceeded to force their way into the president's office and dissuaded security from following them by holding a knife to his throat. When a negotiator doubted their conviction they sliced off a piece of the president's ear.

Then, in the ultimate act of protest, one of the parents committed seppuku, the ritual act of suicide that mostly died out with the Meiji Restoration in 1868. It took an astonishing amount of bravery even in the days of the samurai, when there were world-renowned swords for the incision and, when the agony became too much, a second to slice off your head. A sushi knife and the time it took to bleed out were all the protestor had.

I turned from the report when confronted with this. I'd always been impressed by Fathers4Justice scaling landmarks dressed as superheroes in order to make their point. Their audacity suddenly seemed meek.

Until this time, the press had been strangely quiet. But the kidnap and maiming of a plant president, followed by the self-administered gutting of a small-town accountant, made it a story that was impossible to ignore.

Pressure mounted until both the plant and KanEnCo presidents resigned. Yet this wasn't the same as accepting liability. They stood down 'because of unfortunate circumstance and errors that resulted in the regrettable communication of information not wholly accurate'. The company still denied responsibility and the pace of the Japanese legal system meant a ruling would be at least a decade away, the final decision after appeals, most likely two.

So the parents came at them from a different angle. Collectively they bought single shares in KanEnCo, a move that granted them entry to the shareholders' meeting. Blindsided, the board was berated and humiliated for over an hour.

This finally led KanEnCo to action, but not the action the parents' group had hoped. Suddenly they started to fall victim to more 'unfortunate circumstances'. One parent was maimed in a hit-and-run, another mugged and beaten close to death. They suffered random vandalism – bricks through windows, faeces in letterboxes. They were trailed by footsteps as they walked home at night. Still they persevered.

The next year's AGM was different. This time fewer protestors got in – the meeting was already near full, despite their having been at the gates before it began. Once inside they realised why. A collection of hard-faced men, not dissimilar to those who had been harassing them, were already there. The infamous *sōkaiya*.

The sōkaiya were a side-shoot of the yakuza who specialised in industry shakedowns. They demanded money of Japanese corporations against the threat their AGMs would be disrupted or embarrassing information leaked. Conversely, they could be used by companies to have dissenting voices drowned out. There was hardly a major company not caught in their web.

This sōkaiya was linked to the Takata-gumi.

I stopped reading. Takata would have known I would come across this. I wondered why he'd direct me to a scandal that led back to him. It didn't make sense, and from what little I knew of him that was out of character. Puzzled, I went back to the reports.

At the next AGM, the protestors were immediately drowned out in a torrent of threats and abuse. The meeting was suspended when a protestor responded to a sōkaiya who promptly broke his nose with a punch. Other sōkaiya waded in, security intervened and the board ended the meeting 'regrettably early'. They issued a bland statement that looked forward to a more successful one the following year.

How they qualified success wasn't made clear. But the next year the sōkaiya didn't even wait for the protestors to speak. The meeting ended after just three minutes, an AGM record in Japan. That brought things to the present day.

I sat back. This had to be what I was looking for but I could see no connection to Tomoe and even less to myself.

What, who and why? That's what Takata had said.

The 'what' appeared clear to a point, barring any further twists. Something crooked had happened at the Kamigawa Plant and Takata had got involved, either right at the beginning or when the escalating troubles alerted him to an opportunity.

The 'who' didn't seem much more challenging – there was Takata and then the KanEnCo board and the Kamigawa Plant president, whose actions suggested guilt. But I didn't think Takata would set such a clear line of breadcrumbs to a destination so easy to find. That meant it was unlikely things ended with them. I'd need to find who was lurking in the background. Once I had their names the 'why' would hopefully become clear.

I recapped the players. A gangster – Takata – and a corporate man – I decided to go with the KanEnCo president as the Kamigawa Plant boss reported to him. They were major figures. If anyone was orchestrating events behind them he would have to wield considerable clout. Who could complete the unholy trinity – a gangster, a businessman and . . . ?

I googled 'politician' and 'KanEnCo' and he came up top of the list. The energy minister. He'd recently assumed the post after a year's enforced break from cabinet for accepting bribes –

it wasn't entirely untypical for a political career in Japan.

I considered it. He was clearly capable of involvement and he was certainly in the right job. But it didn't sit right. This had all begun before he was in office and he'd shown no signs of any manoeuvring to date – the plant inspections may have been a whitewash but the painters appeared to come from within the regulatory body itself. The only thing that might have fingered him was if he had a financial interest in the affair.

My problem was I had no way to find out. The resources of the internet might be almost without limit but my technical ability didn't match up. And without hacking into the minister's bank account I couldn't think of a way of discovering his possible stake. Unless . . .

'He's not in,' said a gruff voice.

'Do you know when he's going to be back? Should I try the Ginza office?'

'No. I'll make sure he knows you called. If he wants to talk to you he'll call back.'

The phone went dead.

Rather than have me spend hours ferreting for old information, it would have made more sense for Takata to tell me what he already knew. I could then search for what was still to be found out. As this logical course of action was so clearly out of the question, I decided to be proactive instead. I doubted the politician would be keen to grant an interview, but I was sure others would be happy to have an international voice take an interest.

'We've been incredibly lucky – Eriko has been in remission a year. It's been far harder for some of the others. There've been two funerals just this month.'

I cringed. I couldn't be certain which side I'd land on in this affair but the initial signs weren't good. Lying to someone so harshly affected made me feel like I'd reached a new low.

I was in a small town far removed from the bright lights and bustle of Tokyo. Eriko's parents clearly took pride in their home but an apartment that compact inevitably felt cluttered, even with only household necessities and a few children's toys.

'I'm so sorry. The whole thing's horrific. I hope you get the justice you deserve.'

'That's kind of you to say,' she said and touched my arm. 'I hope the details haven't upset you too much.'

I needed to move the conversation along before my self-loathing became too much to bear.

'Can you tell me what you think's behind it? I mean, was it a catalogue of errors and botched cover-ups, or do you think there's a bigger conspiracy at play?'

I'd been welcomed to ask questions like this because, as I explained to the local journalist who put me in touch, I worked for Energy Without Affect, consultants for a fossil-free future. We were reviewing the best and worst alternatives throughout the world. The parents' group could put forward a case for why nuclear should be included in the latter.

'I'm sorry, but I can't answer that – it's a question we're still asking,' she said. 'It could be that it was just another KanEnCo incident, and for the most part these have been down to incompetence rather than anything else.

'They assumed there wouldn't be an earthquake here and scrimped instead of spending money preparing for the worst. When it went wrong they panicked. They didn't want to be blamed. They thought if they kept the plant running and made repairs when the attention was off them, everything would turn out all right. But events spiralled beyond their control. They're getting nasty because they're scared. They don't know what else to do.'

It was a very balanced account from someone who had been going through hell.

'But . . .'

I looked at her. 'You're not convinced?'

'Something feels strange,' she said. 'It feels like there's something else, something still to be found out. But I just don't know what it is.'

Although she must have become practised at masking her emotions I could see it was a thought that had been consuming her for years.

'Is there anything in particular that's made you suspicious?'

'A million things. There are so many rumours, so many possibilities. It's enough to drive you mad.'

She broke off. I desperately hoped I'd end up on her side.

'One of them goes back to when they were planning the plant, in the early nineties, before my husband and I moved here. As you'd expect, there were all sorts of studies and surveys to make sure the area was right. There are stories they found something then, that there was something funny about the process, something wrong with the project from the very start.'

She gripped the handle of her cup so tightly her knuckles went white.

'But that's it – a rumour. And one that doesn't have details let alone proof. It's not exactly the breakthrough we need.'

It wasn't. But it was something, and if Takata was true to his word, I'd be able to find out what it was.

TWO

'Dickhead. What do you think you're doing playing detective without keeping us informed?'

I'd only got a few stops into the journey home before my phone rang. Kurotaki.

'Kumichō told me to look into things, to be proactive. That's what I'm doing. If you don't like it you need to take it up with him.'

My irritation at being denied the promised support was mixed with guilt at my snooping and made me more strident than was probably wise.

'You motherfucker! You're bold over the phone, aren't you? I'll—'

'I was just doing what I was told,' I said hurriedly. 'I tried to speak to Kumichō but he didn't take my call.'

'You little bitch! What did I tell you about Kumichō? You don't deserve to have him know you're alive. You don't call him up like a schoolgirl when you're in the mood for a chat.'

'OK, I'm sorry.'

'You need something on this, you get in touch with me. If you can't reach me, call Sumida.'

'OK, OK, I will,' I said, my annoyance surfacing again.

'Don't give me attitude, you stupid fuck. You still don't get it, do you? This isn't just to help you. There are people who want to kill you and I've been told to keep you alive.'

I smartened up with the reminder.

'I'm sorry. Really, I will. But in this case I'm not sure it would have been a great idea to have you along.'

Kurotaki acknowledged the point with a grunt. 'We still could have accompanied you down, kept eyes on you there.'

'It seems like you had plenty doing that already.'

'You know what I mean. Next time you want to do something get in touch first.'

I decided to put his word to the test.

'OK, the next time's now. I need to see the ex-president of the Kamigawa plant.'

I reasoned that if there was a conspiracy it could be revealed either by something he could tell me or information hidden in the documentation of the site.

'When?'

'As soon as I can. There isn't much time until the AGM.'

'OK – he'll see you tomorrow. Be at our office at eight.'

'Don't you need to check with him first?'

'Don't question me. Get to the office first thing.'

He hung up. I settled back in my seat and started to doze. My phone rang again, drawing more dirty looks.

'Where the fuck are you?' demanded Sumida.

I was starting to yearn for the days before mobiles.

'I'm on a train.'

'What are you doing on a train? You're meant to be at Horitoku's.'

'What's Horitokus?'

'He's a person. A *horishi*.'

He sounded exasperated. I didn't feel much different.

'What's a horishi?'

'A tattoo master,' he said impatiently. 'Where are you? I'll pick you up.'

'Wait a minute. Why am I going to a tattoo master?'

'You're getting a tattoo.'

'Hold on, if I want a tattoo, I'll get a tattoo. If someone else wants me to get one they can discuss its merits with me first. You don't just arrange it and not even tell me until after the time it's meant to start. It's—' I was lost for words. 'It's just not what you do.'

'Are you finished?' he asked, having paid no attention.

'What?'

'Good. Now shut up and tell me where you are.'

I glanced at Sumida while he drove, the first time I'd paid him proper attention. This was significant in itself – despite being distinctive he somehow went under the radar. He wasn't huge like Kurotaki but at over six foot and broad he was still large for a Japanese man. He carried his bulk athletically, with lithe movements like those of a cat. He didn't have the yakuza crew cut either; his hair was long and bundled on top of his head. Not that this was in any way effeminate – he looked like a Chinese outlaw from centuries past.

I realised my mind was wandering. There were more important matters at hand.

'Why am I getting a tattoo?'

'The boss wants you to.'

'Yes, but why does he want me to?'

'He likes tattoos. You're a yakuza. Yakuza get tattoos.'

Sumida wasn't hugely communicative; perhaps his voice required an output of energy that couldn't be wasted on chit-chat. He was, however, the most intriguing yakuza I'd met. While the others were loud bravado and crudity he kept his counsel, the Michael Corleone to all the Sonnys running around.

'I have to get one?'

'Yeah.'

Perhaps taking pity on me he offered a tit-bit.

'Keep the receipts.'

'What?'

'Make sure you get a receipt.'

'A receipt?'

'Yes,' he said patiently. 'They're tax-deductible as a business expense.'

'Wait a minute – I have to pay? I don't even want one.'

'Whatever. Just remember, they're expensive and it's worth claiming back the tax.'

Curiosity got the better of my outrage.

'How do I do that? Put down I'm the first, unwilling, English yakuza and I'm being forced to pay for a tattoo I don't want as an essential part of my work?'

'I wouldn't phrase it exactly like that in your returns, but essentially yes.'

I was flabbergasted. I tried to think of an analogy.

'It's like a burglar claiming for a ladder after he's robbed a house.'

He took his eyes from the road.

'It's not like that at all. Things have gotten trickier recently but we're still a legal entity. It's perfectly reasonable to claim expenses on the legitimate things we do. I've heard some mizu shōbai clubs have even tried to claim on protection money.'

'And they got it?'

'I don't know,' he replied. 'I can't think their chances were great, but apparently they gave it a go. Anyway, make sure you keep the receipts.'

Asakusa had retained the buzz it had had the last time I lived in Tokyo. Even streets that had seemed rundown and tired now thronged. Small stores grilled *senbei*, rice crackers, out front while their neighbours hawked ceramics, knives, kimonos and other traditional goods. Kabuki stars peered down from lamp-post placards, suggesting here at least they had retained their allure. Altogether it felt as though Asakusa had left the rest of Tokyo to look to the future. Its eyes remained on its Edo-period halcyon days when it had been the entertainment centre of Japan.

Sumida parked the car and we walked through the narrow, bustling streets, the covered ones in particular creating the mood of a bazaar. After making our way from the centre into quieter roads, we stopped in front of a residential block. It was typical of Tokyo's more functional kind, the type that makes one question whether an architect was ever involved.

Its lift battled our weight to the seventh floor.

'Konnichiwa.'

A man in his early twenties was waiting for us. He bowed politely. Sumida barely lowered his head in return.

'Please, follow me.'

As he took us down the hall I wondered again at the transformational effect of Tokyo doorways, the worlds they let you into so often at odds with the utilitarian visions outside.

The walls of the apartment's front room were crowded with photos. I leaned forward to look more closely at one of a sepia-tinted old man who I presumed was Horitoku's master. He was stripped to a *fundoshi*, loincloth, his body an intricate swirl of tattoos.

Impressive as he was, he paled beside the colour pictures around him. There were dragons writhing on skin, more realistic than the legends on which they were based; samurai and outlaws poised to attack, bursting with life after centuries in slumber; phoenixes prepared for fiery comebacks; deities as menacing as their hosts; and courtesans so beautiful they almost compensated for these men.

Displays of virtuosity that were more like special effects than tattoos.

They also seemed very big.

'I don't have to cover my whole body, do I?' I whispered to Sumida.

'Shut up.'

The young man, presumably an apprentice to the master, had just returned with Horitoku.

'Sensei, konnichiwa.'

Now Sumida bowed, and bowed deeply. I followed suit. We received a greeting that was polite but less formal.

'Please excuse us for being late,' said Sumida. 'We will of course pay for the time.'

I stiffened.

'But could I request we extend the appointment? My oyabun is keen for Ray to make good progress with his tattoo.'

Horitoku agreed and they indulged in some pleasantries, Sumida continuing to speak formally, Horitoku replying with the relaxed Japanese a superior is allowed. They briefly discussed the tattoo Sumida was apparently receiving.

'So, did you have something in mind?'

Horitoku had turned to me. He was quite short but had a reassuring solidity and a dapper pencil moustache. His civility and self-assurance made me feel more comfortable than I probably should have.

'I'm not quite sure yet,' I replied – I didn't see any benefit in revealing how I had been coerced at the last minute into being there. 'Would it be possible to look at your work first?'

Horitoku's apprentice was already scuttling for photo albums and folders of illustrations. I looked through them in awe. They were even more magnificent than the ones on the wall. As the designs danced on the flat of the page, I could only begin to imagine how they looked on a moving figure.

A dragon wriggled towards me. It wasn't clear what he was meant to represent. He might have been leering as there was certainly something sinister about him. But it was impossible to be sure of his intentions, as though layers of complexity lay behind the dangerous facade. It seemed appropriate.

'I like this one.'

I turned a couple of pages to see a geisha, or perhaps it was a courtesan. I looked closer and did a double take. It had to be a courtesan, whatever their differences in dress. I knew this because it was Tomoe. Her grace, her charm, somehow even her sparkle had been captured on this illustration prepared for an unknowing recipient's skin.

'And this,' I said, my mood turning melancholy at the coincidence.

Except it proved a lot less coincidental than I thought. A few pages later I saw it; the black fox, dancing and snapping around her ankle. Protecting her, she'd said. I wondered again if I was too late to take its place.

'Where did you get this picture?'

'I took it.'

'You knew my girlfriend?'

'I know her,' he corrected. 'Yes.'

'How do you know her?' I asked, wondering what more of her I hadn't known.

'We can talk about that while I work. Is there a design you want?'

'Yes. The dragon, Tomoe, and her fox.'

He fixed me with a stern look.

'*Horimono*, Japanese tattooing, doesn't work like that. There are rules.'

'I'm sorry, I didn't know. How does it work?'

'You choose a design, and assuming I think it's appropriate, I create it on you. It's not a pick and mix.'

A new turn-up in a week of surprises. I didn't want to be culturally insensitive but if I was going to be tattooed against my wishes, I thought I should at least have a say in what my permanent marking would be. As I pondered how to express this to a man Sumida literally bowed before, Horitoku spoke again.

'The reasons for the courtesan and the fox are clear. Why do you want the dragon?'

'It's a little complicated. It has some relevance to my recent experiences and one or two present threats.'

'Threats? You know dragons usually have protective associations or represent good luck?'

It was yet another thing I didn't know. For me, they represented fire-breathing danger and fodder for Saint George.

'Weren't there some dangerous ones as well?'

There must have been because he concurred, albeit with a little reluctance.

'It's not the way it's normally done, but I suppose you're not a normal customer,' he said, as much to himself as to me. 'Maybe it's worth trying something a bit different this time. It would be nice for your girlfriend too.'

I kept quiet as he mulled the breach in protocol.

'OK, if that's how you'd like it,' he said eventually. 'But I'm going to add a firefox as well. That will be her protection for you.'

I wasn't sure how that worked, but the way things were I'd take whatever help I could get.

'Please,' he directed me towards a towel-draped foam mattress laid out on the tatami floor. 'I have to get the stencils but then we're ready to start.'

'We don't need to discuss it further?'

'No. From now on you just lie down.'

Despite my reservations, I had faith he knew what I wanted better than I did. He probably didn't, but I needed someone I could lean on, someone to trust.

*

'But of course I know her,' he said, not acknowledging the sharp intake of breath and the stiffening of my body as the needles first struck. 'We're both of the *ukiyo*, the floating world.'

'What do you mean?'

I managed to get the question out only after biting back a yelp. Talking wasn't made any easier by the fact I was laid out on my front, my chin and forehead propped up on foam blocks to create the best line for my back.

'Ukiyo-e. Pictures of the floating world. She's a master of paper; I'm an artisan on skin. Of course we met,' he said, as though it was the most natural thing.

'But don't you mainly tattoo yakuza?'

I wasn't an expert in horimono, but I knew anyone with traditional tattoos in Japan was assumed to be a gangster.

'It was like that for a while but not any more. The crackdowns mean many want to be inconspicuous and the recession's affected them too. The oyabuns don't pay nowadays and the junior ranks don't have the money to front up.'

He shifted slightly to improve the angle for his attack. The temporary relief only shifted my focus from pain to the overall situation – the enormity of the thought my body was being permanently changed with something I had no desire to have.

'But just because our clientele have sometimes been rough at the edges, that doesn't make it any less of an art. Horimono go back to the early 1800s. Hokusai helped make them popular and it was a series of tattooed outlaws by Kuniyoshi that made them really take off. Kuniyoshi wasn't satisfied just with woodblock prints either. He created designs for horishi and was even tattooed himself.

'So, you see, ukiyo-e and horimono are one and the same. They've been hand-in-hand from the start.'

'I had no idea they had such a grand heritage.'

'Don't get me wrong, it was always a bit rebellious but it was legal, a badge of honour for the Edo-period working class. It was the Meiji government who made it a crime – they were scared foreigners would think it barbaric. After that, you had to break the law to get one and that put some people off. The stigma remained even when the Americans legalised it post-war.'

He said all this above the noise of the tattoo machine that was making a disconcerting whine behind my head. It pitched slightly higher when moving between me and a thimble of black ink at my side, then buzzed with the anger of a hornet when the needle was driven into my skin.

In less sensitive areas it felt like someone had jabbed me with a toothpick and was dragging it sadistically across my back. In other places it felt like a probe had been attached to my nervous system, sending my body rigid other than the uncontrollable twitching of my toes.

Horitoku was entirely oblivious to the effect.

'The yakuza connection only came about because of the gangster movies in the sixties. They always had a chivalrous hero strip down to battle his adversaries at the end. People didn't associate horimono with yakuza before then, but afterwards it was the first thing they thought.

'It turned out the yakuza loved all of this and the numbers getting tattooed absolutely boomed. Now, I'm not going to complain about the people who pay me, but if you want to identify when horimono's image problems started, you need look no further than then.

'It was never just about them though,' he added. 'Firemen, artisans, tradesmen and geisha all have traditions of getting horimono. They kept coming too.'

He stopped talking as one area seemed to require a particularly keen focus, as though he was not just inserting ink but trying to drill down to the bone.

'There are many cultured minds who've supported us. Like your girlfriend. That's why I gave her her tattoo.'

He paused from his needle torture momentarily, giving me the opportunity to respond.

'Why was the fox her protector? She never told me.'

Come to think of it, I'd never asked. I'd just thought it looked incredibly cool.

'It was the *kami*, the deity, of Yoshiwara,' he said. 'Katsuyama-chan wanted a protector just as her predecessors had.'

He delivered this information as though it were matter-of-fact.

'What – who?'

'Katsuyama,' he said. 'You know about the original Katsuyama?

'No.'

'Katsuyama was the first great tayū of Yoshiwara. Yoshiwara was one of the three main pleasure quarters of Edo Japan.'

The last part I knew. It was everything he had said before it that had me confused.

'Initially, the courtesans of Kyoto and Osaka were considered the greatest, the most refined. Katsuyama was the first to turn eyes to Yoshiwara.

'She wasn't even a courtesan originally. She was a bathhouse girl, an entertainer in the competition outside Yoshiwara's walls. But she was so beautiful, so charismatic, that people came from all over to see her. Her whims and fancies would spark fashions and start artistic trends.'

He wiped at something I hoped was excess ink rather than blood running down my side.

'But the bathhouses weren't popular with the bordello owners. They weren't strictly legal so the authorities didn't care much for them either. One day, there was an almighty ruckus at Katsuyama's bathhouse and they took the opportunity to close them all down.

'Katsuyama's stock was so high by then that The Great Miura, the most prestigious of all the Yoshiwara houses, took her on as a tayū. It was unheard of for someone to be promoted straight to the highest rank.'

Something had been nagging since I'd spoken to Tomoe.

'Weren't they were called *oiran*?'

'Oiran were a lower grade of courtesan that came later. They came to prominence when standards dropped and the tayūs faded away. They're the ones you see most often in the prints.

'Anyway, when Katsuyama made her entrance everyone came out to watch. Even the other tayūs stepped onto their balconies, convinced she would embarrass herself or at least secretly hoping she would. But she raised a storm.

'At the time, courtesans often wore their hair down. Katsuyama bound hers up with a white ribbon and the fashionable ladies of the day immediately took on the style. It's still named after her now. Careful!'

He made this last comment because I'd turned my head.

'Yes, your Katsuyama paid homage to it but there was more to her than that. You know Japanese arts often have succession names? You've got the Utagawa line in ukiyo-e, the Danjūrōs in kabuki, the names of the sumō stablemasters. It was the same for courtesans. But in over three hundred years there wasn't anyone to live up to the name Katsuyama. Ka-chan was the first.'

I wondered how many people were intimate enough to call my girlfriend by the affectionate 'chan'. My stomach tightened as I wondered if Horitoku had been more than a friend.

'What happened to the original Katsuyama?' I asked, partly to take my mind from the thought but also in case there were any clues.

'Well, for the good there was in Yoshiwara there was also bad – the courtesans were indentured and that isn't anyone's idea of fun. But Katsuyama was different. She came to Yoshiwara on her own terms and somehow dictated when she'd get out. No one knows what happened to her, but three years after she first graced Old Yoshiwara she was gone.'

It was a nice story. Unfortunately, it wasn't much help.

'And what do you know about Tomoe, or Katsuyama II?'

'I know that when they decided to resurrect the tayūs, they searched the length and breadth of the country and found the most beautiful and cultured women in Japan. And that even then Ka-chan stood head and shoulders above the rest.'

It was touching – if I closed my mind to their activities beyond the arts – but it wasn't exactly what I meant.

'What do you know about where she might be now?'

He stopped abusing my back for a moment.

'I'd love to be able to help you. I'd do anything if I knew where she was or there was a way I could find out. But I've told you all I know. I saw her three months ago at an ukiyo-e exhibition and I haven't seen or heard from her since.'

*

'OK, that's the outline done,' he said, getting up and stretching. 'We'll start on the shading next time.'

'That's it – just the back?' I asked, pleased the assault was over but feeling sore and strangely tired.

'You can get more done if you like but your boss wanted something started quickly. So we'll begin with the back and you can take it further from there.'

'No, no, that's OK. The back's great,' I said, relieved, although a part of me was disappointed I wouldn't be totally transformed as the men in the pictures had been.

'You'll get a slight fever and you're going to be tender for a few days. Take plenty of showers and put on a bit of lotion to stop it drying up. I'll see you at your next appointment.'

I almost took my cue to leave but I couldn't help myself. As much as I liked him and had strangely enjoyed the preceding hours, the thought had been gnawing at my insides.

'Tomoe, you, er . . . ?'

He regarded me for a moment and then saw where I was going.

'No, our relationship wasn't like that.' The rebuke was clear in his voice. 'We were fellow artists, we admired one another, but our relationship was professional. Any feelings beyond that were like those of a father and daughter.'

'Of course, I'm sorry – my mind's all over the place. I shouldn't even have asked,' I said, delighted that I had. 'See you next time.'

I was surprised to bump into Sumida having a cigarette by a no-smoking sign outside.

'You didn't have to wait for me – I'm good to get home on the train.'

'I don't think so,' he said as we walked towards the car. 'You're a valuable commodity and anywhere there's a risk – like at a horishi's slap-bang in an area notorious for yakuza – you're to be accompanied. So anyway, what did you get?'

I explained, only to find that he'd stopped.

'You told him to change his designs?'

'No, I just asked him to combine a couple.'

'And he didn't throw you out?'

'I was very polite about it.'

He shook his head and started walking again. 'You've got a thing for trouble, don't you?'

He continued before I could protest.

'He's a cultured man but you need to watch your step – Horitoku Sensei's scarier than most yakuza. For my first three years he didn't even speak to me. I'd go in, wait for him to wave me over and then lie down so he could work. To him I was just a canvas paying for the privilege of his art. And don't think I complained. He's close to Kumichō – he did his bodysuit way back. You don't mess with Horitoku Sensei. I've heard some scary stuff.'

Before he could explain why I should be terrified of the first person I'd met recently who I thought might be kind, we got to his car. It was a dark blue Nissan Teana without darkened windows, pimped-up alloys or any other ostentation, which made it entirely unlike the average mid-ranking yakuza's car.

'What is it that makes me a valuable commodity?' I asked, returning to Sumida's original point. 'I don't want to undersell myself, but I can't think of any way I'd be of use to the Takata-gumi.'

'You won't get many arguments on that. There must be something for Kumichō to take you on-board but for the rest of us you're just a pain in the arse. No offence.'

I was offended. I'd been trying to keep my head down precisely to avoid pissing off a group of scary gangsters.

'But I've hardly even been to the office. Apart from you giving me a lift today, I haven't been much trouble have I?'

'It's not you personally, it's what you represent. You know about the situation with the Ginzo-kai?'

'Who?'

He looked at me to see if I was being serious.

'Shit, you really don't know anything.' He shook his head. 'The Ginzo-kai are the biggest yakuza group in the country.'

'I thought that was us?'

'No, we're the biggest in Tokyo and eastern Japan. The Ginzo-kai were founded in Kobe, but about ten years ago they decided they wanted to expand east. It didn't go down too well with us or the other gangs.'

'Surely you could just kick them out?'

'That would be a great idea if they weren't nearly thirty thousand strong. There've been a lot of clashes but they're too big to simply boot out.'

'So what's the situation now?'

'They have bases in Tokyo, and while we don't get along, we coexist. You've got to realise there's been a lot of pressure from the law-makers in the last five years. If we have an all-out war everyone suffers.'

'But what's any of this got to do with me?'

'They're the ones that tried to get you. They're the ones we're protecting you from.'

This was getting ridiculous. I was insignificant, a very average English teacher. I hadn't even been worthy of my girlfriend. How could I be a central figure in the battle between Japan's two biggest gangs?

'But I'm Takata-gumi now. We have to coexist, you said.'

'You're right, but for whatever reason they seem keen to get hold of you and it looks like they'd been willing to suffer some disharmony for that.'

I didn't like the way that sounded.

'But you're just the tip of the iceberg,' he continued. 'Because of you things have got more tense and that's uncomfortable for everyone. But it was bad even before you turned up. Until this year the Ginzo-kai had been sticking to the spots they had but recently they've been encroaching on our turf. For some reason, instead of dealing with them, Kumichō's been holding us back. That kind of thing makes people restless and then you come along – not much fucking good for anything as you put it—'

'That's not quite what I said.'

'—and it's like adding insult to injury. We've got the other yakuza laughing at us.'

I didn't know what to say. It wasn't great for my self-esteem. I had an unpleasant thought.

'Kumichō's position isn't under threat, is it?'

He thought for a moment, a moment longer than I would have liked.

'No,' he said finally. 'It's too early yet. But it's not a good situation. We're getting squeezed by the Ginzo-kai and people are starting to twitch. Something's got to happen and it needs to happen quick.'

I mulled the possibility of my protector disappearing to leave me between two packs of dogs.

'What do you think about it?'

'I think Kumichō's the smartest out of everyone,' he said after a pause. 'If he ever gets taken out it won't be because of something as obvious as this. So for my money, he must have something worked out – for us and for you. But I don't know, I'm still young in the business and there's a lot for me to learn. He's the man to learn from so I'm happy to sit back, watch and wait.'

Sit back, watch and wait while the most powerful gangsters in the country plotted to capture and kill me. I was extremely unhappy to do the same. Unfortunately, I didn't have a choice.

岡野金右エ門藤原包秀

父ハ物頭　禄二百石

包秀ハ二男にして幼き時花岳
寺の門ふ入て僧となり その名を
玉秀といふ兄九十郎 病死活のち
還俗してより 九十郎と えし
主家凶変のをり 父金右エ門老豪
なるがら大石ふ志ゐひ盟約の列ふ
入うと へども 歩行 志ぢいすらば
よりて息九十郎を金右エ門と
改名させ良雄ふ
志ろう〜む包秀
父ふらうりて忠孝を
　　　全くせり

刃回逸剣信士　行年三十一才

THREE

We sat without speaking. Kurotaki stared blankly ahead as he drove with characteristic aggression through the morning traffic. I sat mute, cowed in the presence of one of Tokyo's most-feared men.

'Good album,' I tried.

'Ellington,' he responded.

'So, you like jazz as well?'

It was a two-hour drive – I thought any conversation would be better than silence.

'Of course I do – I like all good music.'

He gave a quick glance sideways to gauge if it was worth going on.

'He was the master. Everyone thinks of his orchestra, the catchy tunes and legendary musicians. But he could turn his hand to anything. His best stuff came at the end of his career, when he had a less quintessential big-band sound.'

He was the strangest man I'd ever met. I wondered again whether the gruff exterior might be a cover for a more reflective soul. Delicate types probably didn't get far in the business but perhaps a hidden sensitivity had allowed him to rise to his position. Maybe it was the weapon he kept concealed and pulled out only when really required. I started to wonder if we might even form an oddball partnership in the end; a good yakuza, bad yakuza team.

'So, it's a terrible thing this whole Kamigawa incident, isn't it? When I was speaking to that mother yesterday, I found it hard to imagine what they've been through, the stress and pain they must have suffered. To have the strength to keep going – you've got to admire them for that.'

I saw his jaw clench and the muscles twitch as he turned his gaze from the road. He swerved suddenly to the side and slammed on the brakes.

'Listen, you limp-dick motherfucker,' he roared, grabbing the front of my shirt – I decided it wasn't the time to point out the inherent contradiction. 'You're a yakuza now. You're Takata-gumi. I know I'm meant to protect you, but if you ever speak like that again I'll beat you until you wish you were dead.'

I sat bolt upright, muscles rigid. I was too afraid even to flinch.

'We're yakuza, we risk getting punched, shot or stabbed. Boxers get head-butted. They get hit below the belt. You live by a nuclear power station, you risk getting fucked up. Those are the fucking breaks. Even if they weren't, that's nothing to do with us. What happens to them is their business. Mine's to help you. Yours is to get information. So go and do it and stop whimpering like a little bitch.'

He slapped me around the head. It was like being hit with a padded anvil.

'Get a hold of yourself. Man the fuck up.'

Despite the litany of evils apparently behind him, it was a relief to see a different face after two hours' stony silence, silence that was somehow amplified by Duke Ellington's (late-period) soulful jazz. We'd been shown into the chairman's office after going through endless security clearances and having our IDs checked numerous times. It turned out he'd returned in the new position some months after resigning as president. I wondered whether he'd changed offices.

'Pleased to meet you,' he said with a smile, reaching forward to shake my hand. 'As a fellow advocate of fossil-free energy I'm sure we'll have plenty in common and much to discuss.'

My introduction, courtesy of the Takata-gumi, clearly had him less wary than he'd have been with other NGOs. Released from the tension of the car I was able to return his smile and shake his hand.

'Now, how can I be of service?' he asked. 'You'll have to excuse me, but the speed with which the appointment was arranged means I'm light on the details and don't have anything prepared.'

He was certainly smooth. At a glance, it would have been easy to mistake him for a traditional Japanese head of business: stern, self-assured and used to his every word being taken as law. But the mannerisms of a man who had worked internationally were also visible through a layer of schmooze applied to the stereotypical Japanese boss. He also had a compelling ear I was trying hard not to look at. Or rather, the part of the ear that was no longer there – a missing lobe that looked like it had been very smoothly cut.

'Well, our study involves a holistic review of all fossil-fuel alternatives,' I spieled, the marketer's preferred language of bullshit quickly coming back. 'We're doing this as groundwork for a cohesive recommendation on how to advance a post-fossil-fuel environment in a financially viable way. We're strictly energy source neutral, of course, but I don't think it would be giving away any secrets to say I envisage nuclear forming a large part of the mix.'

I shot him a conspiratorial look.

'However, in addition to looking at best cases we need to work with those who have overcome challenges they couldn't have foreseen. I want to learn from people like you, people with experience of tackling the impossible, who can help us envisage the most unlikely of scenarios and prevent them in advance.'

I wondered if I had laid it on too thick but his manner suggested he wasn't a stranger to sycophants.

'I'd be delighted to assist you, but perhaps you could be a bit more specific about the ways in which you think I could help.'

'Well, you've clearly done magnificent work in turning the plant around since its difficulties,' I began. 'But I think when doing a review of this sort one really needs to look at everything from the bottom up. Ideally, we'd have complete and transparent exposure to events and decisions from day one. This would enable us to get the full benefit of hindsight and see things that couldn't have been spotted at the time.'

'Certainly,' he replied, with the ease of someone used to deflecting far better interrogators. 'We have the surveys, the topographical reports, the plant blueprints and so on, all in the final files. Much of it is a matter of public record but I can certainly arrange access for you to see the rest.'

'Thank you, but I've been through most of them already,' I lied, deciding to take a punt. 'However, in my experience, I've found the drafts often reveal even more than the final versions. You know how it is – sometimes contributory information gets filed away or details are lost to the polish of the final report.'

And there it was – the tiniest glimmer of a lowered guard. He gave an almost imperceptible glance at Kurotaki, who I turned to see give the slightest shake of his head.

'I'm afraid you've lost me there, Clarence-san,' he said. 'Of course there were drafts, and of course the final one is the most refined. But detail isn't lost or hidden in the process – the presentational techniques make everything more clear, not less. I should point out though that while we keep almost all of the data and drafts, twenty years down the line we may not have every document that contributed to the final report.'

But I'd stopped paying attention. I was looking at Kurotaki, who was pretending he hadn't noticed I was.

'I saw that look,' I said to the side of his head. 'I was told I would be given all the help I need, but there's clearly information I'm not being told or documents I'm not going to be shown. Kumichō told me I would get whatever I need, but you're letting him lie to my face.'

The chairman was wrong-footed by the change in tone. He tried to regain control.

'I resent the implication. You're being told nothing but the truth. I'm even offering you the chance to access all of our data – out of goodwill, not any compulsion, I should add. Don't lose the opportunity to bad manners.'

I ignored him.

'This is bullshit. There's hardly any time and you're going to let a day be wasted by him fucking me around.'

Kurotaki's head snapped to face me.

'Watch your mouth,' he hissed through gritted teeth. 'You're embarrassing yourself. Get a grip, apologise, and hope the good chairman is still willing to help.'

I stood up. 'I'm done. I've got no more questions.'

Kurotaki tried to eye me back down.

'Thank you very much for your time, Mr Chairman,' I said, turning to offer blandishments. 'As Kurotaki-san said, I hope you'll accept my apology – I'm extremely passionate about the energy industry and sometimes my enthusiasm can overflow. I'm terribly sorry if I've caused any offence.'

I don't know if my apology would have been accepted – I'd already started walking towards the door. Kurotaki had no option but to offer his own hurried apologies and follow me out.

We stalked back to the car, both fuming at the injustices we perceived we'd been done. I shouldn't have been surprised that Kurotaki was the one to act upon his. He waited until we were out of sight of security. Then he lifted me by the throat and slammed me against the side of the car.

'You cunt bitch motherfucker,' he roared in my face, spittle spraying, eyes bulging, his skin flushed red. 'You ever fuck me over like that again and I'll cut out your fucking tongue.'

But something had snapped in me too, triggered by the realisation that the only thing that could keep me alive was being held back by the people who'd told me to seek it out.

'So go on then. Beat me until I wish I was dead,' I spat his earlier words back at him. 'This is bullshit. It's a waste of fucking time. If you're not going to let me do what I need to, you might as well get rid of me now.'

I regretted it instantly. My anger was released with the outburst and the void filled with all-consuming fear.

Kurotaki's face contorted further and he drew back his sledge-hammer of a fist. I closed my eyes as it whistled towards me, opening them only when I heard glass smash instead of my nose. He held me by the throat a second longer and then threw me against the car. He glared, and I could see in his eyes the things he wanted to do. But instead of acting on them, he picked a shard of glass from his knuckle and stomped to the driver's door.

'Get in the fucking car.'

It was the last thing he said, and the atmosphere on the drive back was as chilly as the air that blew in at my face.

FOUR

I was at a new dead end, but this time it felt like the way back had been blocked off as well. Now I wasn't inches from being obliterated I seethed with injustice again. I'd done what was asked of me and I'd weaselled what I could from those who were in the right. But if the yakuza – the ones supposedly on my side – weren't putting up their end of the deal, I couldn't see what else I could do.

And that worried me. If I was a bone of contention in a simmering gang feud, I needed to have value to the Takata-gumi for me to be worth their protection. If I was useless in the area they'd identified me as useful, the logical response would be to hand me to their rivals at an appropriate time.

I didn't like the idea of being useless. I needed to come up with something quick.

There was no point doing further research. I was on the right trail – looking for another would have been a waste of time. The problem was my path had been blocked, and tempting as it was to accept that, doing so wasn't an option that boded well. But for the life of me I couldn't see what else I could do.

Unless . . .

My unconscious threw a thought at me that was as welcome as the others it had recently bowled. I tried to evade it but as soon as I put my mind to something else it would skulk its way in there as well. To make matters worse, it had a twisted logic, a line of argument that was difficult to resist. It may have been near-suicidal but it appeared to be the only way to escape a more likely death.

I took a stroll in Shinjuku Gyoen Park to help clear my head. Around me, people clustered by maple and ginkgo trees took pictures of the yellows, purples and reds of the autumn leaves. As I kicked through fallen piles I remembered walking through the park with Tomoe during *hanami* – the time the cherry blossoms bloom. It seemed apt. At the time I'd been enjoying a fresh start, my life full of opportunities bursting into flower. Now they'd withered and would soon be falling away.

Tomoe had been particularly affected by the arrival of spring, and was as bouncy as a kitten in the wind. She'd insisted on walking every corner of the park in order to savour its rebirth.

'Come on, Ray-kun, we need to plan some trips, fun stuff, things to look forward to.'

'Sounds good – what have you got in mind?'

'I don't know, maybe we could go somewhere in August when it gets too hot. Then do something in the winter to break up the cold.'

She grabbed my arm and skipped around me, her energy as intoxicating as the alcohol consumed at a cherry blossom picnic. As always, I'd been the more cautious of us.

'All right, let's do it! But maybe we should just book something for summer now. Winter's ages away – who knows what we'll be up to by then.'

She stopped and tilted her head to the side. Her eyes seemed to seek something in mine.

'You think too much,' she said with a hint of sadness. 'Then you worry, then you wait to see how things pan out. Live like that, and before you know it life's dictating to you. You need to follow your instincts more, Ray-kun. Set your own path.'

She tiptoed up, gave me a kiss and squeezed my bum in a most public and un-Japanese way. She'd then sauntered off with a smile and a saucy look back.

I was now left with a particularly expensive trip to Thailand that looked unlikely to be fulfilled. Despite this, I remained sold on the philosophy of setting my own path. If I was to live up to it, I would need to make some hard decisions in the coming days. Decisions that would force me to confront my instincts and fears.

A quiet time in Kabukichō is a contradiction in terms. Even if there's a lull in the noise, the flow of people never stops. But if you get there on a weeknight, around 3 or 4 a.m., the human traffic is lighter and those enjoying the action have, for the most part, dispersed. The ones able to return home will have done so. Those whose journey requires a bank-breaking taxi will be contaminating a capsule hotel pod with burps, sweats and farts. The remainder sober up and battle hangovers, hunched over bowls of ramen in painfully bright stores.

On this particular night, I was at the row of buildings where the Takata-gumi Kabukichō branch was. I was looking for a way to get to the back.

I don't know why, but Japanese buildings have a gap between them instead of being buttressed against one another as they are in the UK. These range from cracks measuring inches up to a few feet. The one between the Takata-gumi and its neighbour was of the inches variety. But there was a gap of about a foot after an *udon* noodle shop a store down.

For a cat burglar that would have left inches to spare. I darted in during a split second's pause in the swaying human traffic and immediately realised that for me it wasn't nearly enough. I forced myself forwards anyway, trying not to think of what was crunching under my feet. But when I got halfway down the real battle started – a fight against claustrophobia that had me certain I was trapped.

I clawed and scraped my way down the narrowing gap, bursting from it into an alley just as I thought I was going to pass out. I gulped gratefully at the rancid air. I would have loved to take a break to recover. But I couldn't afford to. I needed to get this over with as quickly as I could.

I made my way between the two rows of buildings, dodging pipes and air-con units while looking up in hope. And for the first time in as long as I could remember, that hope was rewarded. The front door may have been locked shut but the toilet window on the first floor was wide open, as it had been when I'd visited during the day. Why wouldn't it be? Who in their right mind would even think of breaking in?

After an ungraceful ascent aided by a drainpipe on one side

and a building an outstretched leg away on the other, I heaved myself partway through the window. An old-style squat toilet sat unhelpfully below, offering no steps down or even a place I could easily land. Thankfully when I launched from my awkward take-off I cleared the bowl. Unfortunately, this came at the expense of my face, which halted my momentum on the door with a crunch.

I pressed my ear against it, too scared even to take a breath. It was highly unlikely anyone had remained locked inside the building but even the thought of being found was enough to make me feel sick. There were no tell-tale signs of movement and my muscles let up slightly from their rigid embrace. I opened the door, just a crack at first, then gradually wider until I was confident enough to edge out. The next challenge to my courage was the kitchenette. It was only when it revealed itself as empty and the main office did the same that my breathing finally eased.

Certain I was alone, I couldn't help but pause at the severed fingers. But despite their morbid allure I knew it wasn't the time to hang around. I turned towards my target: Takata's room.

It was a desperate move but I'd arrived at it rationally. The nuclear issue was clearly of great importance to Takata. He knew more than he was letting on and wanted to use what he had at the AGM. With that just over a week away, I assumed he'd want whatever he had at hand.

The idea of breaking in so I could bring him his own information was clearly ridiculous. But for all he had in his possession it appeared he was missing something, the thing he'd sent me to seek out. And if I could use what he had here to get to that, I'd prove myself invaluable. And that had to be worth the risk. Because the alternative was turning up with nothing and facing the consequences.

So, as dire as it may have been, I felt sure I was doing the right thing. I just had to hope Takata kept whatever he had in Kabukichō. That it provided me with a lead. And that I didn't get caught.

His room seemed bigger and emptier without his presence, although that could just have been the murky light. I started to search for the thing I hoped to recognise when I found it, a plan that had seemed as good as any when I considered it in advance. In practice, it turned out to be less satisfactory. Takata kept the room spotless, the shelves tidily stacked, the desk ordered and neat.

I scanned the shelves first. I even took out a couple of books to check that they weren't false fronts. Finding no joy, I rounded the desk, my heart thumping against my ribs. I pulled at two drawers, more in hope than anything else. Both were locked. I took this as a good sign. He wouldn't have bothered if there was nothing to hide.

There was another positive – the desk was an antique with old-style locks rather than Yales. At secondary school, a few of us had fancied ourselves master burglars in the making. We hadn't progressed beyond using paper clips on small padlocks but we'd become quite adept at this. I grabbed one from the desk-tidy and sat on the floor to re-hone my skills.

It took a few attempts before I got a feel for it again but by this point I was completely absorbed. I'm not sure how long it was before I found the right balance of shape and rigidity, but when I did, I got the satisfying click of the false key slotting into place.

I leaned forward and jiggled it twice to ensure it was solid and wouldn't get warped out of shape. It felt perfect.

Knowing there was no stopping me I started to turn.

I never found out if it would have worked.

I tried opening my eyes but swiftly shut them against the glare of a blinding light. I wondered if I'd reached the end of the long, dark tunnel.

'He's coming round.'

My lids snapped open at the sound of the voice. If it was the tunnel, I'd come out the wrong end. I was slumped on the sofa in the Takata-gumi office, my head rolled against the wall above the backrest, my face tilted towards the overhead light.

'What the hell?'

I put my hand to the back of my head and pulled it away sharply when my fingers came to a swollen lump. I held them in front of me and saw they were smeared with blood.

'Right, motherfucker, you've got some explaining to do. Like telling us what the fuck you think you were doing.'

It could only be Kurotaki. Sure enough, he entered the periphery of my vision just after I heard his voice.

I felt nauseous. I hadn't worked out what was going on yet, so it was likely the result of whatever had happened to my head rather than fear.

'What happened?' I groaned.

Kurotaki nodded to his left and my eyes followed his gesture just in time to see a fist block out the light and crash into my face. My neck snapped back, propelling my head into the wall which made a perfect contact with the bloody egg. I think I passed out briefly, as the next thing I knew a hand was lifting me off my side and sitting me back up.

'I'm asking the questions,' said Kurotaki. 'You're welcome to ask your own and you can go off on any tangent you like, but you should know Sumida here's going to hit you every time you do.'

'I'm going to be sick.'

If Sumida's deft footwork to the cupboard was anything to go by, this tangent was an exception. I threw up in the bucket he pulled out.

Kurotaki wasn't impressed. 'Arrgh, that stinks. You dirty gaijin fuck.'

Whether that was an observation or an indication that Japanese vomit was sweeter smelling was rendered irrelevant by Sumida dumping the bucket in the toilet and slamming the door. I took a lungful of air. My stomach felt relatively normal again and while my head was in agony, the maelstrom of confusion had passed. The problem with that was my memory had returned and I realised how much trouble I was in.

'Are you done?'

I nodded and wiped my mouth with the back of my hand. Sumida put a glass of water in front of me. I took a couple of gulps to wash away the taste but also to play for time.

'So what were you doing?' Kurotaki asked again.

I tried to think of something good to say, but my brain was still rattling around my skull and I couldn't come up with anything but the truth.

'I wanted to find out about the power station. I couldn't think of any other way.'

There wasn't much more to add.

'And you thought you would break into our office? Go through Kumichō's own stuff?'

I nodded, bringing a flash of blinding pain.

'You stupid fuck.'

It was pithy summary and a fairly accurate one too.

He turned to Sumida. 'Get a chopping board.'

That brought me to my senses. If we'd had the summary, this was the time for sentencing and a chopping board didn't seem a good way to start. Sumida went without a word to the kitchen. In panic, I looked up at Kurotaki as I heard Sumida rummage through drawers.

'You couldn't leave well enough alone, could you?' he sneered. 'What, you don't have anything to say? You don't want to shoot your mouth off again and tell me what I can do to you?'

I didn't. I was too busy fighting hysteria. I tried to look at Kurotaki but it was hard to keep my eyes focused on one spot.

'Well, you don't have to worry about me this time,' he went on. 'You're going to take care of this all by yourself.'

At this point Sumida came back and dropped a wooden chopping board on the coffee table along with a ball of thin string. He kicked the table towards me so it came to a stop against my legs.

'Wrap the string around the little finger of your left hand,' Kurotaki said.

'What do you mean?'

He raised his eyes in exasperation and turned to Sumida who honed in.

'OK, OK,' I said, grabbing the ball of string.

I unravelled a length and started wrapping it around my finger.

'What the fuck good's that?' demanded Kurotaki. 'You've got to wrap it tighter than that. You'll know it's right when it hurts.'

'But that'll cut off the blood to my finger.'

He smirked. My stomach sank as any doubts about what was to come next were dispelled.

When I was eighteen, I took a shortcut with a friend through a park. It was after hours so we had to scale the fence at either end. But that didn't concern us – it was something we always did to save the extra five minutes' walk to the pub. On this occasion, I felt something strange as I jumped down. I looked around from my squat and realised it was my arm. It was raised high up behind me, held by the ring caught on the ridges of wire that poked from the frame of the gate.

I only needed one look at the bone gleaming through the ripped mess of my finger to realise I needed to get to hospital, and that it would be best if I didn't look at it again. It hadn't really hurt though. Perhaps it had been so unexpected I was anaesthetised with shock.

Thanks to the NHS and its plastic surgeons, I was not only stitched up but had the feeling in my nerves saved as well. I was told I'd been lucky not to tear off my finger. It was the closest to going a digit down I'd ever wanted to get.

'That's right,' said Kurotaki.

The bottom half of my little finger was cocooned in a tightly bound weave of pink thread. The tip was starting to turn blue.

'You can snip it off there.'

I looked at him, astonished even he could be so blasé until I realised he meant the ball of string.

'I don't have any scissors.'

'That's all right. You can use this.'

I didn't see what 'this' was. I only heard a faint swoosh followed by a whack as something hit the chopping board. The ball of string, now severed from the cocoon on my finger, rolled to the edge of the table. My eyes returned to the chopping board in the middle of which a huge knife was now wedged.

'That's a Kunimitsu *tantō*,' said Kurotaki with obvious pride.

I looked at him blankly, too terrified to show whatever reaction he was hoping to see.

'Kunimitsu was one of Japan's greatest swordsmiths,' he said, sounding irritated. 'He made swords in the thirteenth and fourteenth centuries. They're almost all in museums and collections. That's the closest you'll ever get.'

Quite frankly, I couldn't give a flying fuck about Kunimitsu and the last thing I wanted was to be as close to the knife/short sword/whatever it was as I now was.

'I was only trying to do what Kumichō said. He told me to be proactive. That's all I was trying to do. I just wanted to help out for the AGM.'

I was blindsided with a whack to the head by Sumida but it was open-handed, more sympathetic than a punch but also more offensive. Not that I had any pride left to offend. I was on the verge of tears and probably only one slap away from losing all self-control.

'Shut the fuck up,' ordered Kurotaki. 'The time for talking's over. You've done what you've done. Pull yourself together and take the consequences like a man.'

I took some deep breaths and tried to steady myself. It took a minute before I felt I could speak again without breaking down.

'What do I do?' I asked in a marginally stronger voice.

'Put your hand on the edge of the table by you and leave your finger lying across the board.'

Kurotaki took on a businesslike tone and I was thankful. It made it seem slightly less of an affront to nature and part of a process instead – follow the instructions, get to the end, and move on.

'Take the knife by the handle and stick the tip in the board, a little above the joint of your finger. Then bring it down hard.'

I took another deep breath. It didn't work.

'Do I really—'

'Don't let yourself down.'

I reached towards the knife.

'Don't touch the blade!'

'OK, OK.'

'You don't touch a sword by its blade – the oils from your skin tarnish it.'

'I won't touch it,' I said. 'But it's going to have to make contact with my skin when I . . .'

I couldn't finish the sentence.

'That will be OK.'

I looked at the knife and my mind started to run away from it. What if I wanted to take up the piano again? I wouldn't be able to reach the octave plus chords – perhaps I could do my ring finger instead? And what about medical insurance? I wasn't sure what my status was now that I'd left my job. Even if I still had cover, would it extend to yakuza rituals? Surely they wouldn't pay for someone stupid enough to cut their own finger off?

I tried again to gather myself for what I had to do.

'How badly is it going to hurt?'

'I've never had to find out,' said Kurotaki.

I looked at Sumida who held up the full complement on his hands. He finally spoke.

'Apparently it's not too bad,' he lied.

'The knife,' I said. 'It's—'

'So sharp you could put it on its edge and it would cut through the board and into the table,' said Kurotaki. 'Don't worry about the tantō. Get yourself together, take it in your hands and do what you have to do. It will be all right.'

His tone was more respectful than it ever had been before, perhaps an acknowledgement of what I was about to do, an act finally worthy of a yakuza. Despite that, I couldn't see any outcome to cutting off my own finger that could be summarised as 'all right'.

I picked up the knife by its handle and stared at it, captured by a morbid curiosity for the instrument about to do me such harm. All I could see was the blade. Its hilt was thick, but tapered in a keen line to a razor-sharp edge an inch or so below. It bore no decoration and had no frills or unnecessary curves. Yet despite being designed solely for malice it managed to be strangely beautiful at the same time. But it was a brutal beauty, a beauty that hadn't come from an affectation to please the eye. The crisp lines epitomised form after function. They'd been forged from its thirst for blood.

In this case, the blood was to be mine.

I stabbed the end into the board, closed my eyes and took another deep breath. I opened them and pulled down sharply with all of my might.

The knife sliced through my skin like it was nothing and made light of the cartilage between the bones. Then it stopped. And it was when it stopped I realised the moment's delay of pain had only been that. The muscles in my body went rigid as the first wave hit. Sweat started to pour from my face. I fought to keep my breath within me as I feared it would come out as a scream.

I looked up at Kurotaki, my eyes wide.

'That's all right,' he said. 'It happens. The joint can be sticky. Take a moment and then give it another go. Get on your knees if you think you can get a better angle from there.'

I slipped off the edge of the sofa onto my knees. I braced myself and then put all of my weight onto my right hand to force the knife down. It sank in slightly further and seemed to separate something within the joint. But it still didn't go through.

The intensity of pain multiplied and my breath now came out somewhere between a guttural groan and a roar.

'That's it,' said Kurotaki, enthusiastically. 'You're almost there. You're right in the joint. Give it a wiggle and a final thrust – you'll be straight through.'

My breath was coming in starts and I knew my strength wouldn't hold up to much more. I wiggled the knife and felt it break slightly from the grip of the bones. Pain surged through my body, as though there was too much to be contained in just a small joint.

I slammed down one last time with everything I had. The knife sliced through the mutilated remains of my finger and came to a stop in the board. I let go and looked at the amputated tip, horrified yet fascinated by the sight. I lifted my hand as if it were someone else's and stared at the other end. White bone poked through oozing blood and severed arteries. I retched once but nothing came out.

'I wouldn't do that,' advised Kurotaki. 'It won't help. Just put the tip on this piece of cloth and fold it over like that – that's right – and that. Good. Now have a drink of this.'

He handed me a bottle of whisky. I took three large gulps.

'We'll take care of your finger. It'll go to Kumichō with apologies for what you did. Now wrap your hand in this,' he gave me a drying up towel, 'and go with Sumida. He'll take you to the hospital so you can get fixed up.'

Beyond capacity for thought, I numbly obeyed.

FIVE

He might not have been loquacious but Sumida was definitely better than Kurotaki.

'You made a decent show of yourself,' he said when I got in his car two days later. 'I've seen guys do it better – some are almost looking for an excuse. They'll take off a finger and then finish their drinks before they go, just to make a point. But I've seen others, proper yakuza, do a lot worse.'

He was being quite friendly for someone who'd almost broken my cheekbone and then forced me to cut off a finger. I wasn't sure how to respond.

'Thanks.'

I thought a little.

'You're not affected by it?'

He had no idea what I meant.

'The violence. It doesn't affect you? The things you do. They don't keep you awake at night?'

'It's the world we live in. It's my job.'

He shrugged.

'It's like I imagine life in an office – you worked in an office, right?'

I nodded at the second part of his sentence.

'You had to give people bollockings?'

'Mostly not, but maybe once or twice.'

'It probably wasn't the part of the job you enjoyed, right? It just had to be done.'

Now I shrugged.

'It's a bit like martial arts. When I fight I'm aggressive, I want to land big punches and kicks and knock the other guy out. But it's not personal. It's no different to hitting those punchball machines you get at fairs. It's like everything – you do what you need to for the situation you're in. It's like this guy, I had to cut his hand off the other day—'

'You did what?'

Despite everything, I was shocked by the nonchalance of this aside.

'I had to cut his hand off. Don't worry,' he said, catching my look. 'We didn't kill him – we had a tourniquet – but I was under orders to teach him a lesson, more than just a rebuke.'

He nodded at my hand, whose lack of a finger I would have described in stronger terms than 'a rebuke'.

'I didn't know him so obviously I had no personal issues. I don't even know what he did. But he'd fucked someone over and whoever it was must have been rich or powerful. So he had to be taught not to do it again.'

He looked at me.

'Different trade, different tools, but it's the same as what you did at your work.'

It was an eloquent enough explanation but I still felt there was a difference. I let it go. He was better than Kurotaki, at least.

'So, what are we doing now?'

'We're going to the office,' he said. 'Kumichō wants to see you.'

My stomach turned at the thought.

I don't remember the journey to the hospital except for the pain and Sumida repeating what I should say. I stumbled into A&E with him at my side and he insisted I was immediately seen. I think my condition would have predicated it, but it didn't hurt to have an intimidating yakuza beside me to prevent any complaints.

'You cut it off by mistake making sushi?' the doctor asked as she examined my finger.

I nodded.

'And then fell down the stairs and hurt your head?'

'I was drunk.'

'It's lucky you'd happened to tie it up with string before the accident then, isn't it?'

I was beyond anything but repeating what I'd been told to say or nodding my head. I nodded.

'OK, let's get it cleaned up,' she said with a sigh.

When my 'friends' came by the following day they were turned away.

'You were concussed when you fell,' the doctor said. 'We're going to need you in here another day.'

I was feeling a fair bit better but I still left my response at a nod.

'Look, we both know your story isn't true,' she said in a concerned voice. 'I don't want you going back with those men. Let me help you. Let me call the police.'

I looked at her properly for the first time. She was somewhere in her fifties and her manner suggested she'd had people reporting to her for quite some time. I could imagine it being intimidating but just then she seemed more like a stern mother. I would have loved to have her scoop me up in her arms.

'Really,' I said, fighting the temptation to nestle up to her. 'I'm OK. I think things have been resolved – I'm not in any danger now.'

She didn't look like she believed me but with a full ward of patients it wasn't something on which she could dwell.

'If you say so,' she said, sounding reluctant.

She started to make her way off but then turned.

'You're here for another day. Let me know if you change your mind.'

But I hadn't changed my mind, and when Sumida arrived the next day I followed him to the car, my little finger a swathe of bandages that snaked around the rest of my hand.

'I hope it isn't too sore.'

Takata nodded towards my finger as I sat down.

'It's not too bad,' I said, the painkillers doing little to mask the searing pain.

'I'm sorry I wasn't notified before this happened. It was not in my plans.'

His tone was icy. Considering my reluctant involvement, I assumed his displeasure in this particular instance wasn't directed at me. I thought a pre-emptive apology for anger that was warranted wouldn't be unwise.

'The blame lies with me. What I did was unforgivable. I can't apologise enough.'

'It wasn't your smartest move,' he said, although he looked far less concerned than I'd worried he would. 'But we are left with a problem – beyond your reduced grasp.'

He held up his own left hand, which also included a finger of curtailed ambition.

'You don't have any need to use a sword?'

'Other than when I'm told to cut my fingers off, no.'

'Then I can assure you it restricts you very little in everyday life. It isn't, however, a look normally adopted by foreign workers at well-respected NGOs.'

'I would have thought it slightly unusual.'

'We'll have you fitted with a prosthetic of course,' he said, looking thoughtful. 'But even if we could get it ready in time, you won't have healed enough to wear one. Let's see how you're looking nearer the AGM. Either we'll do the whole hand in bandages like you have a sprain, or put a plaster cast on it and pretend you broke your hand.'

There was a knock.

'Come in,' said Takata.

Kurotaki entered, looking strangely subdued.

'Ah, Kurotaki, you wanted to speak to Clarence-san?'

Kurotaki came up to where I was sitting.

'I want to apologise for the other night,' he started. 'I didn't give appropriate thought to the implications of my behaviour and its effect on the organisation. I will endeavour to improve my conduct and act in a manner more befitting of my position from now on.'

He bowed deeply, turned and left the room. I looked at Takata. I couldn't have been more bewildered if Kurotaki had given me a hug.

'As I said, your loss is not beneficial to the Takata-gumi,' he said by way of explanation.

'And his finger?'

I was making reference to some familiar-looking bandages that swallowed up Kurotaki's hand.

'You see, this is what I have to put up with. I rebuke someone for making another commit *yubitsume*, a practice you know I don't like. And what response do I get? These ridiculous customs are so deeply engrained, the only way he can think of showing his remorse is to hand me his finger in turn.'

He shook his head.

'And the apology to me?'

'That comes from the heart too. You see Kurotaki, in his own way and with his own logic, believes completely in the yakuza of lore. Honour of thieves, protector of the common man, all of that. It's just that he's as confused as a mafioso who prays to God and then commits all sins known to man.

'Anyway, there's a saying: "If the oyabun says the passing crow is white, then all must agree." So even if he thought he was right, if I tell him it was wrong, then by everything he believes in, it was wrong.'

I wondered at the relationship between them, one who had absolute faith in all the myths and tenets, the other who believed in nothing at all. Two completely different men who had nonetheless found understanding and mutual respect. Albeit with a few bumps along the way.

'In this case, I don't think my views on the colour of fauna come into play. He realises he made a mistake. So you can take the apology as genuine.'

He pursed his lips.

'Nevertheless, it might be prudent to show some sensitivity towards him for the time being.'

I nodded. I had no intention of putting his sincerity to the test.

'Right, let's move on.' He looked at me closely. 'While I appreciate your enthusiasm, you may have become a little more proactive than I intended when we last spoke.'

'I didn't know what to do. I felt I had what I needed in my grasp but then it was pulled away,' I said, words tumbling out now I could finally speak to him. 'I know what I did was unacceptable and I apologise. But it was the only thing I could think of to do.'

He massaged the little finger of his left hand.

'You're in too much of a hurry. You think everything has to happen at once. It doesn't. It's like fishing – you reel the fish in a little at a time. If you yank at it you lose your catch.'

I hoped we weren't returning to riddles and metaphors. I just wanted a straight explanation so I could do whatever I needed to stay alive.

'It's like I said before, Clarence-san, things happen around you. There are plenty of people in the world who can react to events. But the catalysts, those who effect action – people like you – are rare. That makes you valuable. Unfortunately you seem unaware of your ability and see failure where there is, in fact, success.'

'I succeeded?'

'The right people are now aware of certain activities – you've done your job.'

'But I didn't get to the bottom of the scandal.'

'I already know everything there is to it,' he said, as though it were obvious I wasn't meant to find anything out from the start. 'That wasn't the point.'

'But—'

'Thank you for your efforts, Clarence-san. Now take the opportunity to rest. Allow your finger to heal, and recover from what must have been a traumatic couple of weeks. I'll see you again before the AGM but please, refrain from doing anything else. When the time's right, you'll be fully briefed.'

He gave me a pointed look.

'Your job now's to rest. Nothing else.'

Not long before, a week without physical and verbal abuse would have been par for the course. Now it seemed as close to paradise as I could get. I just had to hope that at its end, having apparently done my job, I could avoid death and not have to worry about hell.

SIX

Dreaming of the Floating World 2

A gust of wind sent a brilliant cluster of red maple leaves spiralling past her as she looked from the balcony onto the main parade. They would be replaced by cherry trees in spring, peonies in early summer, then chrysanthemums before it all started again. Only in Yoshiwara could one street be the perfect place to view every season.

She looked down and saw the usual mix of people as afternoon passed into evening – tourists gawking at the famed quarter, eager to see but lacking the money or desire to taste its fruits; writers and artists emerging from a hard day's work or a particularly long night; and merchants, dandies and samurai filtering in for the business that was the pleasure of the night.

She stepped back into the room, slid the door shut and thought it through again. It was the best course of action. She couldn't wait for others in hope.

'Michiko,' she called out to the apprentice.

The patter of feet quickly echoed from the adjoining room.

'Yes, Onēsan?'

'Mi-chan, I need to ask a favour of you. But I must warn you, it's not an ordinary task. If you don't feel comfortable I'll understand. It concerns my father.'

'I'll do whatever you need,' said Michiko without hesitation. 'What is it you'd like me to do?'

Katsuyama smiled. She'd been lucky with her apprentice. When Michiko opened her mouth it was usually to speak sense, and scheming and sycophancy were not among her traits.

'I know you're close to Kaoru's apprentice,' she said, referring to the only tayū in Yoshiwara who could come close to her own allure. 'Despite the fact your mistresses fight like cat and dog.'

Now Michiko smiled.

'That's right. Namiji was in Yoshiwara when I arrived. She helped me settle in.'

'I'd like you to speak to her,' said Katsuyama. 'Lord Genpachi favours Kaoru. I want to know if there's been any loose pillow talk between them. Can you do that for me?'

They both understood the significance of the request – Genpachi's dispute with her father's lord had led to her family's downfall. Theirs had been a hatred passed down from their fathers. It had concluded when Genpachi out-manoeuvred his foe and had him stripped of his land, his title and everything else he possessed. He had been forced to shave his head, retreat to a temple and live out his days as a monk.

If he had been made to commit seppuku his retainers and their families would have had to do the same. But they were lucky; his lesser punishment meant those who could find new positions were employed by other lords. The others, although now rōnin, were at least still alive.

For Katsuyama's father it had been different. As senior retainer it had been decided his punishment should be more severe. His land *was taken, his stipend removed and he had been banished from within sight of the castle walls. A proud and distinguished samurai, he had been reduced to working the land to eke out a living for his family. But the land had been ungenerous in its returns. That was when Katsuyama had taken her new name and gone to Tanzen.*

Then her life had turned on a twist of fate. When the first shōgun consolidated the country, the samurai became warriors without a war. It had left them frustrated and quick to be drawn into fights. As they lost their status as protectors, ordinary townsfolk's deference to them decreased and their own self-confidence grew. The two factors combined for a perfect storm and one had erupted in Tanzen. Its refurbishment in blood and gore gained infamy nationwide.

The bathhouses had borne the brunt of officialdom's consequent wrath. But while it had spelled their end, it had marked a new beginning for their most famous employee. Katsuyama had moved to Yoshiwara the same month, bought in on a contract that would feed her family for a significant time.

'Of course,' said Michiko. 'Is there anything in particular you expect to hear?'

'No. I mean, I don't know. I can't think who else would wish ill of my father so I have to believe Lord Genpachi is involved. I don't expect him to discuss the matter with a courtesan, but there may have been conversations that seemed unusual or people mentioned she hadn't heard talk of before. Please try to find anything that stands out.'

She stood as two assistants adjusted her kimono, plain white until painted with a swirl of flowers, birds and clouds at her favourite artist

Moronobu's hand. Her hair she insisted on finishing herself, tying the wide white silk ribbon in its jaunty loop to the right.

'Hold the mirror a little further up please,' she requested of one of the assistants.

She cocked her head, wiggled her hips and then smiled to let them know it was just right.

'Is everyone ready?' she asked.

'Yes, ma'am, except Michiko. No one knows where she is.'

'Don't worry about Mi-chan. She can catch up.'

As she spoke, Michiko burst into the room, her face flushed. Katsuyama cut in before she could blurt out anything better said when they were alone.

'Mi-chan, get yourself ready. We can talk on the parade.'

They made their procession from her residence to the ageya, the houses where only the highest ranked courtesans entertained. In front, a male servant held a lantern and led the way. Behind were two maids who could double as entertainers depending on the number and desire of her guests. Obasan was at her left, there as a chaperone to take care of Katsuyama's interests and those of the house. And to her right, Michiko, included for her innocent repartee and the energy of youth.

Michiko had been sold by her impoverished parents when she was nine. She would have to work until she could repay the sum; no easy matter considering its size and the expenses endlessly accrued. Yet in many ways she was lucky. She had escaped starvation and done her duty by helping her family do the same. She had also been attractive and spirited enough to be bought by a leading house.

Katsuyama shivered as they passed small alleyways to the left and right. In these, the workers' servitude swallowed the best years of their lives. The girls who worked in their bordellos weren't courtesans. Their training wasn't in words, culture and art. They were prostitutes confined within their houses, who served customers at their owner's desire and suffered brutality at his hand.

Michiko would learn from her and become a courtesan of the highest ranks. Then she would have the chance to pay off her contract or have it bought out by a client instead.

Katsuyama's attention returned to the parade. Crowds had gathered for her as they always did. On a whim she kicked her heel a little harder and the red silk of her inner kimono swirled up to reveal the white skin of a rarely seen thigh.

'So, Mi-chan,' she said, through barely moving lips. 'What is it you have to tell me?'

Michiko pretended to support Katsuyama's arm so she could turn slightly and speak unseen.

'You know Mizuno, the rōnin who now owns a dry goods store in Nihonbashi? Apparently he met Lord Genpachi in Yoshiwara not more than a month ago. For part of the evening all the servants and cour-tesans were sent from the room.'

It was intriguing. Theoretically, all from street-sweeper to shōgun were equal within Yoshiwara's walls, but it was still unusual for a daimyō, a lord of Genpachi's standing, to consort with a merchant, a person of the lowest social class. And Mizuno was curious in himself; after being reduced to a rōnin no one knew how he had progressed so swiftly to his astonishing wealth.

The question was how to find out more. But it was a question for another day. The procession had reached the ageya, its sumptuous facade resplendent in the sun's evening glow. She needed to bring *herself back to the present. She would return to this quandary the following day.*

The screams reverberated through the house and brought Katsuyama rushing down the stairs. Servants crowded around Michiko, who was as quiet as they were loud. She sat unmoving and ashen-faced.

'Mi-chan, what is it?' she called out above the furore.

Michiko was unable to say anything but held out her left hand. It was covered in blood.

'Call for the doctor at once and bring water and cloth to my room.' Katsuyama softened her voice and put her arm around her apprentice. 'Mi-chan, come with me.'

Upstairs, they sat on the tatami by the low table. Katsuyama held the young girl to her and gently stroked her hair. She had wound a piece of cloth around the base of Michiko's finger in order to stem the bleeding. She'd then washed and wrapped the wound. Just the very tip had been sliced off, leaving a straight edge where it should have been round.

'Mi-chan, what happened?' she coaxed.

Her apprentice snuggled into her.

'I went back to talk to Namiji, to see if there was anything else I could find out. But we were overheard. Kaoru was furious. I was dismissed but I snuck back around the side. They beat Namiji horribly and told her she'd never work for them again. They're going to sell her to a brothel, even though there are good houses that would happily buy her out.'

Michiko sobbed. She'd retained some of her innocence but not enough that she didn't know what lay ahead for her friend.

'But what happened to your finger, Mi-chan?'

Michiko looked up at her and then back down at her hand as though she had forgotten anything was wrong.

'I was returning from their house when I was grabbed and pulled into an alley. One man held me from behind and another brought out a knife. He told me that I and any others should leave our enquiries alone. If not, he would take my hand the next time and if that didn't stop us he would cut out my heart.'

Katsuyama hugged her tightly.

'I'm so sorry, Mi-chan, I had no idea anything like this would happen. But you needn't worry – there won't be a next time. I'll take care of everything from here. As for your friend, I'll do all I can to prevent her going to a brothel, even if it means extending my own contract to buy her out.'

Michiko hugged her back but Katsuyama scarcely noticed; her mind had already moved on. They had miscalculated badly if they thought she, a samurai, would be scared off at such little threat. Now she knew she was on the right trail there would be no holding her back.

SEVEN

I woke with a start, strangely excited by images of a slender thigh. I struggled out of bed and made my way to the shower, stepping in only when it was piping hot. As a way to clear my mind it came second only to walking and I was sorely in need of the help. Sure enough, as the jet of water hit me, I was rocked by a thought.

What if everything led to Takata?

If my dreams were me trying to work out asleep the things I couldn't while I was awake, had I created this evil character from Takata? Perhaps in real life there wasn't another conspirator. Maybe I was seeing things that weren't there – or, more likely, things Takata had planted in my head. Even if there was someone else it would make more sense for him to be a pawn in Takata's game – Takata wasn't the kind of man to follow another's lead.

The thought was unsettling. If he was misleading me on this, he could be lying about Tomoe as well. Maybe he had taken her. If he had, it wouldn't make sense to have me nosing around in earnest. That could be why he was holding me back. This thing about catalysts and the AGM – it might be smoke and mirrors. It was more likely I was being kept as a bargaining chip, or bait.

A week's rest suddenly seemed a lot less relaxing.

Removing the plastic bag secured around my throbbing left hand, I dried myself awkwardly and tried to work out what I should do. I had no more options than I'd had at the start.

Then something came to me so obvious I didn't know why I hadn't thought it before. Sakura. Was that it? Was that what the dream was about? Was she the courtesan with all the answers?

Now I knew more of its background, the route into Senzoku-yon-chōme, or Yoshiwara as it had been, took on a different light. Rather than entering as I had previously and exposing myself to the streets' eyes, I skirted around the side and came to the road leading to Matsubaya from a less conspicuous route.

It had been four o'clock when I first visited and with the half-hour wait for Sakura that should have meant it would be around 4:30 when she arrived. I pulled down my cap, keeping my tell-tale hand in my pocket, and tried to wait as unobtrusively as I could.

Dusk was drawing in and with it the early-evening autumn chill. I almost missed her as I hunched away from the breeze.

'Sakura-san!'

She turned, startled.

'Sakura-san, I came to visit you a few weeks ago – do you remember?'

I moved forwards, trying to looking as unthreatening as one can emerging from a concealed spot in an alley.

'I just wanted to ask you a couple of questions. They're about my girlfriend. She's gone missing and I think you can help.'

She hesitated a moment and then stepped towards me. 'Yes, I remember you. We had fun.'

I blushed. It had only been a few weeks but things were so different now.

'Yes, we did.'

'So what are your questions? Please don't let them be about people I can't talk about.'

My stomach sank. I hadn't been thinking. Or at least I had, but only about myself. If she told me the things I needed to know she'd be putting herself at risk. The risks so far had shown themselves to have precipitously high stakes.

'Can I just ask them? Then you can decide if you can answer or not,' I said. 'I'm desperate. I don't want to get you in trouble but I might be able to find my girlfriend with your help. Nothing you say will get back to anyone, I promise you. No one will even know that we spoke.'

She looked at me but didn't say anything. I took that as a cue to go on.

'In the last month or two, has Takata of the Takata-gumi come around here?'

She responded with a question that did nothing to answer mine.

'You know this isn't a Takata-gumi area any more? It was taken over by the Ginzo-kai in summer.'

I pulled my cap lower. I wasn't sure how this affected things overall, but it was certainly more uncomfortable in the immediate term.

'Look, I have an appointment in a minute – they might even come this way. Give me your number and I'll see what I can do. I'd like to help if I can.'

She was in the kind of profession where crafting one's emotions to please others was a fundamental part of the job. But I got the sense her sympathy was real. I typed my number in her phone and gave myself a missed call. She gave me another look – I wasn't sure if I saw pity. I wondered what she knew.

'I'll call you, I promise. Take care.'

She gave me a peck on the cheek, and then turned and walked briskly towards her work.

The phone woke me at 2.30 a.m. – I suppose you have to allow for the different hours soapland girls keep.

'There were three of them,' she said by way of a greeting. 'Takata-san and two other men.'

Her words cut through my grogginess.

'Do you know who the other men were?'

'No. But one of them, I'm sure I'd seen his face before – maybe on TV.'

'And the other?'

'It was definitely the first time I'd seen him.'

'Do you know why they were meeting?'

'No. I wasn't even supposed to be there. My boss was meant to serve them – she knows Takata-san from when they were young. But she couldn't come in – she'd had a fall and hurt her hip. She asked me to take care of them instead.'

She paused and I tried to work out what this meant and how it could help.

'It seemed a strange place to meet – like I told you, this isn't a Takata-gumi area any more.'

'And you've got no idea what they were talking about?'

'None at all. I just took them to their room and served refreshments. They burnt something though. They asked me to bring in a bin and some matches and there was ash in it when they left. They'd opened a window but the room still smelled.'

I shuffled into a sitting position, hoping things might seem clearer from there.

'And the man, the one you'd seen before, did it look like he was Takata's senior?'

'No. When they spoke it was as equals. When they entered the room they debated who should take the head seat. They ended up leaving it empty.'

Another answer that made nothing clearer.

'And the other man?'

'He definitely wasn't their equal, but I don't think he was an employee or anything like that. He looked awkward, I don't know, wary.'

'Was there anything else? Anything unusual, anything that made you think?'

'No. I'm sorry.'

I rubbed my eyes. I needed to think this through with a clear head. It seemed like valuable new information but it pulled in different directions and I was struggling to see how it could help.

'Thank you,' I said. 'I'd like to do something to show my appreciation but I think it's better if we pretended this call didn't happen. You should delete my number. I'll do the same with yours.'

She paused, as though debating something.

'You're sweet,' she said. 'I hope you find your girlfriend and everything works out.'

She hung up and I deleted her number. The only *sakura* in my future would be the cherry blossoms next spring.

I lay back and tried to work my way through what I'd just learned. Takata wasn't the undisputed leader but nor was he being led. I didn't believe the KanEnCo boss was his peer, so who could the other man be? I wondered if I should go back to politicians again.

A chill swept over me. Maybe it was the Ginzo-kai boss. Maybe they were in this together. That would explain why they met where they did and why they did so on equal terms. It would also make it more likely I was being used. More likely I'd be discarded when I was no longer needed.

Perhaps Takata was the real power behind the Kamigawa plant troubles and was using them to extort money from KanEnCo. I might be a smokescreen – a distraction to take attention away from him and make it look as though the Takata-gumi and Ginzo-kai were at odds.

Now I was wide awake, enlightened by information that turned everything murky, each new fact confusing rather than making things clear. It took me some time before I got back to sleep.

EIGHT

Dreaming of the Floating World 3

'And I wish you were wearing it now. You know you excite me in a mawashi,' *she said of his sumō-wrestling apparel.*

He broke into a smile despite his best efforts, undermining the baleful reputation he had forged for himself, first on the streets and then in the dohyō *ring.*

'Ka-chan, you can't say things like that with so many people around.'

Yamaryū *gestured around the room. In response she gave a look as risqué as her words.*

'You know courtesans favour rikishi *sumō wrestlers. Why shouldn't I admit to it? Especially for the most powerful and handsome in the land.'*

He smiled again, for despite her flattery there was truth in what she said. He'd fought his way up from street corner sumō. Tsuji-zumo *bore resemblance to tournament wrestling but had major differences as well. Eye-gouging, throttling and roughhousing a man's most masculine parts meant some tsuji-zumo could be no more refined than a brawl.*

But he'd started life impoverished and it had been his way of hauling himself up. Having established himself as the king of tsuji-zumo, he'd been called for by a daimyō lord with the strongest stable of wrestlers in the land. He'd found legitimate sumō even less challenging and had swept aside rikishi from Edo to Osaka and beyond.

'Ka-chan, it isn't what you say but the way you say it,' he argued. 'Although in truth it's usually both. Somehow you manage not only to get away with it but have us fall at your feet as well.'

'But not so soon I hope,' she replied, refilling his sake. 'The night is still young.'

She lay beside him the next morning.

'We've known each other a long time and you've become my most regular visitor,' she said, trailing a finger around the sinews of his shoulder. 'We have a relationship that's closer than just courtesan and client, I think.'

'All of which is true,' he agreed with a grin. 'And unless it's too outrageous I'll do whatever favour you're about to ask.'

She smiled back, turned his head and kissed him. 'You see. You know me too well.'

She paused to consider her next words.

'This may be too much though, so please hear me out before you agree. It may put you in danger. That's the last thing I want but I'm desperate and I don't know what else to do.'

He turned towards her, no less dashing for the sleep-dishevelled state of his topknot.

'You are, of course, aware of the recent mysteries surrounding my family. I have reason to believe that Lord Genpachi may have been involved. From looking into him, Mizuno of Nihonbashi has *appeared. I could have thought it a coincidence, but the reaction to my discovering these things was unusually severe.'*

'This is related to Mi-chan's accident?'

'It is, which is why I know it's dangerous to seek anything else out. But I'm limited in what I can do. Neither man comes to me as a client; Lord Genpachi for our history, Mizuno because he's a man I have always declined. So my investigations are exhausted within the quarter and I can't leave to learn anything outside.'

'And what do you think I can find out?'

'You're retained by a daimyō. In the course of your work you visit other daimyō, meet their wrestlers and perhaps some of their staff. I was hoping there might be one or two people you trust, and if there are, that you could make subtle enquiries of them.'

He stretched.

'Ka-chan, I have another hour before I leave. Asking a few questions pales beside the pleasure I'll have in that time with you.'

She smiled, reached over and kissed him again, lingering longer this time.

'But the hour will be mine to enjoy – it seems I gain twice.'

'I trust you're as well as you look,' said Yamaryū when he returned from his trip.

She flattered him back with interest and he smiled.

'My wit's not enough to best you with compliments so I'll tell you what I found out instead.'

'Was there much?'

'Unfortunately not. But hopefully enough to lead you to information that can help more.'

He shuffled on the cushion that was failing to cope with his bulk.

'You were right about the connection between Genpachi and Mizuno. Genpachi has apparently borrowed a considerable amount of money from him. So in that regard, their liaising shouldn't be a surprise.'

Her brow creased ever so slightly.

'But their reaction to your prying suggests there's more to it than that. Unfortunately, I couldn't find out what this is but I may have found a way that you can. Despite kabuki's official disfavour, it appears Genpachi has developed a secret taste for it. He's been bringing actors to perform at his residence. Chitairō is especially favoured – he's been boasting about his proximity to power as a result. Speak to him. He should be able to tell you more.'

Her frown deepened.

'I thought you'd be pleased.'

'I am – thank you. It's just . . .'

She stopped a moment to take the scowl from her face.

'I know how popular he is but there's something about Chitairō that makes my skin crawl.'

'So,' he said. 'The grand courtesan herself. To what do I owe the honour?'

She recoiled within but managed to maintain her facade.

'Oh, but the honour is mine, Chitairō-san. With every courtesan falling over herself to see you, I'm grateful you could spare me the time.'

They both knew she didn't like him and had rejected his requests for appointments three times before. Enough to be clear it was not coincidence, more than enough to ensure no further enquiries were made.

'I know you're not a man whose charm and charisma is limited only to the floating world,' she flattered, 'but one whose influence has carried him far beyond Yoshiwara's walls. I was hoping I might

prevail upon your knowledge and benefit from your sage advice.'

She had racked her brains for a more delicate way to get the infor-mation – a chance meeting or a shared interest from which the con-versation could evolve. But there was no alternative. She had avoided him since the day they met and they had nothing in common on which to start. Her only path was through risk. She would need to be blunter than she would like, and ready to react.

'A tayū benefiting from a lowly actor? We're still seen by many as prostitutes advertising our wares to the unrefined. How could I be of assistance to you?'

'But you're speaking to a Yoshiwaran,' she said. 'One who appreci-ates kabuki and knows there are no crimes in pleasures of the flesh. Such debates are beneath you in any case – you're the greatest actor of the day. I believe your wisdom is sought not only by courtesans but by the most exalted figures in the land.'

His eyes brightened as he glimpsed the direction the conversation was heading.

'You have an interest in my acquaintances?'

'There may be one in whom I have reason to be intrigued.'

'And who would that be?' he asked, wanting to hear it from her mouth.

'It was just some nonsense and gossip I heard, but it piqued my interest,' she said. 'That Lord Genpachi has been frequenting the quarter with Mizuno. A most unusual pairing, I thought, and being of a curious mind I was tempted to ask someone who would know more.'

'You came to the right person,' he replied. 'But with so many lines to remember in my profession, my memories have to fight for attention inside my head. They can become blurred. Fortunately they seem to clear after rest.'

'Is that so?' she countered. 'And my thoughts are so much sharper before being jumbled with sleep. At the risk of tiring you, I was wondering if you might be able to recall anything now?'

'Perhaps I can. Lord Genpachi, let me see . . . yes, of course, I was at his residence when Mizuno came to visit just two weeks ago.'

He paused to elicit a response.

'But that's no more than I already know,' she said, playing her part.

'Yet I was as intrigued by this odd couple as you,' he continued. 'Fortunately, I'm on good terms with the maid of Genpachi's favourite consort. I spoke to her during a break in last week's show.'

The breaks in kabuki could last anything up to a couple of hours depending on whom the actors were choosing to break with. Women had been banned from the stage to prevent it being used to promote more lucrative pursuits. But male actors showed no less proclivity to the most ancient art. Chitairō may have been entertaining out of pleasure, not business, but Katsuyama had no doubt his information came from pillow talk.

'It appears Lord Genpachi is only in debt to Mizuno in repayment of the debt Mizuno owes him.'

A poet as well as an actor, thought Katsuyama with irritation.

'And what debt is that?' she asked in her sweetest voice.

'The debt he owes for setting up his business. When he was forced to become rōnin, Mizuno was fortunate to retain Genpachi's favour. Unbeknownst to others, they have an acquaintance that goes back to childhood. It was because of this that Genpachi helped him back on his feet.'

It didn't solve anything but it was interesting, a lead that might bring about more.

'Thank you for your kindness,' she said, relieved to conclude the meeting so painlessly. 'Your reputation for knowledge and good grace is well deserved.'

'I'm honoured by your praise,' he replied. 'But in this instance you may have underestimated me.'

'Why is that?' she asked, alert to the possibility of more substantive news.

He made a show of stretching.

'For a full recollection, I really think I would need that rest.'

It was first time she had bowed to another's wishes. That would have been cause for resentment in itself. But to have her suspicions of his character confirmed, to endure his affronts to her dignity, be subject to his lack of respect – that demanded revenge.

He rolled over, heaving for breath.

'You are all they say. The wait only made it sweeter.'

'You too are everything to be expected,' she replied, the knowledge he would die for the day's actions the only thing that kept the chill from her voice. 'I hope your memory is suitably refreshed.'

'It is,' he said. 'But it may bring you more questions than answers.'

She waited out his dramatic, thespian pause.

'Genpachi and Mizuno may appear strange bedfellows but you now know the reason. There's been a far more unusual visitor to Genpachi. Not only for the differences he's had with the daimyō, but for his history of closeness to you.'

'I can't think who you're referring to,' she said, her defences rising.

'The old ally of your father's lord. Your favoured client,' he said, taking pleasure in dragging the moment out. 'Lord Ezoe.'

NINE

I woke deeply unrested. My head seemed to be spinning whether awake or asleep, the tunnel I was in getting darker. I thought again about trying to escape. If I could be tracked down buying a plane ticket, I could always get on a train. I tried to imagine how that would pan out. It would probably take a month going stir crazy in a small-town ryokan before my money ran out. Then I'd be forced back to face music even more unpleasant than the present tune – if Takata wasn't planning to kill me already, he certainly would be by the time I returned. I decided not to get a train.

I kicked a cupboard door in frustration and regretted it instantly, although the pain distracted me from my finger at least. I was tempted to look but the doctor had told me to leave it alone. Judging by the oscillations between numbness and pain I guessed it was still some way from healing.

I looked around me. Rest and relaxation isn't easily achieved when you suspect you're on a countdown to your own murder. It's even trickier when stuck in a studio flat. Even if I wasn't going to do any more sleuthing, I needed to get out.

I jumped on a Yamanote Line train without thinking and soon found myself in Shibuya. I couldn't face the crowds at Scramble

Crossing so I turned right under the tracks and made my way into Nonbei Yokochō – Drunkard's Alley – instead.

I clambered up the steps at the end of the row of bars into Miyashita Koen. I remembered the park before it had been renovated, when the astroturf pitches had still to replace haphazard patches of gravel and grass. I'd watched trainee baton men there once, being drilled in the tool of their trade. From overseeing car parks to maintaining order at roadworks, legions of them were considered essential to health and safety in Japan. In reality it was a government ruse to keep people in work. If the UK was as generous in its employment, I'd have been told to hire assistants instead of getting the sack.

But the thought wasn't bitter. I liked the pride taken in Japan, whatever the job; the fact you could talk to people rather than automated machines; the taxi drivers with their automatic doors and lace-covered seats. I liked the friendliness beneath the formality; the way people got drunk in the evening and dismissed their behaviour the following day. I liked their art and their sports, their history and culture. As I strolled along, the walk became testimony to my love-in with Japan.

And my love for Tomoe.

That took me by surprise. I hadn't considered her in those terms before.

I'd left the park and was walking towards Harajuku, down Cat Street with its fashionable stores and funky boutiques. The last time I'd been there was with Tomoe. We'd strolled along in the late-morning sun, her arm tucked tightly through mine. She'd been teasing me, telling me I was in for a day of shopping instead of the brunch she'd promised when she called. The half-smile always seeking escape had broken into full beam at my indignant response, shining so brightly that to passers-by I was thrown completely into shade. But she'd been blind to them. The smile was only for me.

While I'd loved every minute I'd never thought it was love. Perhaps I was commitment-phobic but I think it was as much a consequence of being a foreigner, the thought never far away that at some point I'd return home. Whatever the reason, I'd never taken the emotional step. Considering everything that had happened and everything I'd found out, it seemed highly inappropriate to do so now.

A tear trickled down my cheek. I wiped it away quickly and checked to make sure no one had seen. All of a sudden I felt completely alone, more so than I'd ever felt before. And then I realised that I was. My friends in Japan thought I'd gone home, and I'd fobbed off my family telling them all was well here.

A month ago I would have had Tomoe to console me. But that was no longer the case. Now all I had were my fears for myself. And my fears for her, wherever she was.

I slumped in front of the TV when I got home, hoping for something comforting to watch. NHK was showing the sumō *bashō* and it was nearing six o' clock. That meant the two *yokozuna* grand champions would be entering soon. On cue, the cameras focused on Hakuho as he swaggered to the ring, a Mongolian who had been destroying all before him for years. Then there was even more excitement for Tatsuzan. He had just been promoted, the first Japanese yokozuna in over a decade. Dashing despite his menace, he carried his muscular bulk with surprising elan.

And that's when I realised. I would have loved to be the strong-man but it wasn't me. Tatsuzan was the rikishi in my dream.

I arrived while it was still dark, a large bottle of sake in my hand. I could already hear the sound of the rikishi inside, their joint shout followed by the synchronised *shiko* stamp of their warm-up routine.

'I'm sorry, but we don't accept visitors during competition times,' said the boy as he slid the door open.

While the senior rikishi may have looked intimidating on TV, he was more like an oversized baby with his round belly and spiky, dishevelled hair. His chunky mawashi looked like a giant nappy.

'I completely understand,' I said. 'But I was hoping to give this to the *oyakata* when he comes down – we have a mutual friend.'

I thought it better to lie and pretend I was there to see the coach – I imagined the yokozuna was subject to constant attention. Baby Rikishi hesitated, a naïve mistake.

'Really – I'm friends with a good friend of his. He'd be far more upset if you turned me away than if you let me in.'

I felt guilty but it didn't stop me shouldering partway through the door.

'I'll be incredibly quiet – you won't even know that I'm here.'

He let me in and I slipped off my shoes and slid across the floor to a low platform on the right. I received some curious looks but I wasn't concerned – they were the juniors in the *heya*, the sumō stable where they all lived and trained. They had to start and finish their practice early to allow the seniors extra sleep.

It was an hour later when the bigger guns started filing in. The intensity of training immediately stepped up. Mountains of muscle and flesh pounded into each other, propelled from tree trunks for legs. They were accompanied by a soundtrack of deep, sickening slaps, the kind of sound you feel as much as you hear. The shock-waves surged through the dohyō into the stage, sending shudders up through my spine. Over and over they crashed into one another. Sweat and blood flowed freely as new welts and bruises piled on old lumps and scars.

Suddenly the room quietened and for a moment everything stopped. I looked over and saw Tatsuzan, massive even by the standards of the giants already there. Then, as if on a hidden signal, the carnage resumed. Baby rushed to help Tatsuzan from a yukata kimono as big as a tent. He nodded towards me. Baby started to speak but didn't get beyond a few words before Tatsuzan turned and started to make his way over. He moved with a swaggering grace but the ground still shook like the approach of the T-Rex in *Jurassic Park*.

'You have a friend in common with Oyakata?' he boomed.

'Well, actually, no,' I said, my voice as comparatively small as I was to his size. 'It's my girlfriend. And she doesn't know the oyakata. She's friends with you.'

At that point, even more than the moments leading up to it, I very much hoped it was true.

'Hey, Fatman!' I yelled at the TV in a moment of exuberance. 'I'll take you down with my Ray Clarence one-punch special. POW!'

I mimed my imagined knockout move with a vigour I hoped would compensate for its lack of style and technique.

Tomoe giggled.

'Ray Clarence one-punch,' she mocked. 'I could probably beat you up.'

I proved her wrong by putting her in a half-nelson but she still wasn't particularly impressed.

'So you can beat up a girl,' she said, in contempt of my strongman pose. 'You'd still get destroyed by any rikishi.'

'You really think so? Look at them – they're all quivering fat.'

'There's fat on them but it's muscle underneath. Look,' she pointed at the TV. 'Look at his legs and shoulders. They're even more impressive when you see them in the flesh.'

'You know rikishi?' I asked, intrigued by yet another in her endless array of new facts.

'My parents were friends with the parents of Tatsuzan,' she said, his name not catching as he was yet to hit the yokozuna rank. 'We knew each other when we were young.'

My dream suggested they were closer than that, although it was a flimsy premise on which to base any assumptions. I wasn't happy at the thought of this alpha male spending time with my girlfriend, but now a small part of me wanted it to be true. Tatsuzan was intimidating even before he thought me a madman babbling about imaginary friends. And at that moment, he was all that I had.

'I'm Chōshi Tomoe's boyfriend,' I said, and waited for the inevitable look of surprise. He was subtle at least.

'Is she OK?' he asked with obvious concern. 'Do you know where she is?'

It was my question. I tried another.

'You already knew she was missing?'

'Of course I did. She's like a sister to me.'

I allowed myself an inward smile.

'In any case, we both live in the floating world. We hear what happens to one other.'

'Do you know why she's missing then?' I asked, hoping the floating world's suspended grapevine might help.

Before he could answer, a deep, grumpy voice rumbled across the room.

'What's going on? Why have we got a gaijin with us, upsetting training and disturbing Tatsuzan?'

The oyakata was an ex-yokozuna himself and the authority he'd carried didn't seem to have dissipated since he retired.

'It's OK, Oyakata,' Tatsuzan assured him. 'He knows a friend of mine. He just wanted to come by to wish me luck and bring a bottle of sake for you.'

He wheeled around with the sake. The oyakata looked at it, pleased despite himself. He grunted appreciation but the feelings of gratitude didn't seem to last long.

'Well, now you've given your best wishes, my yokozuna needs to train – he has a bashō to win.'

Tatsuzan turned back to me. 'I need to get going or he'll chew my ear off and most likely tear you apart. Meet me at Ryōgoku Kokugikan after today's bouts. I'll arrange things – just tell them you're there to see me.'

According to Sumida I was as easy to follow as a child so I'd been as evasive as I could when visiting the sumō beya. I took a similarly roundabout route to get to Ryōgoku Kokugikan Stadium, changing trains more than I needed to and darting onto the final one with only seconds to spare.

I was ushered in as soon as I said my name – if the Kokugikan was sumō's temple then Tatsuzan was its god. The attendant led me into the building, through the entrance hall and then around a corridor where cheering from the last bouts of the day could be heard. Abruptly he pulled me to the right and down a flight of stairs. I came out of the door at the bottom to find myself in the stadium's hallowed inner grounds.

It was a different world to the one above, a land of giants where anything less than massive was positively small. Its inhabitants lumbered through passageways that struggled to contain them, announcing themselves in advance through the sweet-scented camellia oil used on their elaborate hair.

As I did my best to avoid being crushed, I heard grunts and slaps from a doorway. The attendant indicated I should enter, then turned and expertly wove his way off.

Inside, a rikishi was thrusting his palms at a thick wooden pillar that shuddered at every strike. To his right, a long platform of tatamis was split by a thin passageway in its centre. It was empty except for a few rikishi readying themselves for home, and Baby, who was waiting for me.

'Sorry if I got you in trouble earlier.'

'That's OK,' he grinned. 'I get shouted all the time – it actually feels better when there's a reason.'

Before he could say anything else, something in the atmosphere changed and a murmur of voices grew to a clamour outside the door. It opened, and a sweaty Tatsuzan squeezed through the wide frame. He nodded at me while he was towelled down, his chest heaving as he fought for breath.

'Did he win?'

'Yes. He's got a perfect record so far!'

Baby's excitement was palpable but it had different foundations to mine. Tatsuzan had been clear he didn't know where Tomoe was, but he'd said enough to suggest the floating world might. If it really was so well connected, surely I could hope I would soon see her again.

My heart sank. Was that it?

We were in a small restaurant near the stadium eating *chankonabe*, the hotpot dish favoured by rikishi that's reasonably healthy when eaten by the bowl instead of the bucket. It had been a promising start.

'Tomo-chan came to me a month or two ago,' he said. 'She told me about her father and wanted to find out if there was anything I knew.'

'Why would you have known anything?'

'Sumō might not be as popular with the younger generation,' he explained. 'But it still is with the old guard, and they run things in Japan. They support sumō in all sorts of ways – it's not just about turning up to the tournaments. They sponsor us, take memberships at heyas and so on. We meet them and get to hear things as a result.'

'And did you know anything? Could you help her?

'I knew a little, but not very much,' he said, as he emptied another ladle of chankonabe into the oversized bowl the owner seemed to keep especially for him. 'But now I'm worried it was enough to get her in trouble and that her disappearance was my fault.'

'But if it was something you said that caused her to go missing, you must have some idea of where she is.'

'You don't think I'd have done something about it if that was the case?' he said sharply, showing irritation for the first time.

'I'm sorry,' I said, and his expression softened at my dejection. 'I've been worrying about her so much I can't think straight.'

I tried to exhale my disappointment and started again.

'What was it you told her? And why do you think it got her in trouble?'

'At the last bashō in September, the head of the Takata-gumi dropped by the changing rooms.'

He returned a fish ball he'd been about to scoop into his mouth.

'You know who the Takata-gumi are?'

'I've heard of them.'

'Their oyabun, Takata Eiji, I don't think I'd trust him but to talk to he's a reasonable guy. We chatted a while but after five minutes or so Fujiwara Daisuke popped his head around the door. It's like that sometimes; powerbrokers come in, celebs – some days they all turn up at once. Anyway, he asked if Takata would mind stepping into the room next door to have a word with a mutual friend. That was it for a while, but after a few minutes I heard raised voices and whoever the other person was stormed off. Takata, cool as you like, stuck his head back in, apologised for the disturbance and wished me luck in my bout. But I had to wonder about the other guy. I mean, what kind of man raises his voice at Takata Eiji?'

It was the question I wanted him to answer. Wasn't it the sort of thing the floating world was supposed to know?

'Why do you think this had anything to do with Tomoe's disappearance?'

'Because when she came to me asking questions, I told her about it. You know what she's like – once she has her mind set on something there's no way she'll let up. And a couple of weeks after I told her, she was gone.'

'What do you think she did?'

He looked at me.

'She must have gone to see Fujiwara. And whatever she found out must have got her in trouble. I've tried to contact him but he won't speak to me – we've had some difficulties in the past. I can't have pressure put on him either – he knows powerful people too.'

It had been bothering me since he first said the name, but there had been so much else to take in.

'Who is Fujiwara Daisuke?'

He looked at me incredulously.

'You don't know him?' he said. 'He's an actor. Haven't you seen any of his films?'

TEN

'I'm afraid he doesn't know anyone of that name,' she said politely. 'Perhaps you have him confused with somebody else.'

'No, it's certainly him,' I said. 'Would it be possible to try again? Cho-u-shi To-mo-e.'

'I'm afraid that was the name I gave him and he had no idea who she was. I'm sorry I can't be of any more help.'

She was cutting me off, and with it ending the trail and blocking my path to Tomoe. I'd probably only got this far by being a gaijin, an unusual, intriguing voice on the other end of the phone. She seemed keen to get back to more standard enquiries.

'But perhaps—'

'Thank you for calling, I'm so pleased you enjoy his films,' she said, and hung up.

However much of a proactive catalyst you are, there are limits to what you can do when a film star brushes you off. The only thing I could think of was to go through the Takata-gumi but there were two problems with that: one, I'd been told very clearly to stop catalysing and get some rest; and two, it seemed Fujiwara Daisuke was on the side of whoever had the will, inclination and power to face down Takata. Using the Takata-gumi would likely bring more trouble than help.

It wasn't just the logistics of getting through to Fujiwara that troubled me – I was disturbed by the fact I was trying to reach him at all. To this point, my dreams had made a strange kind of sense – my brain sifting through the insanity that had overtaken my life. But I wasn't a movie buff and when I did go to the cinema I usually settled for Hollywood fare. I hadn't heard of Fujiwara. I didn't have any experiences involving actors. Recently I hadn't even seen any films. So dreaming about an actor was already odd. Having one enter my life – or avoid doing so more precisely – was unsettling in the extreme.

The phone rang.

'Hurry up, we're outside.'

'What do you mean? This is my rest week, Kumichō said.'

'Rest at Horitoku's – your appointment's in half an hour.'

I cursed as I hung up. It would surely be easier for everyone if they could just give me advance warning. I grabbed my jacket and made for the door.

I went to the passenger door of Sumida's car and my heart sank. I got in the rear instead and was met by one of Sumida's understated greetings and the silent back of Kurotaki's head. The tension didn't lessen when we set off – Sumida's taciturn nature wasn't the ideal foil for gliding through mildly awkward situations, let alone times like these.

Kurotaki appeared to be simmering quietly, but after a few minutes he decided to break the mood with his unique brand of charm.

'What's this shit?'

'"Grateful Days" by Dragon Ash. It's a hip-hop tune from way back.'

'It's shit.'

Sumida was unmoved. 'When you do me a favour and give me a lift, you can play whatever you want.'

Kurotaki grunted, his need to let out his bile ominously unfulfilled.

'Fucking slut.'

I had no intention of responding. I wanted nothing to do with him.

'Fucking slut!'

Sumida finally reacted to the implicit demand for a response.

'What?'

'That slut over there.'

Kurotaki pointed over the crossroads we were held at towards an elegant Japanese girl and her well-dressed gaijin boyfriend.

'What else can you say about a girl that lets herself get fucked by a gaijin? Dirty whore. No offence.'

The last words were directed at me and just as intended there was offence. I bristled at the slight levelled my way, the gaijin he was really referring to. But my real fury was for Tomoe and the slur aimed at her. Having failed to protect her in person, my urge to defend her honour was more powerful than I would have thought. I battled against it and this time managed to swallow my anger before it raged to my mouth. There was nothing I could do now. I needed to put my feelings aside until a time I could act.

'You can let me out here,' grunted Kurotaki, getting out without another word and slamming the door.

I moved to the front seat and seethed in silence.

'So, have you found out what you need to, for whatever you have to do?' asked Sumida, interrupting my thoughts of revenge.

'Apparently,' I said, my anger latching on to this festering irritation. 'Although I don't know what I'm supposed to have found out and I have no idea what I'm going to be made to do.'

Sumida smiled. I assumed it was at Takata's guile rather than my plight.

'Don't worry about it – he'll have all the angles covered. Just keep watching him. You'll soon know.'

'How long have you been a yakuza?' I asked, suddenly curious about him.

'Nine years,' he said. 'I joined from a biker gang. We were a bunch of arseholes, to be honest. We didn't give a shit about anything – we did whatever we wanted to do. But you can only get away with that so long without stepping on other people's toes. I was caught dealing meth in Takata-gumi territory. They slapped me around a bit and told me I could join them, leave town or be killed.'

'And what do you want? I mean, how long are you going to keep doing this?'

He looked puzzled by the question. 'Forever – who else is going to employ me now? In any case, I get girls when I want them and make as much money as I can spend. Why would I want to change? There are plenty of opportunities in the yakuza as long as you've got balls and a semblance of a brain. I keep my head down and my eyes and ears open. I'll be ready when my chances come.'

He fell silent again. He was probably as surprised as me by how much he'd said.

'What about Kumichō? How did he get to where he is?'

'Kumichō? He's old-school.'

His attention was caught by a fleck of dust on the dashboard that didn't exist. He brushed it away.

'He was born around the end of the war. You wouldn't believe it to look at him now but he came up in hard times – he had to fight for everything he's got. Back then there were hardly any guns, it was all hand-to-hand, vicious stuff, and Kumichō was meant to be the most ferocious of them all. There are all sorts of stories. He's meant to have ripped the voice box out of one guy and gouged the eyeballs out of another, all in the same fight.'

I shivered. I felt I now knew more about Takata than I needed to, but Sumida was like a monk breaking his vows.

'Then he got put away for a murder. It wasn't actually him – it was the boss of the time, Dewaya's, back when we were known as the Dewaya-kai. But taking someone else's sentence was a good way to earn your spurs, especially if it was the kumichō's – you'd get a certain promotion for that. I think he did it for other reasons though. Apparently, there was a lot of internal positioning as Dewaya grew old. Kumichō thought he'd let them weaken each other with in-fighting and clean up when he came out.

'When he was released he took his own sub-crew and moved through Tokyo, kicking out anyone who stood in his way. With his success, the fear-factor and everything else, he wasn't challenged when Dewaya stepped down. That's when we became the Takata-gumi.'

So Sumida was keeping his counsel while he learned, but he clearly had his sights set higher for when Takata was no longer around. He might have been below Kurotaki at that moment but if I was going to put money on anyone for the long-term, it would have been him.

'Come on, get out – we're here,' he said, interrupting my thoughts. 'You've got a four-hour session. Look out for me when you're done.'

I just about held back a string of obscenities. It turned out that while the outline had been inked with a machine, the shading was to be done by *tebori,* literally to 'hand-carve'. Horitoku didn't go as far as chisel into me but considering the tool he was using he might as well have. It looked like a slim, flat-ended paintbrush, but in place of bristles at its tip, needles were bound to a metal stem with red silk thread. He punched it into my skin with alarming speed and as he jabbed and flicked the tool made a disturbing sound, somewhere between the click of knitting needles and a barber's scissors' snip. It felt just like being stabbed with a needle-tipped paintbrush.

'The girl,' I said, looking for distractions. 'Make her pretty please. As close to Tomoe as you can.'

He stopped.

'Of course she'll be pretty,' he said sharply. 'She'll be the most beautiful girl you've ever seen. You think you've got an amateur on the job?'

I apologised. It was the horimono equivalent of questioning Hokusai. Even if I wasn't obliged to show respect where it was due, the conversation with Sumida was fresh in my mind.

'I just meant that ukiyo-e, it was incredibly beautiful, but, um . . . they never managed to make the girls look quite as good.'

'Maybe they had different criteria for what they considered beautiful then.'

'Maybe. I still can't help thinking they were better at mythical creatures and landscapes.'

'Well, keep pondering on that and don't concern yourself with me,' he said as he resumed the assault. 'I'm tattooing the likeness of Ka-chan – I wouldn't make her anything less than perfect. She'll be so beautiful you'll wish you had her on your chest so you could see her every morning when you shave.'

It was good enough for me.

'By the way,' I started again with an unasked question from my last visit. 'Do you know why Kumichō is making me have a tattoo? Not that there's any reason I shouldn't,' I added hastily. 'It's just you said fewer yakuza are having them now so they can't be as easily identified.'

'Maybe he thought you needed some encouragement to identify yourself,' he replied. 'But he loves ukiyo-e and horimono in any case. I did his bodysuit and he often drops by to see the latest work.'

The thought made him wistful.

'It's a shame, the decline in yakuza clients. I could relate to them, I understood what they did. Everything's changing. An "IT consult-ant" started coming recently – I've got no idea what that even is. He seems a nice enough guy but I can hardly understand a word that he says.'

He drifted into his reveries. My focus was on pain. Rather than becoming numbed my skin seemed to hurt more with fatigue, the instrument of torture not only needle-sharp but now red-hot as well. I craved the short pauses between attacks where excess ink was wiped away with a soothing damp tissue and became increasingly despairing at their end. A thought distracted me.

'Do you know Fujiwara Daisuke?' I asked, wondering if the floating world winds might allow their whispers to drift my way.

'No,' he replied bluntly. 'Why?'

249

I deliberated a moment. I was talking to a man who did tattoos for the Takata-gumi and was close to Takata himself. Opening up didn't seem to be the best way to keep something quiet. Then again, there was something about him that made me think he could keep a confidence, especially if he thought it would help Tomoe. I didn't have any other ways to get a break.

'I wanted to speak to him. I think he's linked to Tomoe's disappearance.'

He grunted and stabbed my back.

'I know of him but I don't know him. The kabuki actors are still part of our world, but the TV and film guys – they've got one foot out.'

'Ow!'

I reacted to a particularly brutal attack on my shoulder blade. He ignored me and jabbed at the same spot again.

'Now, why would you think he's part of the business with Ka-chan?'

He might have had my limited trust but I wasn't going to expose Tatsuzan.

'His name came up.'

'Well, if I'm not mistaken he's under the management of the Tasogare Talent Group,' he said.

'That's right. I tried calling his agent but she wouldn't put me through.'

'Mm. Well, be careful how you go there – they're owned by the Ginzo-kai.'

There they were again. Every place I wanted to go seemed to have them waiting behind the door, something that was particularly inconvenient considering they topped the list of people who wanted me dead.

It suggested it may have been their boss at the sumō meeting. That made sense – I imagined he was one of the very few people with the clout to argue with Takata. It also implied they were no longer on good terms. And if your enemy's enemy is your friend, this might mean Takata didn't want me killed. It was a rare ray of light, especially now I knew his methods of dealing with people he did want to harm.

'So why didn't you get through? You strike me as a resourceful kind of guy.'

'I'm a gaijin nobody, he's a superstar. If he doesn't want to speak to me, what can I do?'

'Why didn't you get Ka-chan to help?'

At times it seemed like I was on a different wavelength to everyone I'd recently met.

'I'm sorry, I don't understand what you mean?'

'Your girlfriend is one of the most admired and respected people in the floating world. You might be inconsequential, but the name Katsuyama opens a lot of doors.'

ELEVEN

'I represent Katsuyama II. Would you please have Fujiwara-san call me as soon as he returns.'

There wasn't much she could do faced with the newfound authority in my voice. This wasn't the request of a nobody. It was an equal making a demand.

'But—'

I cut her off by leaving my number.

'Please have him call me as soon as he can,' I said and hung up.

Two minutes later my mobile rang.

'I'm told you represent Katsuyama-san?'

'That's right,' I said brusquely. It was petty but I'd had enough of being the begging boy – someone else could make an effort for once.

'And what is it you want with me?'

'I'd like to meet up. There were some loose ends left when Katsuyama went away and your name's come up more than once. I thought I should check with you before things went any further.'

It was a gamble but either he had enough of an involvement to be worried by this or he didn't, in which case there was no point meeting up.

'It's not going to be easy,' he said, sounding blasé. 'My schedule's incredibly busy. When were you thinking?'

'Sometime this afternoon or the evening at the latest – it needs to be soon.'

We'd see how relaxed he really was.

'Wait a moment,' he said, not sounding particularly happy at the demand.

I heard him cover the phone, muffling the voices that followed.

'This evening then,' he said. 'Come to my place in Omotesandō.'

I took a right out of the station down Omotesandō Dōri and then turned left, away from the designer boutiques and into quiet side roads. They were similar to the others in this castle-town of a city, but differed in their refinement and expense. Fujiwara's place was hidden at the end of an alley that came off a crescent. It had a particularly luxurious air.

I rang the bell and after being quizzed briefly I was buzzed in. The gate opened to reveal a small but well-proportioned garden surrounding a building that oozed money rather than charm. A maid was waiting at the door, and after fussing over me for a moment, she led me through a white-walled hallway into a large, coldly minimalist room.

'Thank you for coming at such short notice,' said Fujiwara, rising from the sofa. Considering I'd been the one who demanded the meeting, it was an obvious attempt at gaining control. 'Can I get you a drink?'

There was nothing one could immediately single out for criticism. He was handsome, his hair was perfectly styled and his clothes looked like they came from all the right shops. But something about him was too obvious, as though he took his tips from watch ads in glossy magazines. I may have backed down to Takata and Kurotaki but I wasn't going to defer to any alpha-male business from him.

'I'll have a glass of cognac,' I said. 'Hine, if you've got it, but if not something else nice. It's been a long day.'

He tried to give me a strong look but it wasn't up to recent standards. I ignored it and he nodded to the maid who scurried from the room.

'So what it is you want to clarify?' he asked in a more haughty tone. 'It's been a busy day for me too and I have further appointments after yours.'

Again there was nothing I could put my finger on, but it seemed as though with this his true colours shone through. Or perhaps it was me. He wasn't only film-star good-looking, he was talented – I'd checked him out on Wikipedia – and there was a possibility he'd slept with Tomoe as well. Jealousy doesn't make for a good judge. I decided I disliked him all the same.

'Katsuyama-san came to see you before she went away,' I said.

'She did,' he agreed.

'She wanted to talk to you about the sumō meeting,' I added, hoping the fewer blanks there appeared to be, the more he'd fill in.

'She did.'

He wasn't really playing his part.

'So why were you there with him?'

He looked at me slightly intrigued. Perhaps it was a different line of questioning to Tomoe's.

'My agency had a couple of ringside boxes and offered one to him. Their relationship's been getting stronger recently and I suppose they wanted to encourage that. His meeting with Takata was already arranged, but I think he felt it would be more natural to go backstage with someone like me.'

'Someone like you?'

He looked at me in exasperation.

'An actor.'

I looked back blankly.

'Actors, rikishi, artists, writers – we're all part of the floating world.'

I smiled. He didn't know he only had associate status.

'With me being part of the ukiyo, it was only natural I accompanied him behind the scenes.'

This was all well and good but it was getting me no closer to knowing who 'he' was. Asking would have given my ignorance away.

'Why's his relationship been getting closer with your agency?'

'It's been that way since Kōda died. I imagine it will be until another *kuromaku* appears.'

Christ. Instead of the name I needed, I was hit with a barrage of other information. Now I needed to look into 'Kōda' and find out what a kuromaku was.

'Onishi had visited the studio before but very rarely. It was only when Kōda died that he started to come more often. He'd meet Yabu – Tokyo boss of the Ginzo-kai – there.'

Finally, among all of this, he had a name. Onishi. But it didn't make sense. Why would the Education Minister be mixed up in this? His only claim to fame I knew of was his controversial revision of the history curriculum. Short of having the Chinese bomb Pearl Harbor it was difficult to see how it could be portrayed in a more nationalist light.

'You're close to Onishi then?' I asked, trying to keep him talking.

For a split-second his studied mask of nonchalance slipped and a look of terror flashed across his eyes. Almost immediately, he reorganised his face.

'I wouldn't say close; we're acquainted. But anyway,' he hurried on, 'in a break I took him to the changing area where he met up with Takata. And that's it. That's all I know – your people know a lot more.'

If that was true, what had worried him into meeting me?

'But I don't know exactly what happened at the meeting.'

'Your boss does. You can ask him.'

'He's a busy man. And maybe he would tell me something different to what you told To— Katsuyama. So can you tell me what you told her please?'

But something had changed in his expression. Whatever he had thought I had on him, he no longer believed I did.

'Maybe your girlfriend had more persuasive methods of interrogation,' he said, straight-faced but with a smirk in his voice. 'I don't think you'll match up, so perhaps you should find time with your boss.'

His taunt worked too well.

'Don't blame me for your girlfriend's profession,' he said, flinching as I sprang to my feet. 'I only slept with her. It wasn't down to me.'

It was a strange choice of words but they only jarred later.

'But she didn't want to sleep with you, did she?' I said, my lip curling. 'You've got all these starlets and groupies after you, but deep down you know it's for what they can get from your fame. Then you met someone who had no need for it, the kind of person whose response would tell you whether you have any meaningful appeal. And she didn't want you, did she? The only way you could maintain your self-pretence was to take advantage of her when she was desperate.'

'You don't know anything. It wasn't the—'

He stopped himself.

'No, go on, finish what you were going to say. Surely you're not scared of me?'

He sneered. 'Look at you. What, you think you're some kind of big-shot because you've got the Takata name? Good luck. See how long that lasts. The gaijin-gumi are on their last legs. Takata's even started running to the police. So no, I'm not scared of you.'

I saw him give a faint nod towards the doorway, presumably at the maid. I didn't pay it much attention because I'd sat down and was unravelling the bandage on my hand.

'You see that,' I said, holding it up. 'I did it to myself. I'm not the first and I won't be the last, but until you've cut off your own finger you can't appreciate what it does to the way that you think.'

I felt something cold spread through me. It took the fire from my temper but made my anger more clinical.

'I've never been in the slightest bit violent – I even used to get squeamish watching films. But when you take a knife to your own finger, when you cut through your own flesh and bone, it does something to the way you see things and the way that you act. Now it wouldn't bother me to see someone get hurt. I honestly think if I had to, I could grab something like that pen there and stab a person right in the eye.'

I don't know who was more chilled by what I said, him or me. But before either of us could react his mobile went, its ringtone repelling the electrified air. It seemed to activate something in him. He pulled it from his pocket and bolted from the room.

I was much slower to react and when I did it was to curse. His nod to the maid and then the phone call moments later – they weren't likely coincidence. The last time I'd been in a meeting similarly interrupted, I'd ended up flying out the window of a moving car.

It was only when I reached the front that I realised an unconventional departure might have its complications, but the thought of the man-monster from last time gave me the boost I needed and I hurled myself over the gate. As I hurried down the alley I tried to work out which way to go at its end. I assumed they'd come the same way I had so I decided to turn left. A glance to the right affirmed the decision – a car with blacked-out windows was parked fifty metres away.

It was hard to believe they could have got there that quickly but I wasn't going to leave it to chance. I kicked into a sprint up a small winding road, then kept going straight where it curved away. I vaulted the walls of the apartment building's garden, rejoining the street on the other side.

I paused to work out my position. If I followed the same line I thought I'd be on course for Gaien-nishi Dōri. I took off again and before long the sound of cars in the distance suggested I was right. But the triumph of my bearings was short-lived – the street narrowed to a path that ended in small steps abutted by a high wire fence. I looked back. I couldn't see anyone following, but if they were, running towards them didn't seem a great idea. I turned back to the fence, swore at it once and started to clamber up.

On the other side it was just a short jog to the main road, which wasn't too bad even with the ankle I turned on the drop down. But despite it looking like I'd made good on my escape, my instincts were yet to be convinced. When a taxi pulled up, I pushed my way in almost before the passengers had a chance to get out.

I ducked below the line of the window. The driver gave me a quizzical look.

'Yoyogi, please.'

If I was being tracked I assumed they'd look for me in Takadanobaba rather than at Tomoe's place.

When the car had gone a few hundred yards I felt confident enough to sit up. I was tempted to close my eyes and revel in temporary safety, but I couldn't afford to relax. I needed to fit the new information into place.

The third man was Onishi, the Education Minister, but I could see no reason for him being involved. He clearly was though, and possibly more than he would have liked due to the death of Kōda, the kuromaku who'd passed away.

I googled the term. Originally, it had referred to the wirepuller who manipulated the kabuki stage with a black curtain. Now it meant a fixer, the link between the yakuza, business and politics.

So the normal balance of power had been skewed. Without a middleman, Onishi had met Takata in person, evidently not to the most cohesive effect. Considering Onishi's apparent relationship with the Ginzo-kai, this shouldn't have been too much of a surprise.

But Takata was so wily I remained suspicious. One had to be ready for double-deals and manipulation whenever he was involved.

Perhaps he had aligned with the Ginzo-kai against Onishi, or maybe he was trying to turn Onishi against them.

It still didn't answer the question of why Onishi was involved.

I stared out of the window at some of Tokyo's less picturesque streets, their drab grey and the autumn drizzle at one with my mood. My mind jumped to what Fujiwara had said about Takata going turncoat. It surely couldn't be true. But if he had, and everyone knew, he'd be in trouble. And if he was in trouble my situation would turn sticky pretty fast too.

It was unrelenting. Anytime I found anything out it only revealed a lot more I didn't know. Every time I spilt my blood for an answer, more questions and the probability of more punishment arose.

The taxi let me out at Tomoe's. I went up to her flat thinking it would comfort me, but her scent was fading and that depressed me instead. I curled up on the sofa and held one of her jumpers to my face. I needed to be with her, to feel her body tight against mine.

I thought of the times I'd lain on this spot and stroked her calf as she walked by; kissed the nape of her neck as she cooked; or shared the gentlest embrace as we drifted to post-coital sleep. I had to believe I'd do those things again.

But I knew if I was going to, it wouldn't be without a fight. And I knew I wasn't up to it alone. Even if she wasn't here I was going to need Tomoe's help. I would have to borrow her passion, her fire and her strength.

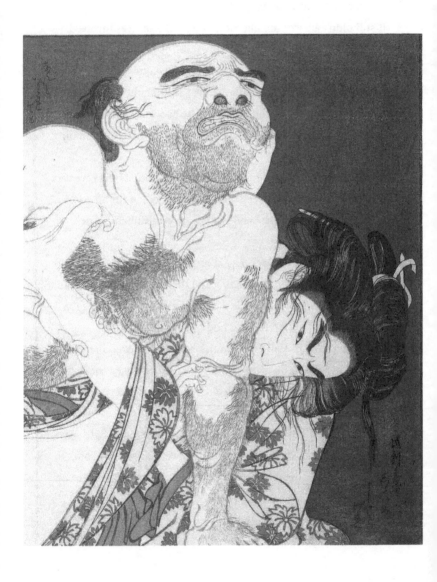

TWELVE

I couldn't help but stare at his hands.

'You want another drink?' he asked, misreading my pre-occupation.

'No, I'm fine. Thank you.' I took a sip from my glass to make the point.

'You've been busy for a resting man,' he said.

'I have?'

'I thought so. Haven't you?'

This would get silly if neither of us committed. I tried to think what Takata was most likely to know. Sakura. I felt a stab of irritation. It was all very well her making big sympathetic eyes, but it wasn't much good if she betrayed me straight afterwards.

'Well, I did remember a detail I thought I should check on in Senzoku—'

'And you thought your easy charm and your way with the flowers of the floating world would outweigh my influence? That she'd help you and not report back?'

That pretty much summed it up.

'Well, no, I just thought it was something I should follow up on in case it could be helpful to us.'

He didn't say anything, he just kept looking at me, waiting for me to reveal something else he already knew. I tried to decide what it was. It had to be Fujiwara – I'd taken too much care when meeting Tatsuzan. I wished I'd been more consistent in my subterfuge.

'I spoke to Fujiwara Daisuke the actor as well. Tomoe once told me they were acquainted so I thought I'd see if there was anything I could find out from him.'

'And was there?'

'A little, but I think I got less than you already know. We had a slight falling-out – I had to leave more suddenly than I'd planned.'

'I heard. You were better at escaping your protectors than you were at covering your tracks on the way. But your haste was judicious – Ginzo-kai men turned up shortly after you left.'

The thought of being caught by them felt like a stone dropped in my stomach.

'Was there anything else?' he asked, maintaining his eliciting gaze. I decided I wouldn't bite this time.

'No, that's it – I had to get some rest in after all.'

His eyes danced. He didn't believe me, but I don't think he knew about Tatsuzan. I also think he quite enjoyed the fact. It was a challenge, something different from his day-to-day.

'You're becoming quite enigmatic, Clarence-san,' he said with a slight smile before becoming serious again. 'But we need to get down to business – your role in the KanEnCo AGM. You'll find there will be sōkaiya at the meeting. That's not something for you to be concerned about. They're affiliates of ours and have been advised of your presence.'

I appreciated the fact I wouldn't get a beating but I recoiled at the thought of being on the same side. My mind went to Eriko's mother. How could I turn up with her enemies after she'd taken me into her trust?

'I don't believe it will be a particularly long meeting,' Takata continued, and as he would be determining its length there seemed a good chance he was right. 'And I think the protest groups may find it difficult to have their voices heard. I would like you to put a question to the board, however.'

He paused a moment and took a sip from his glass.

'I'd like you to ask the president for the Ishikawa Report.'

I waited for further instructions. He took another sip.

'Is that all?'

'That's it.'

'What is the Ishikawa Report? Is it something to do with the planning process behind the plant?'

The point of my investigations, I didn't say. The source of much of my pain.

He looked at me, his eyes probing.

'Why do you want to know?'

'It's at the centre of everything. It unravels the whole affair.'

'Maybe,' he said. 'Or maybe just some of it. But you haven't answered the question. Why do you want to know? Do you intend to do something with the information? Or is it just curiosity that's making you ask?'

I hadn't thought of it in those terms. I'd focused on getting to the heart of things. I didn't have a plan of what I would do when I arrived.

'I can only answer that when I have an answer to my question,' I said. 'I can't plan for what I don't know.'

Something else came to mind.

'Why did you have Kurotaki stop the plant chairman from showing it to me?'

'It works to both our benefits for others to see you as a loose cannon I'm trying to rein in.'

I'm sure it benefited him but I didn't see how it worked well for me – it sounded more like I was being used in a dangerous game. He didn't offer anything else so I returned to his question.

'Well, anyway, if it led me to Tomoe then yes, I'd do whatever I have to do.'

'Of course, Chōshi-san,' he said with a faint smile. I took it as wistful.

'You weren't . . . ?'

I blurted it out without thinking. He looked at me with sharp eyes.

'I have a wife.'

'Of course, I didn't mean to suggest . . . It's just . . . I'd heard that sometimes it isn't considered cheating if it's paid for.'

'That's not how I feel.'

His eyes were black stones. Any warmth or charm had disappeared from his voice.

'To be frank you dishonour your girlfriend with your doubts. You make yourself unworthy of her.'

Had my fear allowed it, I would have felt piqued at the rebuke for doubting my girlfriend – the one who had sold herself for sex.

'Your girlfriend was in a position that was not of her choosing. Yet she excelled in its cultural aspects and took only the most limited clientele in its more personal side.'

The words chimed with something I'd heard before.

'What do you mean, "not of her choosing"?'

He looked surprised.

'She didn't tell you?'

'Tell me what? We didn't have much of an opportunity to discuss her job before she disappeared.'

He refilled my glass.

'You'll need to remain calm while we discuss this – no matter the provocation. I won't accept any outbursts.'

It wasn't a good way to start.

'You know, of course, that your girlfriend is a lady of outstanding beauty.'

I nodded.

'From the start of her career she was just as well regarded for her work in the arts. But there are shadows even in the floating world. Those who lurk in its dark corners were drawn to her light.

'Tanzen was still new then and while the idea of reviving the tayūs was a good one, finding the right calibre of employee was hard. That isn't to say that they hadn't taken on some illustrious figures, but Chōshi-san was special and they were desperate to get her on board. However, as you are aware, she is a strong-willed young lady. She refused their offers however much money they dangled in her face.'

He looked at me carefully. I sensed there was something horrible to come.

'Now her father—'

'Her father's involved in this?'

I still imagined him as a whistle-blower or some such.

'Her father's business abilities were at the opposite end of the scale to Chōshi-san's gift for the arts. He borrowed money to make good on the losses he made, but good went after bad. If you follow the trail from moneylenders, you'll find there aren't too many degrees of separation from men like us.'

I had my qualms about being included in the grouping but I wasn't about to interrupt.

'The trail of money in Chōshi-san's father's case led to the Ginzo-kai, and as you know, the Ginzo-kai were backers of Tanzen.

'You must realise it's impossible for debts in our industry to be forfeited or else everyone would default and that would lead to the system's collapse. But as a yakuza, one can benefit from being open to creative settlement. It was clear to the Ginzo-kai that in this case they owned a debt they couldn't recoup. At the same time they were chasing an asset they were unable to gain. By bringing the two together they thought they could do the impossible and achieve two seemingly unachievable aims. So they offered Chōshi-san's father a choice.'

I didn't want to hear it.

'If he didn't make up the difference within a week he would be stripped of every asset he owned down to his last set of clothes. He'd be left to live his life in destitution, and at a random point in the future he would be killed. And it wouldn't be a quick death. Alternatively, he could persuade his daughter to enter Tanzen's employment.'

'He sold Tomoe out?'

I couldn't believe it. She was his daughter. She was all that remained of his dead wife. My mind jumped to the abuse I'd heaped upon her. She'd only been doing it to save her dad.

'Yes,' said Takata. 'But it's a bit more complicated than that.'

'What do you mean?'

The question was instinctive. I wasn't sure I could handle anything else.

'Chōshi-san's father was a weak man – I can only think her virtues come from her mother. He didn't refuse the Ginzo-kai as a father should. But he didn't have the mettle to tell his daughter of the price he was to make her pay for his own mistakes.'

'I don't understand.'

'He went through with the deal. But he didn't speak to Chōshi-san – he left her recruitment to the Ginzo-kai.'

'But she'd already turned them down. Why would she suddenly accept their offer without a reason?'

'She'd refused Tanzen. The Ginzo-kai employ more robust methods of recruitment. They persuaded her to join in the end.'

I closed my eyes. I had a horrible idea of what was coming next.

'How did they "persuade" her?'

'Ray-san, I think you know. I'm not sure the details will help.'

'I need to hear them.'

'They raped her.'

Visions of Tomoe I didn't want to see forced themselves in front of my eyes.

'They told her that if she didn't work for Tanzen they'd send the pictures to her father, her employers, her friends – anyone she'd ever met and anyone she ever would. And they told her there was a threat to her father's life, a threat she could negate.

'But Chōshi-san's father was a proud man, which is ironic considering how few of his life's endeavours warranted pride. He insisted they didn't tell her he'd agreed to it. But he was disgusted by what he'd done and what she'd become. His way of dealing with it was to cut her out of his life.'

His eyes became bottomless again.

'There's no need to mourn his passing.'

I sat without moving.

'Dignity and rape aren't concepts that can sit together,' Takata went on. 'But they were as respectful as it's possible to be. The girls tricked over from Asia are gang-raped to break them in. With Chōshi-san there were no goons. I don't know who was responsible for her initiation but I'm told he was more refined. She was to be their most valuable employee. They did what they had to to have her sign up, but they did it in a way that would cause the least harm.

'But there was obviously a limit. They needed her to have sex with someone not of her choosing and they needed to have it on film.'

The clinically planned precision of a business rape.

'Your Chōshi-san did her ancestry proud. She had to be subdued in the end. When she came back to her senses she bit off the man's nipple. Unfortunately it wasn't enough to escape the consequences of the day.'

He refilled the glass I'd just knocked back.

'A tayū is not to be confused with a prostitute at any time, but you should understand Chōshi-san deserves disapprobation least of all.'

I didn't say anything. There was nothing I could.

'I'm sorry; I assumed she'd have told you, or that you'd at least know the gist. I'm aware it isn't easy news to absorb, but I'm afraid you need to deal with it quickly. There'll be a time to reflect but that time isn't now. You can't afford to look back. You need to focus on the future and on what you can do to help Chōshi-san now. The first step towards that is at tomorrow's AGM.'

I sat slumped with my head in my hands. It was all very well saying I should reflect on it later, but that was like destroying someone's home and telling them to think it over after a good night's sleep.

'Please don't abandon me too.'

Tomoe's words from our fight. The last time we spoke. Having discovered her father's treachery, she'd gone wherever she was thinking I'd turned my back on her too.

'Boohoo, the little pussy bitch is having a cry.'

I looked up from the sofa. The office had been empty, its inhabitants out tearing the legs off children or whatever they normally did. That's where I'd slumped.

'For fuck's sake, he really is,' continued Kurotaki. 'Pull yourself together cocksucker – you're a yakuza. It's not a job for poofs.'

I wiped at my face with the back of my hand, hating him for intruding on my grief. It only spurred him on.

'Hey, we didn't finish our conversation the other day.'

I said nothing and made to leave.

'The one about sluts. It reminded me of something. I know the guy who broke in your girlfriend. He said she moaned like a thousand-yen whore and was begging for more when he was done.'

The next thing I knew I was face to face with Sumida, his right arm pressing my left to my side, his left struggling to control my right. He'd intervened to deflect its swing. At its end was a heavy glass ashtray, the one I'd picked up from the table as I leapt to my feet. The weapon I'd swung at Kurotaki's head.

Having been caught flat-footed, Kurotaki was starting to rage back, trying to rip away the sandwich filler that was Sumida as he attempted to restrain the fury on his other side.

'Out.'

One word from Takata and Kurotaki was contained. He turned and stalked from the room. Something had snapped in me though and I continued to rail at the empty space.

'Get a hold of yourself,' ordered Takata, anger starting to rise in his voice.

I struggled a last time and then the fight left me as quickly as it had come.

'Get him a taxi – and make sure he gets in it and the driver knows where to go. Then come to my office. I want to know what that was all about.'

Sumida bowed.

'And you,' he turned to me. 'What did I tell you? Do you want to save your girlfriend or fight the people on your own side? Pull yourself together. How are you going to do what you need to tomorrow if you get yourself killed in a fight?'

He turned back into his office and slammed the door.

I tried to do as he said in the taxi home but I couldn't cope, it had all got too much. A couple of months ago I'd been a normal guy with a normal job leading a normal life. Now this.

But it wasn't just my circumstances. When I threatened Fujiwara I hadn't been shocked by what I said, but by how genuine I'd been. And just now. If I'd hit Kurotaki flush with the ashtray it would have hurt him badly, maybe even killed him. I felt deep down I was the person I'd always been but at the same time something in me had changed. My actions were those of someone else.

My mind went again went to Tomoe. My beautiful girlfriend who had been defiled. The soulmate I'd betrayed in her hour of need.

Until that point I'd thought that if I could keep going things would have to get better, that they couldn't get any worse. I was starting to realise this wasn't necessarily true. The world in which I found myself had unlimited potential for horror and pain. I had a chance to claw my way out and that would start with the AGM. But I couldn't help thinking that if things were to get better it would only be after they got much, much worse.

PART THREE

ONE

I could see the crowds from down the street. A group was waiting in front of sliding metal barricades that blocked entry to the front of a grey skyscraper. Facing them from behind the barriers was a line of security guards. Surrounding them on the other side were journalists and camera crews who were resisting the efforts of further security men attempting to corral the entire group into an orderly mass and prevent them spilling into the road.

On the opposite side of the street was another group, slightly sparser in number but making up for it in noise. They were being led by a man with a microphone in an increasing intensity of anti-KanEnCo chants.

It was from this side that I approached, my hand bandaged in the style of a man who has hurt his wrist rather than cut off a finger. No one paid me any attention – after all, I was just a passing gaijin who couldn't be involved. At the last minute I cut across the road, weaved through the crowd and flashed the pass Takata had provided. The security men quickly wheeled the barriers open and closed.

I was through almost before anyone noticed, certainly before any cameras could be pointed at me. But a pair of eyes had caught mine. They'd smiled in greeting and then looked confused when I couldn't hold their gaze. The last sight I had of Eriko's mother was her face changing from confusion to horror as her mind worked through the possible reasons I was being let in.

I was stopped by tense security men at two more cordons before I could enter. I imagined they had experience of the recent AGMs and were looking forward to the day with as much enthusiasm as me.

Once I'd presented my pass at reception, I was taken to a lift and shown to the tenth floor. I got out to see clusters of thick-set men squeezed into ill-fitting suits that their muscles and beer bellies seemed likely to burst from before the meeting was done. I hadn't been to any AGMs before but I couldn't imagine they were typical investors. Their snippets of conversation revealed greater interest in the water business than the Nikkei, and their hungover expressions suggested more than one had been doing active research the previous night.

The smoking area was particularly popular – Tokyo's law-makers having confusingly restricted the practice outdoors rather than inside, to prevent accidents in the city's ubiquitous crowds. It was from here the sōkaiya leader approached.

'Kularens-san?' he said with a slight bow. 'Pleased to meet you.'

I returned the pleasantries and he started his briefing.

'We should be getting started pretty soon. The other shareholders will be let in at eight fifty-five, at which point we'll be allowed entry to the meeting room. As we're here first' – I didn't ask what predicated this treatment – 'we'll have the choice of seats. I'll ensure you get one right at the front.'

I nodded and thanked him.

'The meeting will commence at nine with a statement from the president. After that the floor will be opened to questions.'

I nodded again to show I was keeping pace.

'It's a forum that has generated some passion in recent years,' he said delicately, as bored thugs around him yawned from their exertions of the previous night. 'So it's possible things could get heated. In that case, the meeting will end prematurely. However, I believe you have a question that needs to be asked. We'll ensure decorum is maintained for the time it takes you to do your thing. Is that all clear?'

I assured him it was and he went to have another cigarette, it having been at least five minutes since his last. I went back to the question that had been running through my mind since I wrenched it from the events of the previous day.

What was Takata's plan?

Just as I'd finally got in reach of the 'Ishikawa Report' our conversation had veered off on a dramatically different line. I couldn't be sure if this had been an intentional diversion or not.

But I'd done as Takata had said. I'd returned home and, unable to close my mind to the thoughts running amok, I'd gone to bed early, surprising myself by how quickly I'd fallen asleep. In the morning, instead of letting my emotions roam uninhibited, I'd formed a barrier around a sole task: doing whatever I needed to do at the AGM.

What I couldn't close my mind to were the thoughts of what Takata expected from this. The KanEnCo board surely wouldn't be happy with my question and it seemed strange that Takata would want to upset the people paying him. But perhaps he didn't intend to; it might be a move to wrong-foot the protestors, a way to lure them into his fire.

Either way, it looked like I was to be a catalyst again, and in my experience that usually ended in pain. At least this time the people likely to mete out the violence were on my side. The thought that I wouldn't be on the receiving end was comforting, but brought with it a stabbing sense of shame.

The sōkaiya leader shot a couple of staccato '*hai*'s into his phone as he walked towards me. He nodded.

'We're on.'

He turned and shouted 'Let's go!' to the room.

He took first place outside a door on which the meeting details were pasted and indicated I fall in behind. The rest of the sōkaiya lined up after me, their bored expressions replaced by grim game-faces with a current of violent excitement underneath.

The lift door pinged and the first of the protestors emerged. The tension immediately ratcheted up. They were escorted over by security men who placed themselves between the two groups. As more of their number started to pour from the lifts the cat-calls started. I turned away. I didn't want any part in this, but if I had to be involved I just wanted to get in, ask my question and get out.

The door opened and the pressure from the queue forced the sōkaiya leader and me through, barrelling us into the man opening it and truncating his welcome speech. The conference room had the requisite soullessness of any corporation or large hotel. There was a long desk at the front backed by tall windows that were masked with muslin curtains to avoid any distractions from outside. In front of the desk were two banks of seats that went ten or fifteen rows back, each with about ten chairs either side of a walkway.

The sōkaiya leader led me to the front and we sat down. About half of the sōkaiya followed and filled in around us. The others hung back, encircling the protestors when they sat, leaving them an isolated island in a hostile, black-suited sea.

Blue-uniformed security men stood at the edges of the room, their faces anxious as they fidgeted, their backs pressed against the walls. Instead of the usual murmurs of a large crowd I could hear the sōkaiya niggling the protestors. Their indignant responses were met by gruff insults and threats.

A door at the front beside the table opened and the volume of the crowd increased. A group of ten or so men entered one after another and took their seats. Sour-faced, they were all over sixty, as soulless as the room and distinguished by hair that appeared to grow more jet-black with age. I looked at the president ten feet in front of me. His mouth was so puckered you'd have thought he survived on lemons and sour milk. He was the one I was to direct my question to.

'Please. Please! We're ready to start.'

An official tried to quell the noise from the front right.

The president looked around the room with disdain. I imagined he was recalling days when the AGM had been filled with investors. Anyone with conventional interests had decided to make do with the annual report – this battleground posing as a meeting wasn't for them. The president waited for silence before he made a start.

My mind wandered the moment corporate jargon began to spiel from his mouth. But I think he was no happier to be there than I was. He wound up his speech quickly in anticipation of an early escape.

'So now we'll take questions from the floor.'

A cacophony of voices rose from the protestors, their calls eliciting an immediate echo of abuse.

'We will take questions in the proper manner,' the president said icily. 'Please raise your hand if you have something to say and you'll be addressed one by one.'

I sensed hands straining up behind me but mine suddenly felt like lead. The sōkaiya leader turned to look at me. The president was also staring, a perplexed expression on his face.

'Yes, please,' he said sounding relieved, and I realised my hand had made its way into the air.

I became conscious I didn't know the form in these meetings, whether to stand or stay in your seat. I got up.

'Ray Clarence from Energy Without Affect,' I introduced myself, and then paused.

'I've been researching the Kamigawa Incident as part of our study on a fossil-free future,' I began, easing myself in. 'The plant has been most helpful already but there is still a source of data we are yet to receive. It would be invaluable to us at EWA, but I think it would go some way to resolving the problems between KanEnCo and its less contented investors as well.'

The president looked at me curiously. Whatever he'd been briefed to expect, I don't think it was this.

'Could you please let me know where I can access the Ishikawa

Report, the independent report written by Ishikawa Manabu on the suitability of Kamigawa as the site for a nuclear plant?'

The president's eyes widened in horror. The room went quiet. The protestors weren't sure what this was but they could sense its significance. The president opened his mouth to speak and then closed it. He tried again but no words came out. Behind me the room erupted, the protestors demanding this new-found jewel, the men in black suits trying to shut them up.

The president looked desperately at the sōkaiya leader, his eyes demanding something be done. He seemed to have forgotten I was in the same family, that they wouldn't do anything to me.

I felt the sōkaiya get to his feet.

'Sorry,' he said.

I turned to find out what he was apologising for just as he floored me with a huge punch. It threw me over the back of my seat and I saw the room explode through an inverted forest of chair legs and legs. Protestors and sōkaiya hurled themselves at one another, chairs and people went flying this way and that.

I lifted my head and looked forward to see the board beat a hasty retreat. I struggled up, thinking I'd be better off upright, only for two fighters to barrel into my side and catapult me over the table at the front. I hauled myself up again, this time more cautious of my flanks, and peered over the top. Somehow amidst the orgy of violence my original assailant spotted the movement. He pointed me out to a security man who rushed over to form a one-man guard.

The rest of security was starting to gain a semblance of control. The women had for the most part escaped. The men were either laid out on the floor or had guards in front of them, blocking their aggressors' path. The sōkaiya were not proving as easily quelled. It took another wave of security to sweep in before order was finally restored.

The protestors were ushered out first except for the injured being treated on the sides. When they'd been seen through the litter of chairs, the guards escorted the sōkaiya, who they showed far greater wariness at being around. I was taken with this group, still with my personal watch.

We'd left the room and were moving towards the lift when somebody grabbed my arm. I started and pulled away sharply. I had no desire to have the nascent swelling on my face balanced with another punch.

'Come with me,' said Sumida.

He held up his hand in gesture to the guard, who didn't look keen to argue the point.

'What are you doing here?' I asked.

The guard took the acknowledgement we knew each other as fair reason to scuttle off.

'We need to be discreet getting you out,' said Sumida. 'It's swarming with reporters out front.'

Aside from the ache in my jaw, I was still feeling woozy from the sōkaiya's punch. I felt quite relieved to have someone shepherd me. I shrugged and let Sumida lead me down the corridor to a fire exit at its other end.

A dizzying number of stairs later we came out in a basement car park, its cloying fumes concentrated by low ceilings and a lack of fresh air. It was around this time I started to feel uneasy. It didn't take long before my doubts were confirmed.

'Get in the boot,' said Sumida.

We'd reached the moment of truth. I'd done what they wanted and they were going to get rid of me. The car park stood empty except for the two of us. I looked for possible escapes. The nearest exit was the stairwell we'd come from, but in my present condition I had to think Sumida would catch me before I could get to the door.

'I think I'd be better in one of the seats,' I said, taking a step back.

Sumida looked at me.

'Don't be a dick. If I wanted to hurt you I could do it any time. You might not realise it, but you just kicked off a shit-storm up there. The press are going to be all over you if they see you now. On top of that, you've just made a new set of enemies. So stop fucking around and let me get you out of here without being seen.'

There was plenty to question in what he'd just said, but one thing in particular pissed me off.

'What do you mean "*I've* just made a whole set of new enemies"? It was Kumichō's question. I only asked it. Surely this country's got to run out of people who want to kill me at some fucking point?'

He either took the question as rhetorical, or didn't want to dishearten me with how many others might be baying for my blood.

'Just get in the car.'

He stepped towards me. I took another step back, but he was close enough to grab me if he wanted.

'You're going in there one way or another. Don't make me force you – it's not necessary and it'll hurt.'

I climbed in reluctantly and he closed the lid with a thud. I was immediately cocooned in silence broken only by the beating of my heart. Then, the sound of the engine drowned it out and the car started to move. I tried to manoeuvre into a less uncomfortable position but the angle suddenly elevated, rolling me backwards in the dark. Just as abruptly, we flattened out and then came to a stop. I heard a muffled Sumida speak – I presumed to a guard – and we started to move again. Shortly after that something changed, either in the vibrations or the sound, maybe both, and I realised we were no longer inside. Within moments there were new sounds, people shouting and thumps on the side of the car. Then we accelerated and the noise died away.

The last time I'd been in a boot was when I was a teenager and there were too many of us to fit in the seats of our group's only car. I'd lost at paper, scissors, stone. I hadn't been too happy about it at the time, and even less so when I found out later the exhaust had a leak and was slowly releasing fumes. But I'd lived. The air was fresher in Sumida's, but I felt my chances of survival weren't nearly as good.

As we drove on my sense of foreboding grew worse. Sumida's reasoning had been plausible, but there's something about being stuck in the pitch-black boot of a yakuza's car that gives rise to doubt. And if I'd been ready to accept an end to things a week or so earlier, I wasn't any more. The situation had changed. Whatever happened in the AGM had sent shockwaves coursing through the affair. I hoped they might shake Tomoe loose. That alone was worth fighting for.

I felt around me. Sumida was a practical guy – there had to be some kind of tool should he break down. Perhaps a wrench, or anything else that was metal or hard. There was nothing. The boot was pristine. There weren't even any crumbs or bits of dirt on the floor.

I felt the car slow and pull to the left. If this was the time of reckoning I needed a plan quick. A random image flashed before me – Mr Chow from *The Hangover*. It wasn't a thought I wanted to be my last and I wasn't planning to strip. But I was equally sure I wouldn't go down without a fight.

The car eased to a standstill and I heard the driver's door open and thud shut. I shifted around and moved onto my back, curling up so I could plant my feet on the floor. Facing the opening, I coiled my body as much as the limited space would allow.

I heard him press the button to release the lock and light streamed in from a crack. He started to raise the lid and the crack grew into an opening through which I saw a strip of blue sky. Then the opening widened to reveal Sumida, his arm raised, his body open to attack.

That's when I leapt.

I sprang at him ripping at his eyes and throat, ready to take advantage of his surprise and pound him into the floor. Then I'd take the keys, start the car and make my latest great escape.

In reality I leapt straight into the registration plate overhang. It smacked a lump into an as yet unblemished part of my head and sent me crashing back into the boot.

Sumida had flinched and staggered backwards when I jumped up. Now he'd regained his balance he fell about in gales of laughter that almost succeeded in putting him to ground where my attack had failed. I'd never seen him so animated but I wasn't in a position to admire his emotional liberation. I was flat on my back again, trying to stem the flow of blood gushing from my head.

'I told you I'm not going to hurt you, you silly fuck,' he said when

287

he stopped laughing long enough to speak. 'Look what you've done to yourself.'

I looked at him through the blood and my fingers and swore at the boot lid.

'Come on – get out,' he said, more serious now. 'You're going to get blood all over my car.'

He helped me out and I looked around. We were in a nondescript car park off a side street. There was no one to be seen. He grabbed a cloth from inside the front and gave it to me so I could clean up my head. When I'd done the best I could he let me in the passenger side, opening and closing the door so I wouldn't mark it with blood.

'Here, use these,' He threw me a pack of wet wipes. 'I thought I'd let you sit in comfort now we're out of the way. If I'd known you were going to attack me I would have left you where you were.'

'Thanks. And sorry,' I said, cleaning myself enough that I only needed to hold the cloth to my head to stop any more blood. 'So what happens now?'

He gave a nod of satisfaction. 'Now the feinting and faking stops. Whatever this is, now's the time the endgame begins.'

The endgame. We sat in silence contemplating it. For him it meant danger, but also excitement and opportunities to learn and gain. I approached it partly in hope but with an equal amount of dread. I held tightly to the thought it would bring back Tomoe but doubts and worries darted in from the corners of my mind. Nothing had come without cost in the last month. What horrors would the endgame bring?

TWO

'Throw some stuff in a bag and tie up any loose ends. I'll be back in half an hour.'

'What?'

'There's too much heat on you,' said Sumida. 'You need to stay somewhere safe.'

'My flat's not safe?'

'Not any more. Get your stuff – I'll be back soon.' He drove off.

Fucking great. My only place of respite was being taken away from me too.

I made my way up and down the small stairway bridge that separated the end of the alley from my block of flats. I went through the entrance of the building and hauled myself up the stairs to my front door. I wondered where I'd be going next. I opened the door, took off my shoes and started to take off my jacket. I didn't do anything else because at that point everything went black.

I came to, face down on my sofa, my legs hanging over the end, my face in a puddle of drool. I started to lift my head but gave up when I felt a hammering pain.

'What the—?'

I put my hand to the back of my head to find a huge bump

oozing blood. That brought it up with a start. The last time something like this happened, I'd found myself facing two yakuza and lost a finger soon after that. But the room was empty. I groaned, wheeled my legs around and heaved myself up. I looked around the room to check again. Apart from the back of my head, there was nothing to suggest anyone had been there at all.

'What the fuck?'

I was in no way happy with the amount of times I'd been hit in the last month but at least with the rest of them there'd been a point. Who the hell knocks someone out in their own flat and then leaves without doing anything else?

I put my hand to my face. It was slathered in dribble. I forced myself up from the sofa and went to the bathroom off the short hallway at the entrance to the flat. I stopped outside it to steady myself on the handle when I started to sway. They'd have to start using my head on marksman sights – as far as I could make out it was impossible to miss.

I opened the door.

And that's when I realised my recent journey had seen me floating in paradise. Only now would I know what it was like to be dragged through hell.

I dropped to my knees, my efforts to steady myself nullified by the sight. I didn't even notice when one of them cracked against the small step, even though it would bother me for another week. It was as though all the feelings and senses had been ripped from me, leaving just the shell of my body behind. A body that was numb and unresponsive. A body almost as lifeless as the one curled in the small space of floor under the basin, between the toilet and bath.

Then the pain hit. It may have started at my knee but I only felt it when it had coursed through my body and taken hold in my heart. From there it rose through my chest seeking escape, clawing its way up my throat. But even though my throat contracted and my head rolled back, and even though my mouth opened and my lips drew wide, no sound came out with the silent scream and the pain remained within.

I looked back at the body, forced by the small space into the foetal position in which it had entered life. A body that had once been a person. A person who had lived a gamut of emotions and had an energy force of their own. An ex-person, who was now just an object under my sink, its previous fluidity mocked by the rigid tangle of limbs it had become.

I was transfixed by it and my paralysis forced me to drink in the full horror of the sight. The white of the body's rubber skin was broken by a shadow of pubic triangle, just visible from the way it was curled. A brown nipple protruded from a breast pressed unnaturally against the floor. And a deep red welt ran around the neck of what would once have been an exceptionally attractive girl. Except now her face was propped forward on its chin, facing me, her death mask holding me with its eternal stare.

I couldn't look away, even though I wanted to more than anything I've ever wanted in my life. But it was impossible to break from her haunting gaze. For as difficult as it was to reconcile the lifeless body with a vibrant, living person, I had no choice.

I'd been looking for the person the body belonged to.

I'd known her.

I'd loved her.

It was Tomoe.

THREE

I retched violently. It broke the spell that had me bound to the floor and rocked me into the wall behind. I swallowed back the sick that rose up. I retched again and jumped for the front door. I couldn't lean over Tomoe to throw up in the toilet.

Mine was the last apartment on the corridor with only the care-taker's utility room beyond. I burst into that, grabbed a bucket and emptied my guts. Or at least I thought I did. After a pause I threw up again. And then once more. I fell back from my crouch, my head bumping closed the press lock in the centre of the door handle as I did.

I couldn't believe it. It couldn't be Tomoe. She had too much life for her to be dead. I closed my eyes. I must have been mistaken. There couldn't be a dead body in my bathroom. And even if there was it couldn't be Tomoe's.

But I knew there could and it was. The sweetest, most beautiful girl I'd ever met was lying cold on my bathroom floor. Never again to brighten my soul with the sparkle in her eyes, never again to melt my heart with the tender warmth of her love.

I knew I had to go back into my apartment, to face her, to see her one final time. I had to go back to make sure she was treated with the respect she deserved before she physically departed the world.

The door rattled behind me and I jumped.

'It's locked. We can check in with the caretaker when he gets here.'

That wouldn't be for another week – he was on leave.

'No sign of the suspect,' said another voice from the direction of my apartment. 'The body's here though.'

The police? How could they have known there was a body in my flat? I'd only found out a few minutes before. And what would they know about a suspect?

No answers came, but before long more people arrived. Radios crackled and official voices spoke in their own languages and codes – policemen, forensics and doctors. I was stuck in a small, dark, windowless room with the acrid smell of my sick; unable to move, unable to leave, able only to think about the dead body of my girl-friend on the other side of the wall.

'OK, if it's all taped up you might as well come down and keep an eye on the building from downstairs.'

The radio clicked off and I heard the policeman make his way down the corridor to the stairs. I looked at my watch. It was nearly six. I had no idea what had happened in the last few hours – it was like my mind had shut itself down. Now it had started up again I needed to pull myself together and work out what I was going to do.

It was easier said than done – my mind was pinballing in every direction. I closed my eyes and went to the most crucial question first.

Who would have done this?

It had to be the Ginzo-kai, with Onishi orchestrating. It made sense – they'd got themselves rid of a snooper and were having her shadow take the fall. I wouldn't be free to do any meddling for decades, and that was only if I escaped being put to death.

But something didn't feel right. How had they found me so quickly and reacted so fast? How could they have known where I was and when I'd be there?

'Throw your stuff in a bag – I'll be back in half an hour.'

The words came back to me. But you hadn't needed to return, had you, Sumida? Whoever it was – probably Kurotaki – was already here. They'd been playing me all along. The coldness, the callousness. Sumida had just been joking with me. Takata had endlessly sung Tomoe's praises. How can you go from one thing to another with such little regard?

I stood up quickly to prevent my mind returning to the 'if onlys' that might have saved Tomoe's life or the images of what I'd seen a few hours before. I needed to focus.

I had two tasks. The first was to get the out of the building and find somewhere the country's two largest yakuza and its police force couldn't track me down. It wouldn't be easy but it was probably the simpler of the two. Because something had changed when I saw Tomoe's body. I had no idea how I was going to do it and the chances were it would be beyond me anyhow. But I couldn't hope for survival as the best outcome any more. It was no longer enough. I had to find out who killed Tomoe. Then I'd either get revenge or I'd go to hell trying.

*

I opened the door of the caretaker's utility room the tiniest crack and peered down the corridor. It was empty. I opened it wider, put my head out and took a lungful of untainted air. All was quiet. I stepped out and tiptoed to my apartment next door. I looked at it and then regarded my feet.

My front door was taped up thoroughly. It might have been possible to open but it would have been a noisy and time-consuming task. I was wanted for murder. I needed to get out of there quickly and quietly and minimise any risks. The only reason I was contemplating one was because of my feet. They were bare but for a pair of broad-striped socks that were acceptable from a sartorial perspective but not suitable for outdoor escapes.

I broke from my hesitation and walked quickly on – it was better to be free in socks than imprisoned in shoes. I made my way past the stairwell, turned left at the end of the corridor and descended the other set of stairs. These led to the front door via an identical corridor to the one on my floor. I imagined the police had scoped the place and were aware of that. What I was hoping they didn't know was if you climbed over the small side-wall at the foot of the stairs, you could edge between my block of flats and the next building to reach a road on the other side. At least I hoped you could. I'd seen the gap before but it was extremely narrow and not part of a normal route.

I burst out the other side gasping for breath and quickly dusted myself down. When I felt I looked relatively normal again I made my way back to the bridge, all the while keeping an eye out for the police. There weren't any. It made sense. If I'd escaped the building as they must have believed, the chances weren't high I'd come back.

I made my way to Sakae Dōri. It was bustling now but I cut straight off it on the other side, weaving through alleys to the main road. I knew there was a chemist with bathroom flip flops on display outside.

I'd have preferred a pair of trainers, but once I'd darted into the lanes on the other side of the road I felt better for having something on my feet. I was out of the immediate danger zone. But if the beating of my heart was anything to go by, I had a way to go before I was safe.

I wanted to get out of Tokyo but I thought the police would be watching nearby train stations so it made sense to give them a wide berth. A taxi would have been a welcome alternative, but if there was a bulletin out on me, my blood, bumps and bruises meant I wouldn't be difficult to spot.

If I couldn't travel I needed to get out of sight and it would have to be somewhere close. The question was where?

I swiped the card key and opened the door. It was as seedy and trashy as I remembered, just ten years more rundown, its air thick with the memories of past occupants' smoke.

I'd stayed after a night out soon after I first came to Japan. I was living in Chiba then, around to the east and down from Tokyo Bay. Once you'd missed the last train, the only thing to do was drink through it and not think about the hangover that would hit you when you woke with a start, having overshot your station on the first morning train.

Or you could pull and go to a love hotel. Which is exactly what I'd done. We'd been at a drum 'n' bass night at The Liquid Rooms in Kabukichō. Once we'd fumbled our way out and into a taxi, she'd told the driver to head to Shin Ōkubo before we locked in an alcohol-fuelled embrace. Quite why we'd gone there I didn't know – I later found out the whole of north Kabukichō was wall-to-wall with love hotels – but for some reason she'd wanted this place. The passion hadn't outlasted our sore heads in the morning. But it had been a memorable enough night for me to have retained something of it in my mind.

It was the kind of love hotel that had little to do with romance. Some cater to couples having a special night out, others to young-sters enjoying the bells and whistles of themed establishments.. This was aimed at the illicit. There was no receptionist or any visible staff – everything was done at a vending machine once you'd gone down the steps and behind the screen discreetly covering the front. It was ideal for a man cheating on his wife. It was equally well suited to someone wanted for murder by the police and wanted for murder by Tokyo's gangs.

I took off my no-longer-best clothes and went into the bath-room, hoping to clean off some of the events of the day. After-wards I towelled myself dry, numbly revelling in my cleanness and the welcome change the smell of soap and shampoo made to sick. I hugged a bathrobe around me and climbed onto the bed.

I longed for sleep so I could escape the horrors that confronted me when awake. But my mind was a mess. While I'd been in danger, it had focused on escape. Now I'd found safety, it forced images of Tomoe at me, images I wished I'd never seen, ones I wished I could banish forever from my brain. As though without them I'd have forgotten the events of the day and my failure to keep my beautiful girlfriend alive.

*

There was a thudding sound, then silence. Then thudding again. I opened my eyes but it was just as dark as when they were closed. I flailed around me, wondering if I was caught up in a new kind of dream. But then the thudding started again and I smelled the smoke and felt the pain in my head and the pain of my loss and I remembered where I was.

'Open the fucking door!'

I knew that voice. But I didn't know how it knew where I was. I groped around the top of the bed, found a light switch and scrambled to the door. I looked through the spyhole. Kurotaki looked even uglier for the distortion of the fish-eye lens, Sumida slightly bored. How had they found out I was here?

Kurotaki leaned forward to pound on the door again, looming in the spyhole. I jumped back.

'Open the door. We know you're in there. We're here to help.'

'Like you helped Tomoe, you motherfucker?' I wanted to scream. But I didn't. Face-to-face I wouldn't stand a chance against one of them, let alone both. Now wasn't the time. I hurried into my clothes and slipped on the flip flops which were even less suitable for what I knew had to come next.

I ripped apart the curtains, pulled open the window and looked down. I was only on the first floor but it still looked formidably high. I heard voices again and someone started fiddling at the door. I decided I was more afraid of them than I was of the height. I gathered myself and stepped onto the ledge.

I landed in a tiny walled alley. My first thought was that I hadn't broken any bones. My second, straight after, was that there was no obvious way out. I looked up and down at the walls on each side, wondering if I was ever going to get any luck. Deciding I'd have to make my own, I scrambled up the back wall then tottered along another that abutted its end. I jumped down when I could go no further and realised, to my relief, that I was on the road on the other side of the hotel.

I glanced over my shoulder just long enough to see Kurotaki appear at the window. The sight gave me the boost of energy I needed. I turned and ran.

I wasn't sure exactly where I was but I knew I needed to get away from where I'd been. I ran blindly, taking a left, then a right before cutting through a playground. I came out into a packed alley and realised I was now somewhere I knew – Ikemen Dōri. If Shin Ōkubo was Tokyo's Little Korea, Ikemen Dōri was its Seoul Street. Its shops and restaurants buzzed with energy, drawing crowds attracted by Korea's recent cachet of cool. I was more interested in the thick cover of people provided by the narrow pedestrian lane.

I weaved through the crush, working through my options as I went. I hadn't been thinking clearly. The hotel might have squeezed within Shin Ōkubo's borders, but it was right on the edge of Kabukichō – deepest Takata-gumi land. They'd probably put out word for hotel owners to watch their CCTV for a bedraggled gaijin stupid enough to turn up.

I came to Ōkubo Dōri. I needed to make some decisions quickly and I had to be sure I made no more mistakes. The next one could see me killed.

I had a head start – I doubted either Kurotaki or Sumida would have jumped out the window, but they wouldn't be far behind. I tried to think of the most logical thing to do, the thing I'd bet on if I were chasing me. North was the scene of the murder, south was Takata-gumi Central. The sensible move would be to head west towards Nakano, or east to Iidabashi. I ruled out both. I'd counter-intuit an escape. I didn't have the guts to go the whole hog and head to Kabukichō so I decided to keep going north. Back to Takadanobaba. Back towards the scene of the crime.

I crossed Ōkubo Dōri and cut down a narrow lane beside a *pachinko* parlour so smoky the fumes seemed to seep through its glass. My brisk pace and the crisp night air helped clear my head. I knew exactly where I'd go.

I was told it was in the nineties, just after the bubble burst, that the change came to Tokyo's public spaces and parks. Waves of blue tarpaulins suddenly appeared, undulating across open spaces like a modern-day mutation of an ukiyo-e sea. Unlike the homeless of England, their occupants weren't predominantly escapees from abuse who found solace then incarceration in drink and drugs. For many it was sheer poverty – the downturn in construction at the end of the bubble hitting labourers particularly hard. But for others it was the pressures of society and their own notions of honour that exiled them from their homes and imprisoned them outside. Their trigger was the end of lifetime employment. On losing their jobs, their response to the shame had been to leave their homes and families and take refuge in the streets – or parks.

It wasn't only in the cause of their plight that they differed. The way they went about their homelessness was dissimilar as well. They commandeered Tokyo's public spaces and constructed sturdy blue tarpaulin tents that they tended with pride; cooking pots hung outside entrances, shoes neatly lined up in front.

But there had been a crackdown while I'd been away and the city had reclaimed much of its land. I wasn't sure where the majority ended up, but I knew one had made his home under the bridge where Koshu Kaido Road separates Shinjuku Station and the Southern Terrace. With rain cover taken care of he'd focused on comfort and warmth. I'd admired his cardboard cocoon whenever I walked past.

I grabbed a load of boxes as I passed a convenience store clearing out at the end of the day. Then I continued on to Toyama Koen Park. It was dominated by the concrete mass of Shinjuku Sports Center and the hard-surface sports pitch in front. But surrounding them were the trees and stretches of grass more typical of a park. And at the edges some doughty tarpaulin men remained.

They operated on a guerrilla basis now, deconstructing their mobile homes during the day then lurking in the perimeters before they set up again at dusk. No one would think anything of it if there were an extra person bedded down. I was extremely doubtful even Takata's network extended that far with its spies.

The choicest spots had already gone, but I found a decent opening on a piece of grass between a bridge, a playground and the edge of a path. I set one box as a base, kicked out the bottoms from the others and concertinaed them into a cocoon. When they were as long as me I took off my flip-flops, put them to the side and slid in. I pulled the last box over my head.

FOUR

Dreaming of the Floating World 4

'I may not have told you everything,' he said calmly, sat cross-legged, his hands placed regally on his knees.

'And what you did tell me may not have been entirely true,' she replied, kneeling on the other side of the table.

Lord Ezoe nodded.

'You're right, but I would ask that you don't hold it against me. You know I respect you too much to think you wouldn't find out. But at the time it was judicious. I needed to continue my investigations undisturbed by other concerns.'

He bowed his head.

'I apologise for any distress this may have caused.'

He studied her but Katsuyama remained as she was. He smiled to himself. Her beauty, her charm, her culture; they all held appeal. But what captivated him was the strength concealed within her, the steely fury she could clinically dispatch. In this she was like Tetsuko, his prized falcon who would plummet from the skies like a stone – ruthless but without emotion, at that moment living only to execute her strike. Had Katsuyama been born a man it would have been a daimyō he sat in front of, maybe even the shōgun himself.

'I presume you are aware I had greater involvement than I disclosed in the circumstances regarding your father's disappearance?'

She nodded.

'And perhaps you know that I have had some interaction with Genpachi and his lapdog Mizuno?'

She noted his disregard for Mizuno but remained quiet.

'You may not be aware that it was me who abducted your father.'

This finally startled her into a reaction.

'You took my father? But why? Where is he now?'

'I did take your father,' he said. 'But unfortunately I was unable to keep him in my care. Please, let me explain.

'The runt who slandered your family held a grudge against your father. But this wasn't the sole cause of his derogatory remarks and their timing wasn't by chance. He was prompted to make them for the response their instigator knew they would bring. I was warned of this, which is why I had men ready to take your father to safety when he did what honour obliged. Unfortunately I was duped. The men I had intercept him were ambushed and your father was taken again.'

'But why?' she asked. 'Who would go to all this trouble? And what good would it do them?'

'Genpachi. I was given the warning by another so no search for a culprit could implicate him. Any trail that didn't lead to me would only reach Mizuno, for it was men he hired who intercepted mine. It would be near impossible for anyone to trace Genpachi's hand in this affair.'

'Except you have.'

'Except I have. But without any proof.'

'But again – what purpose did any of this have? Lord Genpachi has already won his battle with my father's lord. My father meant nothing to him.'

'That's where the situation becomes more complicated,' said Ezoe. 'The restrictive measures the last shōgun forced on the daimyōs are still felt sorely by many. Others, significant names like Mizuno among them, smart from being made rōnin. Since the shōgun died and a boy took his place, there has been talk of putting things back as they were.'

'But there are always whispers of revolts and rebellions. My family's downfall was caused by a personal dispute. It had nothing to do with the shōgunate. I don't see why my father would have been involved.'

'You're right, but others who knew him less well were less sure and times are tense. You see, at the moment there are more than just rumours. There's a plan to overthrow the shōgun. In the course of the rebellion, I'll be killed.'

'You?' she exclaimed. 'Why?'

'Because it's to be led by Genpachi and he knows my power base is independent of him. If anyone was to challenge his position, I'd be the most likely to succeed.'

'Lord Genpachi? But he's on the council of regents until the shōgun comes of age.'

'He is on the council but he finds it irksome that four other voices compete with his. He also dislikes the idea of his power being diluted in the passage of time. So he's taking advantage of this period of transition and using the disaffection of others to further his own goals. He plans to take power for himself.

'First there will be an attack in Shizuoka. It will be made to look like a rōnin rebellion, so none of the daimyō families held in Edo Castle are harmed. But the assault will be more impressive than anticipated and the bakufu will find it necessary to send further men. When they've made good distance, a fire will start on the outskirts of Edo. As you know, a blaze could quickly consume the city. There will be pandemonium and the castle will be left exposed. Genpachi's men will take advantage and attack from within; other forces will launch an assault from outside. Together they will take control.'

'What claim to legitimacy do they have?'

He silently admired the speed of her thought.

'They've turned the shōgun's mother. Genpachi found out about an affair with one of the last shōgun's retainers – she will concede to the illegitimacy of the child. Crucially, the emperor has no affection for the shōgun. He'll back Genpachi in the affair.'

He paused to admire his enemy's plotting.

'It's a good plan. The only way to defeat it is to expose it before its implementation.'

'Is that why my father was taken?'

'Yes,' said Ezoe. 'The senior retainer of Lord Wada, you may re-call, had good relations with your father in happier times. He saw the possibility of redemption and spoke to him in vague terms of the plan.

'But Genpachi is a cautious man. He has men watching men and more to watch the watchers. He remembered that he, not the shōgun, lay at the root of your father's misfortune. He couldn't be sure your father wouldn't reveal the plotting in revenge. He decided to act so he wouldn't have to find out.'

'So my father is dead?'

'Your father is dead,' he confirmed. 'But rest assured, he was allowed an honourable death and his seppuku was exceptional. The cut was deep and wide and he allowed no second to take his head.'

She paused to reflect, her thoughts on the honour not the horror of her father's death. But despite his fearless embrace, the rehabilitation of their family name remained incomplete.

'How may I avenge him?'

He had known the question would come.

'We face a challenge, you and I: you to avenge your father's death; me to postpone mine to a more conducive time. I considered approaching the regency but it would be my word against Genpachi's and when it comes to the council his holds more weight.'

He sipped from his cup.

'I visited him to see if I could draw a mistake or implicate him but I was without success. The only way to defeat him is to catch the plotters as they conspire.'

'And how do you plan to do that?'

'They will meet once more to pledge an oath. As theirs is a plan that needs all parties united, Genpachi wants a guarantee so none can back out should they begin to harbour doubts. The daimyōs' families are kept at the castle as hostages against rebellion – as it has been since the last shōgun so ruled. Were any to be found plotting, their families would be tortured and put to death. By signing the oath, they guarantee this fate should they back out and the plot be exposed. Their only option will be to succeed.'

'You wish to get hold of the oath or find out where it will be signed.'

'That's correct. But I'm not close to either and time is running out.'

His network had done what in most circumstances would have been a superlative job. On this occasion, what they were yet to find out could lead to his death. He looked over at her furrowed brow.

'It's my wish to have you at my side in this matter but I'm yet to think of what you can do from within Yoshiwara's walls.'

'All I can think of is getting information through Kaoru,' she said. 'Both Lord Genpachi and Mizuno spend time with her. At present I can't see a way to do this, but let me dwell on the matter. I'm sure I can find a way to help.'

She held his eyes with her own and he saw that despite her calm demeanour a fire burned inside. She spoke again.

'I don't know if it has any bearing, but the actor Chitairō is sleeping with Lord Genpachi's wife. I imagine it would provide an unwelcome distraction should he find out at this time.'

'I will see the news reaches his ears,' said Ezoe, wondering what the actor had done to fall into such lethal disfavour.

He shivered, suddenly uncomfortable where he sat. He wondered at the cause of his discomfort, whether it was Katsuyama's clinical dispatching of a man, or if the cushions he was sitting on were inadequate, or the temperature in the room too low—

わが庵は
都のたつみ
しかぞすむ
世をうぢ山と
人はいふなり

喜撰法師

FIVE

I woke in an explosion of cardboard boxes. I peered around me and my eyes met those of an old man. He looked as though he'd been on his early morning walk but was now stopped dead. We stayed as we were, both unsure of what was going on.

My situation slowly came back to me. I was sleeping rough in Toyama Koen because I was a gaijin yakuza on the run from my gang, its rival and the police. It didn't make much sense but I had an explanation. The old man looked like he couldn't think of one. I shrugged and gave him a morning nod. Taking it as the closest to a rationale he'd get, he nodded back and went on his way.

I remained as I was. Tomoe had lodged herself in my mind, opening a door to a fresh wave of grief and remorse. I struggled to escape its weight. I couldn't afford the grieving process yet. That could only come when I'd done what I needed to do.

I couldn't sit long in a pile of cardboard boxes either. Apart from anything else I'd soon freeze. I reached for my flip-flops. They weren't there. In a country where lost wallets are handed in to police stations with the money untouched, someone had stolen my temporary shoes. I got up cursing and started to make my way gingerly through the park.

Winter was approaching and I caught the first edge of an arctic wind. Supposedly they blew down from the north. In reality they slapped you flush in the face whichever direction you went. Walking around in inappropriately thin clothes with, or in this case without, flip-flops got me thinking. Even with their dedication to hot pants and miniskirts, the girls of Tokyo still wore overcoats in winter. The only people dressed with less thought to their conditions than me were sumō rikishi, or the junior ones at least. They had to wear thin cotton yukata and wooden *geta* sandals all the way through the year.

'Yeah?' rumbled Tatsuzan into the phone.

'Hi, it's me, Ray,' I said. 'I'm in a bit of trouble. I don't want to draw you in, but it's to do with Tomoe and I need help.'

'What sort of help?'

'I need to be picked up from Toyama Koen in Takadanobaba. Then I need somewhere to stay for a few days.'

'OK,' he grunted without hesitation. 'Whereabouts?'

He might have been a bit scary but he was a good guy.

'South entrance.'

He calculated for a moment.

'I'll be about twenty to thirty minutes,' he said and hung up.

Feeling slightly better, I bundled up my boxes and left them beside a blue tent gently vibrating with snores. Then I headed to the south exit and the convenience store that was close by. I walked out of the park and stepped from the corner onto the road with the store. At that point I stopped.

A police car braked to a standstill a foot short of where I'd been about to step.

I looked through the windscreen. The policeman looked back. His eyes scanned downwards and I became very conscious of the tarmac under my shoeless feet. I started to calculate the chances of walking past without being stopped. The policeman picked up his handset, his eyes still fixed on me. His pillion pressed surreptitiously at his seat-belt release.

I stopped thinking about my odds.

I took a step back, wheeled around and began a fast walk back the way I had come. I heard the sound of a car door open behind me. I gave up on the fast walk and broke into a sprint.

I've always been reasonably pacey but the thought of a lifetime in jail had me moving like Zola Budd on speed. In no time I was back at the bridge. I darted under it, crashed through some shrubs and came out on the asphalt by the sports hall. It felt like I covered it in a couple of bounds because I soon had the north exit in sight. Beyond it were the lanes of Takadanobaba. I could lose myself in them.

My eyes on freedom, I hurdled the barriers at the entrance of the park. I failed to notice the police car that had been streaking along the road beside. I became aware of it when I heard its tyres screech, milliseconds before something heavy and hard smashed into my thigh. I flipped onto its bonnet and I must have been launched off its windscreen, because the next thing I knew I was flying through the air.

The momentum of my landing sent me into an unintentional stuntman roll. It ended with me face down on the tarmac by a small parade of shops. I lay stunned, the wind taken from me. Or at least I thought it had been. Moments later a knee thudded into my back and forced the last vestiges from my lungs.

'Move a muscle and I'll snap your fucking arm in half.'

My left arm was twisted painfully up my back alongside the right and I felt cold metal snap around both wrists. The owner of the aggressive voice then hauled me up by the scruff of my neck and turned me towards the car. He opened the back door as his red-faced partner caught up from the chase and gave my head a good whack against its frame as he threw me in.

'Things haven't worked out. Best you don't reply. Good luck in the bashō.'

I deleted the text as soon as I sent it. It was as much as I could do to pick the phone from my back pocket and type with my hands behind me, glancing over my side. Hopefully he'd understand – the last thing I wanted was to drag one of the few good guys of late into the mire.

But now I had to worry about myself. The Japanese penal system can be surprisingly lenient on some offences but on others it's indisputably harsh. Murder sat in the latter category. I was pretty sure they would look with particular disfavour on a gaijin entering their land and extinguishing one of its cultural lights.

So even though every plan to date had ended in disaster, I needed to come up with another quick. And this one had to work. Because I couldn't let myself be led by events. The only place they'd take me would be to my death.

Harnessing the influence of the Takata-gumi was no longer an option. They were probably lining up a prison hit on me right then. Conventional routes didn't appear more promising. The police wanted to send me down, not save me, and legal recourse didn't seem to offer much hope. I didn't know any criminal lawyers and even if

I found a good one there was no way I had the money to pay them.

I broke from my thoughts. Something didn't feel right. I tried to lever myself up.

'Stay as you fucking are.'

As well as having a similar way with words as the yakuza, the police appeared to hold me in about as high regard. I lay back but twisted so I could look out the window from my position sprawled across the seat. All I could see were flashes of buildings. It wasn't enough to work out where we were.

'Where are we?'

'Shut the fuck up.'

I was uncomfortable about how long we'd been driving. We'd been in Shinjuku ward – it wasn't as though there wasn't a station to take me to there. Perhaps murder cases were dealt with at a specific location, but it felt odd nonetheless.

We turned a sharp corner and pulled to a stop. I looked out the angle of the window expecting to see the characterless outline of a police station. Instead I saw the gilded curves of a temple roof. Alarm bells ringing, I pulled myself upright as the policemen stepped from the car. The door by my feet opened and one of them leaned in.

'Move it. You're getting out.'

Not until I knew what was going on I wasn't. I swung back to my right and kicked out to the left, my foot catching him flush in the chest. He tottered backwards and I made to leap after him so I could knock him out of the way and then run. But just as I was launching myself the door behind my head opened and rough hands pulled me back.

I was hauled out by the driver, who lifted me upright and around, and slammed me hard against the side of the car. But it didn't drain my fight. I used the bounce from the frame to propel myself forward, aiming a head-butt square at his face. As close as I came it didn't connect. And instead of knocking him out it pissed him off. He chopped me with a brutal punch to the stomach that would have dropped me instantly had he not had me pinioned against the door.

He snarled in my ear.

'Make a scene and I'll break every one of your fucking ribs and then work through the bones in your face.'

It was unnecessary. I could hardly breathe, let alone do anything else.

He dragged me around the car to a small temple in the middle of a quiet residential street. It could have been any of hundreds of neighbourhood shrines. There'd be no finding me here.

The other policeman gave three slow evenly spaced knocks on the door. It immediately unlocked and slid open a crack.

'Watch him – he's feisty,' the policeman holding me said as he unlocked my cuffs.

A man who could only be a yakuza grabbed me by the throat.

'The police have their limits. Fuck with me and I'll beat you so far out of shape you'll be able to stick your head up your arse.'

My mind would have boggled had it not been occupied persuading my lungs to pump air.

'All done,' said the policeman as the cuffs clicked off.

The yakuza grunted his thanks.

'Speak to Sato – he'll see you're taken care off.'

He pulled me inside and I heard the police descend the steps and get in the car. He slid the door shut as the engine started. No one would be coming to save me now.

The only light came from gaps in the wooden slats at the windows and it took a moment for my eyes to adjust to the gloom. When they did I saw we were stood by a collection box in front of another door. The yakuza stepped towards it, keeping ahold of my shirt at the chest. He politely addressed its occupant, who indicated we had permission to enter. The yakuza slowly slid open the door.

Sat on the tatami floor behind a small table set for tea was Takata.

SIX

'Clarence-san, thanks for coming,' said Takata, sounding as though my being there was a pleasant surprise.

'The invitation was quite compelling.'

He poured some tea into a cup which he pushed across the low table.

'Please, sit down. You look like you could do with giving your feet a rest.'

I looked at my shoeless feet. Above them my trousers were ripped and my shirt was torn down one arm and streaked all over with blood.

'Thank you, I could,' I said as I sat. 'It would be great not to be on a hit list too if there's anything you can do about that. Or if I am on one, perhaps you could just get it done with instead of having the shit beaten out of me every other day.'

He ignored the sarcasm.

'I'm afraid I can't do anything about your first point, Clarence-san. As for the second, I'll try my best but you have a tendency to find trouble. It makes it difficult to give guarantees.'

'It doesn't sound like there's much you can for me then, does it? You could tell me why you killed Tomoe, at least.'

I may not have had any hope of surviving but I still had some of her fire.

'If you wanted me out of the picture you could have had Sumida shoot me. There was no need to do what you did.'

I felt myself soften as I said it, at the thought of her on my bathroom floor. I fought the vision. I couldn't afford any weakness if I was going to cope in the moments before my death.

'Chōshi-san was not killed by me or at my request,' he said. 'Aside from the admiration I had for her – which I think I've made clear – I very much needed her alive.'

I looked at him closely. I couldn't work out this new angle, what purpose any games could have now.

'What do you mean? If it wasn't you, who killed her?'

'To start with your second question, she killed herself.'

'No!' I said vehemently. 'That's bullshit. Tomoe's death wasn't suicide.'

I was sick of all the lying, especially now there was no point.

'What do you want? If you're going to tell me the truth, tell it. If you're not, do whatever you're planning to do.'

'Clarence-san, I understand you're distressed but I can assure you I haven't lied to you since we met. I've withheld details I felt wouldn't benefit our joint objectives, but what I have told you has been the truth.'

He fixed me with one of his looks but I still had enough of Tomoe's fight left to meet it.

'You're right, Chōshi-san wasn't what might be considered the suicide type. But she did take her life. She was about to be abducted. That would have led to the same outcome but with some unpleasantness in between. By choosing her own time and method she not only avoided this, she prevented her oppressors getting what they were after. And she used her death as a form of seppuku. She died with honour and used her passing as a rebuke to theirs.'

Now his face softened.

'Your Chōshi-san was as admirable in death as she was in life. You should take comfort from that.'

'But why didn't she contact me?'

The thought hurt, whatever my newfound 'comfort'.

'She was already dead. She took her life shortly before you found out she was missing. They froze her body in case they had need for it – as they later found out they did.'

I tried to process this. I was still struggling to come to terms with the fact she was no longer alive. This was a revelation too far.

'Clarence-san, just because her life was taken at her own hand, it doesn't mean she didn't have killers and it doesn't mean she wouldn't want revenge. And if anyone is capable of exacting vengeance from beyond the grave, it's Chōshi-san.'

This cut through my shock.

'What do you mean?'

'You've been of great service to the Takata-gumi for your ability in effecting events, but that wasn't the sole reason I took you in. Chōshi-san cared for you and she admired you. I knew if there was anyone she would have entrusted to assist her, that person would have been you.'

I thought for a moment. I couldn't think of anything she'd entrusted to me. She'd seemed far keener to keep me from being involved.

'But she didn't. She didn't tell me anything.'

I racked my brains to make sure it was true, that there weren't any clues or messages I might have missed. But there weren't. I hadn't had any idea what was happening then and I still wasn't much wiser.

'I don't even know what's going on now – how can I do anything? And how can Tomoe get revenge now that she's dead?'

'Death won't be a barrier,' he said, sounding entirely convinced. 'As for you, perhaps she told you something you need a prompt to bring back. Or maybe she left you a message you're yet to find. However it transpires, you'll be the key to unlock this. As long as we keep you safe, you'll be the one who allows Chōshi-san her revenge.'

It was ridiculous.

'What is "this"? Can you at least tell me what's going on? My girlfriend's dead, I've been beaten and nearly killed, and I'm being chased by gangsters and the police. I think I have a right to know.'

He smiled and held up his palms.

'You're right. I'm sorry but I needed you to seek your own answers. It was essential your actions drew certain responses.'

'You used me against Onishi,' I said, cutting in. 'You wanted to worry him at first, so he'd think there was someone who could pose a threat but someone you might be able to control. Then you wanted to panic him, to lure him out. You used me as bait.'

Even Tomoe did, I thought.

'I apologise for any distress the lack of information may have caused you,' he continued, ignoring my interruption. 'But I promise, I haven't tried to kill you and I certainly don't want you dead. The truth is I need exactly the opposite: it's essential you stay alive.'

The stay of execution brought a lot less relief than I might have expected. My brain was already overwhelmed, and the dangling of life and death before me had become too common to react to normally in any case.

'But as you say, you have a right to know and there's no benefit to you not knowing any more. It may even help.'

He took a sip of his tea.

'You're already aware that something wasn't right with the Kamigawa site. This wasn't known from the very beginning but Ishikawa was a scientist who lived locally and for some reason he had his doubts. He did his own investigation and discovered the site ran directly over a previously undiscovered fault. But by that point, things had progressed too far. The report was buried along with its author, who died in an unfortunate accident soon after he handed it to KanEnCo.'

'How was Tomoe's father involved in any of this? He had nothing to do with the nuclear industry.'

'He wasn't anything to do with the industry, but he was from Shizuoka prefecture where the plant is. As is Onishi. In fact they were from the same town and they knew each other when they were young. When Onishi first started out, Chōshi helped him with campaigning and fundraising. Onishi was a nobody then and took whatever assistance he could get. But when he moved beyond local politics, he only brought the associates he considered beneficial. Chōshi wasn't one of them.

'Chōshi accepted his lot but he still hoped the connection could prove useful later on. He'd helped start Onishi's career after all and he was sure that was worth a favour somewhere down the line. Many years later, when his businesses started to fail, he thought the time had come when he could call it in. Onishi now headed up the LDP's wealthiest faction and had the power to make poor men rich and rich men poor. Chōshi didn't even get a response.

'As his businesses fell about him, he was forced into the arms of moneylenders. He grew bitter. Normally that kind of bitterness just rots at the insides of those it consumes. But Chōshi got what looked to be a break.

'One evening, he was drinking with one of his cronies when a report on the Kamigawa Plant's construction appeared on the bar's TV. His friend was an estate agent and remarked on the swathes of land he'd bought for Onishi years before. He speculated on the mark-ups that must have been made when they were sold on to KanEnCo.

'Chōshi may not have had an eye for business but he wasn't dumb. He got copies of the original purchases and then checked the registry for the sales to KanEnCo. Onishi's name wasn't mentioned but all of the companies that sold the pieces of land could eventually be traced back to him.

'Chōshi realised he might have found Onishi's Achilles heel. But he knew in the grand scale of scandals it still wasn't enough. So he sat on the information he had and quietly dug for more. He had an advantage over the protestors. Passing information to them was the same as taking sides and that could lead to a rapid decline in one's health. The snippets he came across over drinks and dinners were the gossip of unaffiliated parties that could be safely passed on.

'Eventually he got a name. But after Dr Ishikawa's accident, his family developed reclusive traits. However, when Ishikawa's wife passed away, nearly twenty years after her spouse, Chōshi went to pay his respects to the son. He convinced him that should he have the means, he would avenge Ishikawa's accidental passing. He was told Ishikawa had indeed left a copy of his report. The son, now without fear of repercussions being borne on his mother, would be happy to give it to him if he promised to bring down the men responsible for his father's death.'

'So Tomoe's father had been working on this for years?' I asked, impressed by his dedication.

'Of course. You don't tackle a man like Onishi like that,' said Takata, clicking his fingers. 'Chōshi's pride ruined his life in almost every conceivable way. But as a vehicle for retribution it was a formidable trait.'

'But if he had the information, why didn't he hand it to the police or the papers?'

'Who in the police? The ones who brought you to me? And which newspapers? The ones KanEnCo has its advertising accounts with? The ones that contain associates of mine? Or perhaps those that have one of Onishi's many contacts at their helm?'

He paused so I could consider the paucity of options available to Tomoe's dad.

'Chōshi understood this well enough but he also had other thoughts in his mind. At this point, he showed there may have been a part of him worthy of redemption. He decided to blackmail Onishi instead.'

I was familiar enough with Takata not to be surprised by his admiration for the pragmatic approach. But I thought even he might struggle to define it as a balance to Mr Chōshi's sins.

'I don't quite see how that makes him a more worthy character?'

'Part of the deal would have involved buying out Chōshi-san's contract.'

The revelation caught me off-guard. I wasn't sure how it made me feel. It did nothing to make up for his betrayal. It may even have been out of guilt – a selfish act to assuage his shame. It certainly didn't make me feel any sadness for his death.

But thoughts of him weren't uppermost in my mind. What gripped me was the realisation that had things not gone so horribly wrong, Tomoe might still have been with me. Free from her binds rather than dead.

'What happened?'

'He never had a chance,' said Takata bluntly. 'He was a nobody up against forces far too big. He acted as though it was about the money and the release of his daughter, and in some ways it was. But he'd been working on this for years and at its root was his need for revenge. At first that was for being forced into the hands of money-lenders and ruined. Then came the need to avenge his daughter and hit back at those who had made him hate what he saw in the mirror every day. We knew he'd betray any agreement once he had what he claimed to want.'

'We?'

I suppose it was obvious, but my suspicions had been swinging wildly for a month. Once I knew Takata didn't want me dead I'd somehow separated him from everything else.

'You look surprised?' he said. 'You knew we were involved. We were employed to minimise protests and scandals. From that point on, our interests were aligned to Onishi's and the plant's.'

'And Tomoe's father?'

'We met – Onishi, he and I. He gave us the report and it – the original and a copy – was burnt. I think your friend Sakura may have told you this already?'

I ignored the jibe.

'And then?'

'And then his house and office were searched for the other copies we knew he'd withheld. When nothing was found a further meeting was convened. In the course of this, he was persuaded to reveal another copy hidden in a security box.'

I wondered at the 'persuasion' required to make a man give up the fruits of over ten years' planned revenge.

'While this was going on a visit was paid to his lawyers. They decided it would be appropriate to return the copy he had placed in their care for release in the event of his premature death. At this point it appeared that all copies had been retrieved and destroyed. It was around then Chōshi decided to take his life.'

A very assisted suicide.

'So why Tomoe? If all the evidence had been destroyed, it wouldn't have mattered what she found out – she'd never have been able to prove a thing.'

'People tend to become sensitive when matters are this serious. Even if there isn't proof, they don't appreciate someone digging about.'

'Does that include you?'

He ignored the question.

'But the reason Onishi set the Ginzo-kai after her was because she did have proof.'

'What do you mean? I thought you said all the files were destroyed?'

'We thought they were. But young Chōshi-san started asking questions that suggested she had knowledge of their content. That strongly implied they were not. That put Onishi in a panic and he's not the kind of man you want to have panicking over you.'

Before I could point out he was doing exactly that, Takata wrapped things up.

'You're aware of how tragically events unfolded from there.'

He actually looked quite sad as he said it but something wasn't right.

'But you were on his side. And Tomoe came to see you. It seems very convenient that the Ginzo-kai started acting for Onishi at that point instead of you.'

'I see I still don't have your confidence. It's not unwise to view our world with an element of distrust – in fact it's a trait that should stand you in good stead. Chōshi-san was similarly doubtful but for her it had less positive results.'

The smile had faded from his lips.

'We spoke a second time, a few weeks after the first. By then certain things had changed. I tried to convince her that both she and the report would be safer if it were left in my care. But in the circumstances it was difficult to convince her of my sincerity. She declined to pass it to me and I didn't get the opportunity to persuade her again.'

'You'd destroyed all the other copies and killed her father. I'm not convinced you'd have won her over however many meetings you had.'

'The police reports are quite clear – Chōshi took his own life. Even if that weren't the case, his actions prior to his death amounted to the same thing. When you cross from normal life into the world of the yakuza, you choose to live and die by our rules.'

I wondered how that worked for people forced into it.

'Your girlfriend understood that. I think you're aware of it too.'

Clearly there were no dispensations.

'As for the other reports, they were destroyed to prevent them coming out in a manner that would have done us harm. At the time it was expedient – relationships that are no longer cordial were still functioning then. But when another copy became available – believe me, with things as they'd become I would have ensured it didn't come to any harm.'

'Why? Surely you needed them all destroyed? You said it yourself – your interests were aligned with theirs.'

'Our interests *were* aligned but things change. Life leads us down unexpected paths.'

He studied me a moment, trying to decide whether to break his information on a need-to-know rule. I was suddenly unsure I still wanted to know more. I'd half killed myself in search of answers but all they had brought me was pain. I was worried what else I might hear. What other ways my memories of Tomoe could be spoiled.

The thought of her pulled me together. Her death couldn't be left unavenged.

'Onishi and I go back a long way,' Takata started, having apparently decided to break his cardinal rule. 'We met when he was a young, up-and-coming politician and I was a junior in the yakuza ranks. We found we worked well together. I provided assistance in turning out his vote; he opened doors for me in return. I then fed him a cut from the opportunities these created and so it went on. A virtuous circle, or perhaps a profitable one if the choice of words doesn't seem apt.

'But as we made our way up our poles we inevitably saw one another less. Open socialising between figures in our arenas is frowned upon and would have been detrimental to us both. As the literal distance widened we could have drifted metaphorically too. But we were fortunate to have Kōda-san and through him our relationship remained strong.

'Unfortunately he passed away and things changed. Men who float effortlessly between the over- and underworlds are rare. Perhaps a worthy successor will emerge soon but we lacked for one then. Rather than agreeing to a temporary alternative, Onishi decided it was a role he could absorb. That was decades of power corrupting good sense. It made him forget we live in a world of specialities, that the kuromaku is a position only men born to it can fill.

'I tried to make the point but Onishi suspected me of manipulation. As time went on, he became more twisted by power-lust. He turned his back on decades of cooperation and started playing us off against the Ginzo-kai.

'It came to a head in a meeting between us, not long after I first met Chōshi-san – I think you may have heard about it already. Now he's trying to undermine me and have me deposed. That would strengthen his position with the Ginzo-kai and give him far greater influence over us.'

'How can he undermine you? Like you said, you operate in different worlds.'

'We work in different realms in the same world,' he corrected.

'The floating world?'

'We operate in its shadows. Onishi is the storm cloud that blocks out the sun.'

His face darkened as though to make the point.

'As you can attest, we hold influence with sections of the police but there others who give their allegiance to the Ginzo-kai or to him. We started facing problems from them. At the same time, the Ginzo-kai became increasingly aggressive and started to expand into our territory. On top of that a whispering campaign about me was initiated.'

I had an idea what that was about but I felt awkward acknowledging it and gave him a quizzical look.

'We sometimes work with the police. We'll help them bust us for something insignificant and perhaps have someone do a bit of time. It gives them face and keeps the public off their backs – the other yakuza do the same. But recently there have been acknowledgements of my support where I haven't helped, in matters that have been detrimental to the yakuza. I don't need to tell you that the future for an informer isn't very bright.'

He said the last part in his usual easy manner, as though he was discussing a recently developed flaw in his golf swing.

'You don't seem very worried,' I said. 'Isn't this a major problem for you?'

'I suppose so, but I've been in the business a long time – I don't intend to be so easily removed. It's been more frustrating than anything. As I mentioned previously, I was hoping to focus on more constructive aims.'

His mind seemed to wander to his programme for generational change. I was more concerned about what was happening now.

'What are you going to do?'

'They're panicking and that will lead to opportunities. What's more important are your next steps.'

'I don't know what they are,' I said, my anxiety building. 'I appreciate your faith, but I'm not sure you're on the right path if you're expecting the answers from me.'

'Rest up and get your head back together – the answers will come. You've done all right so far.'

'That was different.'

'It was the same. One thing though – you can't go back to your place and you shouldn't go to Chōshi-san's. They'll be watching them both.'

'Weren't they before?'

'We made sure our presence was felt. That made them more circumspect, along with the rumours you were MI6.'

It didn't take much guessing as to their source.

'The gloves are off now though. You'll need to go to a safe house.'

It no longer seemed so bad. I thought of somewhere in the countryside or one of Tokyo's nicer spots.

'We've got a place you can go to in Ikebukuro.'

'Ikebukuro?'

Ikebukuro was a few stops north of Shinjuku. It was as dirty and noisy and just as much hassle but it lacked the compensatory buzz. It also didn't seem particularly safe.

'Aren't there a lot of yakuza in Ikebukuro?'

'There are. And not a single one will have a clue who you are. Forgive my bluntness – I recognise your strong, distinct features,' he said gallantly. 'However, many in our industry have had little to no interaction with Europeans. To them you all look quite the same. It will be less dangerous for you to be mixed in with other foreigners than secreted away somewhere you'd stick out like a sore thumb.'

It made sense but I could think of preferable alternatives none-theless.

'In any case, every time I've told you to rest you've ended up criss-crossing the city like a bloodhound that's picked up a scent. I think it's better to leave you the option to act on your instincts. If we stick you up a mountain there's not going to be much you can do.'

He called out.

'Matsumoto.'

The name rang a bell. The door opened and I recognised my greeter from earlier, now less distinguishable for having cropped his hair from the luxuriant style Kurotaki had abused.

'Thank you, Clarence-san – I look forward to seeing you again soon.'

I realised I was being sent on my way. I got to my feet.

'Of course,' I bowed. 'I hope I'll be able to help.'

With that I was shuffled out of the room and the temple. Despite the odds, free to die another day.

SEVEN

It was hardly surprising it wasn't a journey of non-stop chatter. Our only previous conversation had involved him threatening to beat me into contortions that would terrify a gymnast, and his general demeanour was on a par with Kurotaki's. This time the silence was welcome. I had a lot to take in.

I wanted to think about Tomoe. I suppose I wanted to start the grieving process, to try to come to terms with the horror of her death. But I couldn't give myself over to her because of everything that had just been thrown at me. Some of it possibly by her.

If I was to believe Takata, all the complex strands led to a simple end: the scheming of a corrupt politician and a brutal yakuza gang. Getting retribution was going to be far less straightforward.

I sat back to reflect on what it would involve. I'd be going after whoever forced Tomoe into the water business and whoever drove her to her death. That meant taking on Yabu, Tokyo boss of the Ginzo-kai and guilty on both counts. And Onishi, the puppet master choreographing events from above.

They were two men I should never have known about but for their appearances on TV and in the press. Two men who certainly shouldn't have been aware of me. Yet somehow I'd arrived in a situation where I was to try to take them down while they did their best to kill me. Considering they were two of the most powerful men in Japan, I had to think their chances of success were far better than mine.

I finally had the answers I'd been seeking. Except for one. The one that had been nagging at me from the start. The one that had nearly killed me as I sought it.

What was I going to do?

I fell asleep almost before my head hit the pillow in my sparsely furnished new home. It was getting dark when I woke. I stretched and my bumps, bruises and amputations reintroduced themselves in a sharp shock of pain. Admitting defeat in a brief attempt to get up I rolled over and realised there was one spot of discomfort that had held itself back. A sore piece of skin the size of a horimono courtesan that Horitoku had been filling in.

And for some reason it made up my mind. As outlandish as it was I decided to go with Takata's suggestion. I'd trust Tomoe to provide my answers. I'd put myself in her hands.

It seemed so simple. Sit back, relax and wait for the solution to be placed before me. My plan of action decided, I even managed to drag myself the few feet to the sofa to watch an evening film. When it finished I tumbled back into bed and slept again, this time for the night.

I woke the next morning still far from comfortable but everything seemed to hurt just a little bit less. It wasn't such an effort to get out of bed and by the time I'd showered I was close to feeling refreshed. The problem with my plan struck me soon after that.

Once you're done sleeping, there's very little you can do in a twenty-square-metre flat. I switched on the TV to see a presenter shouting, his key phrases flashing in neon on the screen. I'd been beaten around the head enough recently – I didn't want to inflict equivalent punishment on my sense of sound and sight. I flicked through another couple of channels then turned to my phone for distraction before I gave up on that.

I tried the kitchenette, walking the three strides from the fold-up sofa to a radio on top of the fridge. I bobbed my head to a song briefly but bored of the one that came after that.

I looked around for something else to distract me but I'd exhausted all the possibilities the flat had. I cursed it, without apparent effect, and gave up.

Despite Takata's reasoning I felt far from safe as I stepped into the street. I scanned it both ways but there were only a couple of lookalike salarymen and a few students milling around. I looked harder, wondering where the Takata-gumi man was. I'd been left an emergency number and told there would be someone nearby at all times. I couldn't see any likely candidates but I still had the uncomfortable sensation of being watched.

I headed down the road and then wandered into side streets. Signs for girly bars and massage parlours immediately caught my eye – they were exactly the kind of places to attract yakuza for work or play. The thought sent a shiver down my spine. The lack of stimulus in the flat seemed to have been over-compensated. A happy medium might be better sought elsewhere.

I got off the train at Harajuku and, unusually, felt pleased to have arrived. It was hard to imagine anyone but schoolgirls, shoppers or tourists wanting to get caught in the crush. It certainly wasn't the kind of place to top a yakuza's go-to list.

I let myself be washed by the tide of people down Omotesandō Dōri but soon fought my way off to the left. I was rewarded with instant calm. Twenty metres down the small side road and I was where I wanted to be: The Ōta Memorial Museum of Art.

It was Tomoe who'd recommended it, a small museum housing one of Japan's biggest collections of ukiyo-e. It was one of her favourite places and as such seemed a prime candidate for a venue if she'd had a message for me she wished to hide.

They changed their exhibitions on a monthly basis and I stopped outside to see what was on.

'Flowers of the Floating World – The Courtesans of Yoshiwara'.

This was it. It was too much to be coincidence. Tomoe's message had to be inside.

I came out an hour later soothed by the museum's understatement, made melancholy by Utamaro's languid charm – and just as ignorant of what to do next. For despite the apparent sleight of hand by the gods there was nothing from Tomoe. I had no better idea of how she wanted me to take her revenge.

I sat on a step outside and shut my eyes. Perhaps I had received some kind of clarification, but from my unconscious instead of the Divine. Because it was suddenly obvious. It was time I returned to reality and stopped looking for answers in dreams and messages from the dead. I'd allowed Takata to overwhelm me. I'd let him project his desires onto Tomoe and through her onto me.

Now was the time for it to end. I'd thought of her as a force of nature but it hadn't prevented her from being killed. That alone should have made me see sense. However much she'd seemed to encapsulate life, she'd been as mortal as the rest of us. Instead of trying to lift her above the fact, it was time to let her rest.

Despite it leaving me at a dead end, the moment of clarity brought a kind of peace. That night sleep came hard and fast. I woke as though from a coma ten hours after I'd lain down. But even if I hadn't been aware of it, my brain must have been active while I slept. Because the well-reasoned closure I'd gone to bed with had been discarded with the previous day.

It didn't make sense. This implacable drive was more like Tomoe. But as much as I tried I couldn't rediscover the sense of the evening before. However sound my rationalisation, an internal imposter was leading me another way. Whatever had lodged itself in me was relentless in urging me on.

I decided to head to Ginza – I'd met Tomoe there not more than three months before. She'd sauntered up with a smile brighter than a supernova and a kiss that radiated through me. She'd acted as though there was nothing unusual. I'd had to ask why her hair was set like a geisha's and she was wearing a kimono of clouds swirling around blue-green hills.

'I felt like it,' she shrugged. 'You don't like it?'

'I love it – you look sensational. It's just a little different to what you normally wear.'

She'd just lifted her shoulders again, angled her head and given me another heart-stopping smile. I'd spent the rest of the day in her glow, admiringly despised by male passers-by.

But there were no hidden messages there either. Or in Daikanyama the next day, or Shimokitazawa the one after that. It was no good.

There were memories aplenty but no missives from beyond. I hoped the opportunities Takata was expecting were presenting themselves with greater haste to him. I was at the point of giving up.

The next day, when boredom struck, instead of reaching for my psychic's hat, I grabbed a matinee ticket to the first thing about to start. I settled in as the room faded to black.

EIGHT

Dreaming of the Floating World 5

It was a day much like any other. As had been the day before, the one prior, in fact all of them since she met Ezoe. She could have exploded with frustration but restricted herself to making faces at the cat.

'Mi-chan, what are my appointments for the day?' she asked the apprentice when she'd finished breakfast.

'You have a booking in the early afternoon,' Michiko began.

'Mm, and the evening?'

'The evening's a little more complicated. You were to see a paper merchant but the Izumiya ageya sent their apologies – their premises won't be available for entertaining after all.'

'What do you mean? An ageya can't do that. That client's been waiting months – to cancel now would be unbearably rude. Surely they're not proposing that?'

'I'm afraid they are, Onēsan,' said Michiko. 'Our proprietor was most unhappy. He rushed straight over but they were adamant. He's been trying to find an alternative but with it being so late he hasn't had any success.'

As Michiko was speaking Katsuyama's expression had changed.

'Perhaps it isn't such a bad thing after all.'

'I thought you'd be upset.'

'Mi-chan, as you'll be free this evening, could you find one or two other apprentices to help with a task?'

'Saikaku-sama,' Michiko cried, grabbing at the stranger's arm. 'It's wonderful to see you again after such a long time. I hope you're planning to stay in town.'

'Let go of me,' the stranger barked from under his deep-brimmed straw hat. 'I'm Wada and whether I stay is not your concern.'

Michiko retreated to side of the road and the other apprentices. Uncovering the names of those who preferred not to announce themselves was part of what an apprentice did. Usually it was to pass the time and feed the gossip that sustained Yoshiwara. Today she had a sense her mistress wanted the information for something else.

One of the other apprentices went to inform Katsuyama. Michiko settled back, apparently in playful conversation, but in reality watching the street for any other visitors heading towards Izumiya.

Lord Wada. So it could be true. Katsuyama hurriedly prepared some ink and wrote out a note. Once finished she called for a servant to have it dispatched. It was just a warning so he would be prepared. But if what she suspected was happening, it would be followed by another letter that would require a more immediate and dramatic response.

As the servant departed another of the apprentices arrived with a different name. Fifteen minutes later and there was one more. It tallied with her suspicions but the most important was still missing from the list.

*

'Saikaku-sama,' Michiko cried, grabbing at the stranger's arm. 'It's wonderful to see you again after such a long time. I hope you're planning to stay in town.'

'Get out of my way, you filthy whore.'

With his deep-throated reply, the stranger thrust Michiko from him with such force that she tottered and fell. He and his assistant continued towards Izumiya at pace. But Michiko's relay was already in action, nodding forcefully at the monk selling tea-whisks as she raced to catch up.

'Sir, sir,' the monk slurred as he staggered forward. 'Not only the very best tea-whisk, but a wonderful reminder of Yoshiwara.'

He tripped, falling into the man's assistant who, despite his best efforts, careered into his master beside.

'Let me help you – I'm so sorry for this offensive drunk,' said Michiko's friend as she caught up. 'He's an embarrassment to the quarter. We try to have him barred, but he must have an arrangement with the guard at the great gate as he always finds his way back.'

The assistant was caught between attacking the monk, who was backing away in haste, and bowing at his master as he was steadied by the apprentice at his arm.

'Get away with you!'

The man shrugged the apprentice off and turned his ire on the monk.

'You're fortunate I have business to attend to or I would test my blade on you,' he snarled. The monk retreated even further at the threat. 'If I find you here when I return, you'll be in two pieces before the day is out.'

He stalked towards Izumiya, his assistant hurrying in his wake.

'Did you get a look?' asked Michiko when she reached her friend.

'It never fails,' said the apprentice, flipping away the small mirror she'd held at her side to see under the stranger's hat. 'I don't know who he is but he's the man you were looking for. The one with the mole on the left side of his face.'

'He's here,' exclaimed Michiko as she burst into Katsuyama's room. 'Lord Genpachi, he's here.'

'It's as I thought.'

Katsuyama hurried to her writing table and wrote out a note.

'Mi-chan, I need you to have this dispatched to Lord Ezoe with the greatest of haste. Use Itō, he's the fastest, and tell him he will be paid double if he has the message delivered within the quarter-hour.'

Michiko took the letter and darted from the room.

So it was happening. The events had come to their climax. And they were to reach their conclusion here. For all the searching outside, the walls of the quarter hadn't been obstructing her. The path to retribution lay within. They had those who had destroyed her family entrapped.

'It all comes back to Yoshiwara.'

NINE

Samurai leapt from the darkness, slashing at one another and splattering blood. I started and looked around. A student eyed me warily from the seat beside and I realised where I was. I rubbed my eyes and settled back. Another strange dream, this one sparked by the soundtrack of warriors.

Or possibly not.

The words struck me.

'It all comes back to Yoshiwara.'

Except it wasn't really the words, it was the voice. There was no mistaking it. Tomoe had spoken to me as I slept.

I burst from the cinema into bright sunlight and bolted towards Ikebukuro Station. Or at least I tried. Tokyo isn't a place you move fast – there are too many people and with centimetres at a premium, no one's willing to spare an inch.

But I wasn't going to bow to decorum. I weaved and pushed my way down the street, cursing under my breath and over it but getting nowhere fast. A murder of crows exploded in a black cloud of beating wings, their screaming caws an echo of my desire to bawl at the crowd. Even the jazz blasting from lamppost speakers was frenetic, howling out in saxophonic alarm. But no one picked up on the urgency and my progress remained painfully slow.

The crowds were even worse at the station. I gave up all notions of etiquette, shouldering my way onto a densely packed train whose occupants surged with every acceleration and brake.

It didn't make sense, this need of mine to move so quickly. Tomoe had been gone over a month – an extra ten minutes would make no difference here or there. But I just had the feeling I needed to be fast. The solution was at my fingertips but it felt fragile, as though it could be ripped from me at any time.

'I don't know what you mean.'

That couldn't be right. She had to.

'I don't believe you. Tell me what you know, and not the lies and half-truths Takata tells you to say.'

'I promise – I've told you everything. Nothing else happened here.'

I was back at Matsubaya. I'd taken a risk. I'd come out of the station and run there directly, taking no precautions at being seen. The owner had been unpleasantly surprised.

'What are you doing here?' she'd whispered at the door. 'It's not safe.'

'I have to see Sakura.'

'She's with someone,' she said. 'And there are people in here you wouldn't want to be seen by.'

I think she was genuinely on my side but I was beyond empathy by that point.

'Pull her out,' I demanded. 'I've got to see her – it's a matter of life and death.'

She gave me a sharp look but then her eyes softened just a little. She took me by the arm and led me quickly to a room at the side.

'Wait here, and when Sakura comes make sure you're quiet. If you're heard, your "life and death" will more likely end in the latter, and maybe not only for you.'

Sakura had turned up a few minutes later, wrapped in a yukata decorated in the flowers of her name.

'Something else happened,' I said. 'I know it did.'

'I promise you, I don't know anything else.'

It wasn't going as I'd expected. I decided to change tack.

'Sakura, I like you, but things have happened over the last month that have changed me. If I think I have to hurt you to get the answers I need, I will.'

'Stop,' she said, taking hold of my hands and cutting short what I thought was a bone-chilling threat. 'You're not going to do anything. Whatever's happened to you, I know you're still a decent guy.'

She gave my hands a squeeze.

'I've told you everything I know. Whatever else happened, wherever it happened, I don't know anything more.'

I grasped back as though I might wring something from her hands or at least draw strength. I tightened my jaw to prevent the cry of frustration fighting to come out. The answer had to be here. Tomoe had told me herself. If I was ever going to get a message, that had been it.

'If you're in a rush in Tokyo, the only way to get where you're going more quickly is to leave earlier than you did.'

Johnny had told me that. He also insisted on having a cold

355

shower in the gym as it 'wasn't a place for weakness' and had count-less other pearls of wisdom he was ready to share. But this was a rare occasion when he was right. If you're desperate you can weave your way through some of the crowds, but it's an illusion of haste, as much use as hurrying to the front of a moving train.

'You just have to accept you'll get there when you get there,' he'd advised. 'It's impossible to make up time.'

Except I was going to try. I'd put down 10,000 yen by the taxi driver and told him it was his plus the fare if he could get me to Ningyōchō in ten minutes flat.

'But you have to know. It all comes back to Yoshiwara. It has to be here.'

My voice sounded desperate. Sakura gave me a sideways look, but she knew enough about my recent history to cut me some slack.

'Yoshiwara?'

'I was told I'd find the answer in Yoshiwara – don't ask me how. I think it's unlikely Takata and Onishi did a round robin of soapland meetings and I don't think Tomoe did any entertaining here. So it has to be in Matsubaya.'

She lifted her head at the sound of Tomoe's name.

'Your girlfriend's Katsuyama II, isn't she?'

'That's how some people knew her,' I said, my tone prickly. 'But her name was Tomoe.'

She ignored my pique.

'This area was *Shin*, New, Yoshiwara,' she said.

'Yes, I know – that's why I'm here.'

'Katsuyama I was never in Shin Yoshiwara.'

I didn't know that.

'What do you mean?'

'Shin Yoshiwara opened in 1657 after The Meireki Fire. Katsuyama I was no longer a courtesan then. She only ever worked in Moto Yoshiwara – Old Yoshiwara – and that was in a different place.'

I'd told the taxi driver to head to The Great Miura Hotel. When I'd asked Sakura if anything remained of Moto Yoshiwara, she'd told me most probably not. But The Great Miura and Hamadaya restaurants were the only long-standing establishments she knew of, and they were probably on plots that went back to Moto Yoshiwaran time.

The traffic was thick as we approached Ningyōchō. I was still trying to do Tokyo's impossible, so the taxi driver got lucky just short of ten minutes when I had him let me out one hundred yards from where the great gate would have stood. I cut off the main road into a side street. Based on Sakura's explanation this put me in Moto Yoshiwara proper, within the area a moat would once have closed off.

When I came to a small shrine guarded by two foxes I took a left along a narrow street. Fifty metres down, an ancient wooden gate broke the line of a high wall. Exquisite roofs peeped over it, their swooping tiled outlines giving the impression of rolling waves. It was how I imagined the area's architecture in the distant past. If I were a newly deceased courtesan sending messages through a dead tayū, it would have been my choice of venue for the big reveal.

I passed through the gate and crossed a gravel river on stepping stones that looked like reflections of clouds. Moving through the sliding door of the entrance I found an interior as impressive in elegant grandeur as the outside's ornate lines.

As I took off my shoes, a kimono-clad assistant hurried to greet me in a small-step rush. My head was so mixed up I half expected her to start speaking in ancient Japanese.

'Welcome to The Great Miura. Please let me know how I can help.'

She addressed me formally but the words seemed contemporary enough.

'Um . . .'

I stopped. I was now almost certain I was in the right place but the situation was so unusual I couldn't think of an obvious way to begin.

'Er, I believe a message may have been left for me here by a young lady. She went by the name of . . .'

I weighed the possibilities.

'. . . Katsuyama.'

I wondered how much the receptionist knew of the history of the place. She gave nothing away.

'Katsuyama-sama? But of course,' she said with a smile.

I looked at her look, trying to work out if it was knowing or if she was just being polite.

'Please, come with me to the front desk.'

We walked down the hallway past dark wooden beams and paper doors exploding with colour; birds and flowers bursting from hand-painted scenes.

'And you would be Tokugawa-sama,' she said once behind the desk, showing no sign of nerves at facing a Caucasian descendent of the shōgun.

'Erm, yes, that's right.'

I hoped it was just Tomoe being playful and I shouldn't expect even stranger dreams.

She smiled.

'You're slightly early. Your room's not booked until later in the week. But for a friend of Katsuyama-sama and a man of your stature I'm sure we can find a way around that.'

She took me by surprise. I could only assume I'd unravelled things more quickly than Tomoe had expected. The thought made me feel good. I was starting to believe I really had reached the end, that the final answers would be in the room.

'Would you be so kind as to take a seat while we have the room prepared? Perhaps you might like to peruse the package Katsuyama-sama left for you as you wait.'

My eyes snapped from their glaze and locked on the envelope she held out. I reached for it. This was the moment. Everything would be explained in that file.

TEN

Ray-kun,

I know you must be upset reading this because by the time you do I will be dead. But please try not to be too distressed – every life is different and they all end in different ways at different times. I'll die earlier than I expected, but the time I had was good. And while I'd have preferred to live longer, my death isn't a waste.

I suppose deep down I knew the path I was taking would lead to this, even if I didn't admit it to myself. When I think why I followed it I think of principle, of not being walked over by others. And I think of justice, for my father and for myself. I suppose if you add them up they equate to honour and that seems a ridiculous reason to die, as though I'm living out a samurai drama from the past. Yet at the same time it's the most logical of reasons, because if you don't have any honour or codes to live by, what purpose is there to life?

As for my father, I won't try to express the pain his actions caused me – although I'm grateful I had you to comfort me at the time. But beneath whatever he became, or maybe always was, traces of a decent man remained. He wrote me a letter, as I am doing to you now, so he could speak to me from beyond his grave. I won't bore you with the details but he knew the magnitude of what he did. And while it was too late to make amends, he did what he could to belatedly redeem me from his sins.

For all his good or bad he was my father and I was his daughter and that bond can't be broken or denied. To have him act as a father at the end, and know the man I'd loved still existed within him, helped bring me the peace I need now.

Most people don't get to choose the manner of their death, so to be able to die with honour means in some ways I'm blessed. But my redemption isn't complete – it only will be when past wrongs have been put right. I wanted to do this without involving you but I ran out of luck and I ran out of time. I suspect you may have suffered as a result and I'm truly sorry for that, Ray-kun – I hate the thought of you being hurt because of me.

But I think you appreciate the situation – I hope you do – and I know you're capable of doing what needs to be done. Because you have the strength, the intelligence and the determination. You always did, you just didn't know.

You reading this letter means you know what happened. I hope it also means you've found a way to understand. I'm so sorry I couldn't find a way to explain earlier so our last memories could have been sweeter.

There are, though, still some details you won't know.

Before my mother died, we used to go to a small chalet at the foot of Mount Fuji. I was too small to remember, but I have flashes of nostalgia that make me certain it was a happy time. I'm sure it was the same for my father because we never went again after my mother passed away.

When I found out what had happened to him and I got to the bottom of why, I went back. I knew he wouldn't allow the events to go unavenged. Waiting for me was the letter I mentioned and the documents you will find enclosed with this.

There is a report on the Kamigawa Plant that reveals the safety issues that were identified before construction began. Onishi is on the circulation list. There's also documentation on the money he amassed from the sale of the land and his financial stake in the plant. If you get these in the right hands he will be undone. He'll be the first to fall but Yabu will be left exposed and he'll soon be toppled as well.

Getting them in the right hands won't be easy, though. Onishi is a powerful man and there are very few willing to stand against him. Unless you get the files to them, they won't see the light of day and this will all have been a waste. I'm sorry to place such a burden on you but I ran out of time before I could find a suitable person to trust.

One possibility is Takata of the Takata-gumi – the man you helped me track down. His men were responsible for the death of my father but in a strange way he's not guilty of the crime. I know that sounds odd, but my father's murder was initiated many years ago – to blame Takata would be to blame the gun rather than the man with it in his hand. That doesn't mean he can be trusted – despite his charm he's an extremely dangerous man. But I don't need to tell you this. I know you'll make the right choice ☺.

So now, instead of completing what I need to, I'm asking you to do it in my place. Because the net around me has closed quickly and I can only perform some last, hurried tasks before the Ginzo-kai track me down. Even getting this letter to you is complicated because I know they'll have people checking your post.

I'm putting you in danger again. Doing so has been the hardest dilemma in the many I've recently faced. But in the end I decided to go with my instinct, and my instinct told me you'd do what I couldn't and put the final pieces into place. Like a gaikokujin samurai. My gaikokujin samurai who I can't wait to meet again.

So enough about danger and death – I was my happiest when I was with you so this letter should end with life and love. I loved you from the moment I saw you. I knew instantly you were the one for me. I think you loved me too – I hope you did – although perhaps you didn't realise at the time.

I know sometimes you felt uncomfortable, as though you were the lucky one of us both. But it was never like that. You made up what was missing in me. When I was down you picked me up, and when I was up you made me fly higher still. You made me happy and you made me feel complete. I loved you and I love you and I always will.

Now I have to go. But there isn't a goodbye for us, Ray-kun, so take this as a farewell. Because we will meet again and we'll love each other just as we did. The same and much, much more.

Forever yours, your eternal love,

Tomoe

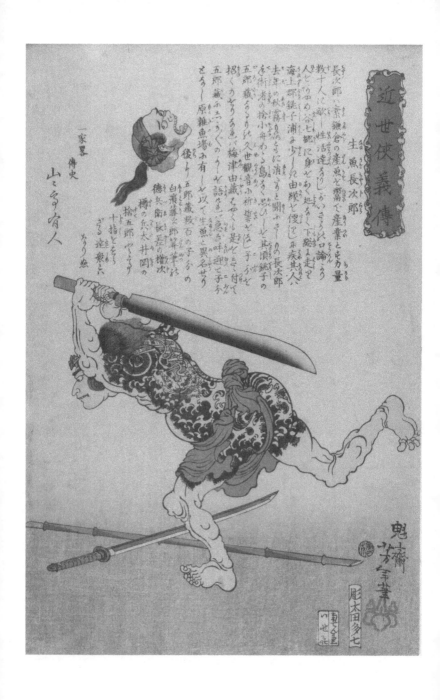

近世侠義傳

生魚長次郎

一家景傳史
山々亭有人

魁齋芳年筆

彫太田多七

ELEVEN

I kissed the letter on the lipstick mark by her name and read it again. When I finished the second time I closed my eyes and felt at peace with the world for the first time in a very long while.

The moment was fleeting. I opened them when I heard the receptionist call my, or rather Tokugawa's, name. Beyond her a beast of fearful proportions, partially contained in a suit, was trying to squeeze its enormous bulk through the entrance door. It wasn't Kurotaki and I'd only seen one other man in Japan that big. He'd almost ripped my arm from its socket, his accomplice had bludgeoned my face and shortly after I'd gone out the window of a moving car.

'Hello, Ray-san,' the monster of the Ginzo-kai called out as his face came into view. 'Fancy seeing you here – it's been too long.'

I was on my feet and running down the corridor before he finished – I had no desire for a repeat of my previous experiences with him. A last glance in his direction showed the receptionist gamely stepping across him to block his path.

Out of the reception area the place was a shoji-sided maze. I slid a door open at random and found myself in the toilets. There was a tiny window above the basins on the other side.

It wasn't difficult getting up to and partway through it, but they hadn't been designed as emergency exits and I had a moment's panic before a frantic wiggle of my hips allowed me to drop head first outside. I rolled to my feet with the momentum of the fall and looked around. Normally I'd have appreciated the ornate courtyard with its stone lantern and picturesque pond. At that moment I just felt trapped by the four walls of sliding doors. I ran to one opposite, slid it open and leapt inside.

'*Dōmo sumimasen, gomen nasai.*'

I fired a volley of apologies to startled diners as I hurtled through the tatamied room. From there I continued my direct line from the Beast, crossing a corridor and bursting in and out of a room on the other side. I found myself in another garden, just as beautiful and just as unhelpful, this one bordered by a high wall. I cursed with a profanity to make Kurotaki proud.

I didn't pause long. It was the wall or return the way I'd come for a match-up with Godzilla's meaner twin. I rocked on my heels then bolted forward, throwing everything I had into the jump. There was a moment of gut-churning fear as my feet failed to get purchase. But then I found traction and managed to kick and clamber my way to the top.

The fall was nothing compared to a first-floor hotel room and I dropped to a crouch, perfectly poised to spring down the alley and make good my escape. But as I was about to, something connected with my head. Something so brain-jarringly powerful that even after a month of cranial impacts it seemed to freeze time and leave my vision surrounded by the jagged edges of a comic book 'BANG'.

After delivering the stupefying punch, its owner's other hand caught me as I collapsed to the floor.

'You dumb fuck,' he said, far less friendly than he had been when greeting me minutes before. 'There are two ways out of this place, the front and the back. What the fuck good did you think it would do you running around inside?'

He held me like prey in his monstrous claw and spoke into the phone in his other hand.

'Yeah, I got him. Meet me round the back.'

His turned his attention to me.

'Try anything and I'll stick a pen in each ear and smack them so hard they meet in the middle of your head.'

It was almost a shame he had to be a rival to Kurotaki – they'd have got on so well.

'I hope you're not assaulting one of the Takata-gumi.'

As though the gods had gifted me the power to will someone into being, his detestable voice rang out.

'Or perhaps you're just helping Ray-san up,' Kurotaki continued. It was the first time I'd heard him refer to me without a curse.

I heard footsteps from behind and knew the feet would reveal themselves as Knifeman's. I lifted my head and saw Kurotaki twenty metres down the alley, aggression oozing from every pore. Sumida stood alongside him, looking as perturbed as one might on an afternoon stroll.

'If that is the case, please accept our thanks,' Kurotaki said with a faint nod. 'Ray-san, why don't you come over here?'

Apart from the fact I wouldn't have been able to stand, let alone walk, I didn't move because of the flesh-covered vice that had me clamped by the scruff of the neck. The Beast gave no indication this situation would change.

Kurotaki didn't say anything else but he started to edge towards us. To my left, Knifeman's feet shuffled into view. It was at this point, as everyone moved to their starting positions, the man-monster realised he wouldn't win the impending fight with me in his grip and reluctantly tossed me to the side.

I slumped against the wall and looked upon the scene. It was like a Western showdown picked up from the last century and dumped in the present-day East. Tokyo's two most-feared men finally facing each other. Two freaks of nature about to discover who had inherited the more monstrous genes. Who would win, the East Asian tiger or the Japanese black bear? Kurotaki seemed confident it would be him.

'I've got this,' he said quietly, his gaze locked on the Ginzo-kai as he spoke.

Sumida's posture immediately relaxed. Not that he'd been tense in the first place, but he took a small step back.

I felt far less at ease. I wanted to scream at Kurotaki. I didn't care about his life, in fact I was sure the planet would be better without it. But his bravado wasn't just a threat to him. If he was killed there wouldn't be much time left in this world for me.

But the situation was too tense to make a sound so I didn't. Kurotaki continued to edge forward. And the two Ginzo-kai readied themselves where they were.

The slow-motion showdown played tortuously on, seconds as

minutes, minutes as hours. Kurotaki's eyes remained locked on the Beast and rightly so. But I was also concerned about the man at his side; the man I knew would be carrying a knife. It was no good Kurotaki taking out his main adversary only to be caught by the weaker link.

Still he inched forwards, now close enough for me to compare him and his double. Two monsters fronting as men, set well above their malevolent peers in meanness and power. It was possible they hadn't met before. But they would have known the other's reputation and had probably anticipated this day. Kurotaki would have been looking forward to it.

Still he pressed on, so carefully you could hardly see him advance. He may have been confident enough to stand down Sumida but he wasn't so stupid he didn't know what was at stake. His body looked tense, but it was the tension of preparedness without being tight. When the moment came it was easy to picture it transforming, like a predator's spring from its crouch, like—

Kurotaki exploded into a blur. Blood splattered the wall opposite, accompanied by a sickening squelch and another streak of blood that slapped my face. I wiped at it, disgusted, but more than that anxious, desperate to see. I needed to know what was going on, who was winning, if I'd emerge from the next few minutes alive.

I saw Kurotaki and his nemesis through a film of blood. They were clasped to one another, face-to-face. Both had expressions of frenzied intensity, but it was impossible to know whose was fuelled by adrenalin and whose by fear. Kurotaki's elbow on the other side was raised unnaturally but his hand was out of sight. I couldn't tell if his posture was aggressive or if he was disabled by pain.

It seemed an age they stood there, but then the freeze-frame broke with another thunderous eruption of blood. Kurotaki stepped back and I saw its source – spraying from the neck of the Beast where Kurotaki had withdrawn his short sword. The precious blade was coated with human oils now, having been buried hilt-deep in the Beast.

Kurotaki released his hold from its shirt. The Ginzo-kai monster collapsed to the floor like a film-prop filled to excess with fake blood. Beside him more pumped from the throat of Knifeman as he thrashed on the floor in the last throes before death. His hand was still reaching inside his jacket for the tool he hadn't been fast enough to retrieve.

I wiped at my face again in absent disgust. I was trying to piece together the flash of movement I'd just seen. One second all three had been standing; the next, two men were writhing in a river of blood.

An imprint of memory showed Kurotaki reach inside his jacket and swing out back-handed to the right. The strike that had almost decapitated Knifeman with its razor-sharp, Kunimitsu-bladed edge. He'd used its recoil to drive back, thrusting the dagger into the Beast's gaping neck. All at such speed they hadn't stood a chance.

I flinched as he seized the front of my top and hauled me to my unsteady feet. He let go, then grabbed me again as I tottered and started to slide down the wall.

'Come on, Ray-san, let's get you back.'

He took a last look behind him and spat at the twitching mass of flesh and blood still struggling against its fate. He dragged me over to Sumida, who gave a brief nod of approval before he turned.

We made our way to where I hoped would soon be a car, Tomoe's letter in my pocket, the file still stuffed down my top. I think I then passed out because I don't remember anything else.

TWELVE

I opened and closed my mouth to work up some saliva – it felt like someone had stuffed in a handful of sand. I started to move my head but stopped when bells started clanging and lights flashed behind my closed eyes. I opened them slowly. Then I undid my previous caution by sitting bolt upright with a start.

The letter.

A nurse hurried into the room and tried to restrain me as I attempted to get out of the bed. I was in such a weak state she had the upper hand even before a passing doctor saw the commotion and came in to help.

'Clarence-san, please try to relax. You need to rest.'

I looked at her. It was the same doctor who'd treated me before.

'I had a letter. It's important – I have to find it.'

'The letter's safe, don't worry. You were railing about it when you were brought in so we kept it right here.'

She opened a drawer by my bed. I scanned the letter anxiously to make sure it was the right one. I relaxed and folded it up.

'When was that?'

'Yesterday. You've been out cold since.'

I gave her a weak smile through my aching head.

'Aren't there any other doctors here? Do you have to do heads as well as hands?'

'I'm very happy sticking to hands,' she said. 'I just took an interest when I saw you wheeled in. So if you're asking whether I'm in charge of your present treatment, no, I'm not. But if I were to make an unqualified diagnosis, I'd say your refusal to find new friends suggests mental rehabilitation is as important as physical therapy in your case.'

She picked up the chart at the foot of my bed.

'Based on this and the conversations I've had with your doctor, physically you're going be fine – for now, at least. But if you keep associating with the same crowd you're going to be back here again. That's if you're lucky. Next time it could be the morgue.'

She looked at me unhappily. I tried to give her a reassuring smile.

'Don't worry.'

She didn't look convinced.

'Honestly, it's all over. Done.'

'Now why don't I believe that? Is it because I remember you saying much the same last time? Or because you've not even been here a day and one of your "friends" has already had to be treated again?'

'What do you mean?'

Before she could answer, there was an announcement over the tannoy. She gave a quick smile and told me she'd check back in. Then she rushed off.

'I've got no idea,' said the nurse before I could ask. 'I just started my shift. But please, you're not ready to get up. Just lie back for the moment. The doctor will be in to see you soon.'

I did as she said and before I knew it I was out again.

*

I woke to the sound of voices, but these didn't have the same professional tone. I opened my eyes a crack and closed them at the brightness. I had another go and two silhouettes took shape. The silhouettes then became people. They turned out to be Sumida and Kurotaki.

'He awakes. Takata-gumi's hero.'

It had been enough of a shock to be called by my name in the alley. Kurotaki referring to me as a hero, even in jest, was a bit too surreal. I looked at Sumida.

'Things moved quickly after you decided to take your little break,' he said.

'Hey,' warned Kurotaki.

I'd never seen him like this. His mood could only be described as bubbly.

'We hit Yabu and his two lieutenants straight after we dropped you off,' Sumida continued, unfazed. 'Combined with the two you led us to, it means we've taken out the brains and brawn of the Tokyo group. They're in chaos. We started moving on their operations the same day.'

'What about—'

He threw a newspaper at me before I could finish.

'Onishi knew Kamigawa could lead to nuclear disaster', I read.

Then the subhead.

'Construction forced through for personal gain'.

I squinted at the body copy, my eyes still trying to find their place in my head.

'Don't worry about it,' said Sumida. 'In short it says he's fucked.'

He strolled around the side of the bed.

'He's done and Yabu's dead. You got revenge for your girlfriend.'

377

'And we got our city back,' Kurotaki cut in. 'After this, the Ginzo-kai will have to make do with scraps. We're back in charge.'

'What's that?' I asked, nodding at the swathe of bandages wrapped around his gesticulating left hand. He shrugged.

'It's nothing,' he said. 'Someone had to make a gesture to the Ginzo-kai bosses in Kobe – not that there's much they can do now. But it's best if we can agree recent events were caused by an over-enthusiastic Takata-gumi sub-group. It gives them face and an excuse not to set up for war. The way things are with the authorities, that would be bad for us all.'

'You need to be careful – for someone who had all ten fingers not more than a month ago you're losing them at a worrying rate,' I said unkindly. 'You'll look like a leper if you keep this up.'

He either didn't register my coldness or pretended not to notice.

'Yep, my hands were a whole lot happier before you showed up, but I'm pleased that you did. If you do want to get into that though, you don't just owe me a finger now—'

'I don't owe you a finger – you lost the first because you owe me one.'

'—you owe me your life as well.'

Much as I didn't want to admit it, he was right. I wasn't going to acknowledge it to him though.

'And here's me thinking I'd given you two, plus Yabu and the others you took care of. It seems you owe me rather than the other way round.'

He might have saved my life but I still despised him. I'd have been happy to take his and call it quits.

'Maybe I do, Ray-san, maybe I do. For the moment let's say we're even,' he said, his upbeat mood refusing to be tempered by my chill. I still wasn't sure if his insensitivity was genuine or just his way of playing the game.

'But we should head off. You need some rest. You don't seem your normal self.'

He moved towards the door.

'By the way, Kumichō wants to see you. There'll be a car waiting for you when you're discharged.'

I ignored him and gave Sumida a nod which he replied to in kind.

They left, and Kurotaki's vacuum seemed to draw the last of the stress from me, sucking it with him and out of the room. It was over. I'd survived. I couldn't say I'd won, but the fact I was breathing meant I hadn't totally lost.

THIRTEEN

Dreaming of the Floating World 6

'So what will you do?' he asked, once the frenzy of events had abated and the roar of excitement dulled to a buzz.

'I think that's a question I should be asking you,' she replied. 'The actions of a regent of the council are of far greater interest than someone as inconsequential as me.'

He stretched with languid indulgence, as if doing so would clear the months of strain.

'I don't think the bakufu would have had your debts annulled if you were as insignificant as you claim. If they hadn't, the first thing I would have done would be to buy out your contract.'

'But they did and so you can't. Which still leaves me wondering what you will do instead.'

'I will do as the duty of a regent demands. I shall endeavour as best I can to ensure our great land is run for the betterment of the shōgun and his people.'

It was said with a straight face that didn't hide the smile that lay beneath. She returned it with an equally impassive look that revealed just as much. But she still didn't tell him her plans and he knew she wouldn't. He doubted he would see her again.

Outside the sun blazed an early-winter glory. A gust of wind tore at the few leaves still held by jealous owners, sending them pirouetting through the air and down the parade. To the unknowing eye all appeared normal, but those who knew the area knew it was not.

Yoshiwara thrived, it survived, on drama. This usually centred on true love breaking through the quarter's superficial romance: courtesans eschewing the rich and powerful for the powerless and poor; love pacts that led to unlikely escapes; and quashed romances and double suicides that left a bittersweet aching in even the hardest Yoshiwaran heart.

The heroines were the courtesans, the greatest revered for their indomitable spirit, their rebellious verve and elan. The heroes were their lovers and clients, but only those who revealed themselves exceptional in gallantry and charm. Through their dramas, collective misery was made bearable by the adventures of a few.

But the greatest of Yoshiwara's stories were usually myths, a fact that was acknowledged by being ignored. Until now, when a story greater than all others had played out before their very eyes, its significance felt not only in Yoshiwara and Edo, but in Osaka, Kyoto and the rest of Japan.

Crowds had lined the streets and clients and courtesans jostled on balconies to witness a squad of bakufu troops surge down the parade. They had advanced to Izumiya without resistance for the plotters had relied on stealth instead of strength for their defence and had left their militias behind.

As custom demanded, they had even handed their swords in at Izumiya's door. One assistant made an attempt to retrieve his when the bakufu samurai burst in. His neck was severed three-quarters of the way through as reward.

They had been led out with hands bound and some heads bowed.

But not Lord Genpachi's. He had maintained his regal bearing, walking proud as the line of lords made prisoners were marched to Edo between a samurai guard.

Within ten days they were dead. But their crimes were too abhorrent for the honour of seppuku. Their interrogations were thorough and abundant in pain. The deaths that followed lingered almost as long, the slow demise of crucifixion ended by thrusts of long lances just before exposure extracted its final toll.

Their bodies were displayed a week more, serving warning to would-be plotters and providing carrion for scavengers and birds. Their families were treated more leniently. They too were tortured, man, woman and child, but in their beheading their deaths were at least swift.

At the end of the controlled carnage none of the plotters' bloodlines remained, their long dynasties at an end. But plenty were willing to take their place, to assume their land and their stipends, their power and wealth.

Men like Lord Ezoe.

But of Katsuyama? Three days after the affair she disappeared from Yoshiwara like a will-o'-the-wisp. And despite its disappointment, Yoshiwara was happy. Truth was now free to be moulded into myth; the constraints of fact removed and the possibilities endless for playwrights and artists to craft.

So it was that in the eleventh month Katsuyama lived and breathed the Yoshiwaran air, and in the twelfth she did not. And while there must have been those who knew where she went, none ever said.

FOURTEEN

'So, Clarence-san, you did it. You avenged Chōshi-san's death. You took on two of the most powerful men in the country and won.'

Takata looked at me with probing eyes. As with everything he said, I couldn't be sure what was genuine and what was loaded to reveal something in my response. I tried to give up as little as I could.

'Thank you. But I think it would be more realistic to say I was a useful pawn. It seems to me you won this particular battle.'

He smiled. It looked sincere.

'You undervalue your contribution,' he said. 'But you're right that the situation has worked out for us both. Let's just say we each have cause for celebration.'

He raised his glass to mine. We were sat in the living room of his house. Unlike the last time it was just the two of us, if you dis-counted the bodyguards stationed outside the room and around the grounds. A gentle breeze blew outside, rustling the last stubborn leaves of a maple tree that refused to accept the passage of time. It was losing its battle and a sudden gust tore another piece of treasure from its spindly grasp.

'So what do you intend to do?' he asked.

'I haven't decided yet.'

He threw me a curious look.

'You're an intriguing man. Although I suppose by now I shouldn't be surprised.'

His eyes searched mine, as though through them he could draw further information from my brain. I held his gaze but kept my mouth shut.

'I make it my business to be able to read people and anticipate their actions, but you've had a capacity to catch me off guard from the start.'

'I'm not sure what you mean,' I said. 'I only got out of hospital half an hour ago. I haven't had time to think.'

'I didn't expect you to give it much thought. My impression was of a more reluctant member of our organisation. I thought you might take the debt we owe you as an opportunity to get out.' He waved a hand magnanimously. 'You would of course go with my blessing, and you'll always be able to rely on our support. We don't hold quite the same influence in your country, but if you needed it I'm sure there would be ways in which we could help.'

I wasn't trying to play mind games with him. I really hadn't thought about what to do next. I'd spent my two days conscious in hospital snoozing, reading and watching TV. I'd revelled in new-found safety. And I'd thought about Tomoe and reread her letter countless times. Despite everything, it had strangely brought me peace, even a faint glow of happiness amid the melancholy thoughts. It had allowed me to remember her alive, to remember us, to break from the visions of her dead. Which made me think.

'Wait a minute. How come I'm not under arrest?'

'Oh, that?' said Takata. 'They ended up doing a post-mortem after all. It revealed that poor Chōshi-san couldn't have had her life taken by you on the day it was alleged.'

My eyes narrowed.

'Come to think of it, the Takata-gumi seemed to escape mention in all of the reports I read.'

He shrugged.

'What do you expect? We provided some security consultation but essentially we were bystanders. In the scheme of things the newspapers appeared to think our fleeting involvement not worthy of note. They were far more interested in Onishi and Yabu.'

Two small examples of the power that came with reclaiming the throne. With his enemies and counterbalances gone, he'd be stronger than ever. It was the kind of thought that would previously have made me shudder but I didn't feel anything now. I'd changed. Or maybe I hadn't. Maybe the person I always was had just been released. It was what Tomoe and Takata seemed to think.

'I'm not sure what there is for me now in England that there wasn't before,' I said, returning to his question. 'I don't know what I'd do with myself if I went back.'

'And you do if you stay?'

'I could go back to teaching.'

'A nine-and-a-half-fingered teacher with a large horimono on his back? I'm not sure there would be many schools queuing up for your services.'

'My finger? Who would hold an injury from a car accident against me? And I'm not planning to teach any classes bare-chested.'

He smiled.

'You don't think the life of a teacher may seem dull now you've been involved in a more . . . dynamic job?'

'Maybe all I ever wanted was happy mundanity.'

He cocked his head and observed me.

'Maybe it's what you thought you wanted, I'm not sure. But I don't think deep down it's what you really desired. The kind of people you're drawn to, the way you went about things when events turned out as they did. Your life wouldn't have led to this if you really were after quiet.'

I wondered if he was right. But I'd backed out of bungee jumps before when I got nervous – it wasn't the kind of thing that suggested I'd been looking for this.

'Well, we'll have to see. I need to take some time out. I might go back to London after all.'

'There are "buts" in your voice.'

Faces flashed across my mind and a nipple that no longer was.

'There are buts.'

Slights and unpunished acts.

'I still feel I have unfinished business. Maybe I'll stay.'

He raised his eyebrows.

'Unfinished business?'

'Something like that.'

I wondered if he got the same sense of satisfaction leaving people hanging on what was left unsaid.

'I mean, I've got to get my tattoo finished for a start. I'll look pretty stupid going around with it as it is for the rest of my life.'

He smiled, and I sensed the smile was from inside as well as on his face.

'If you stay, you'll have to show it to me when it's completed. Perhaps you'll be able to enlighten me on your unfinished business at the same time. The ripples from the pebbles you throw have a tendency to turn into waves. I'd like to be able to prepare.'

I smiled back. He was right. If I did stay it was likely to get just as messy again. But the thought didn't scare me as it once would have. It wasn't just Sumida – I'd been looking and learning as well.

I got up and bowed deeply. He stood and bowed in return. With that I turned and walked from the room.

IMAGES

I have been able to illustrate this book with the wonderful prints featured within thanks to the kind support and great generosity of the following museums, art dealers and printmakers. I am extremely grateful to them all.

Art Gallery of Greater Victoria
Honolulu Museum of Art
JapanesePrints-London
Metropolitan Museum of Art
Minneapolis Institute of Arts
Mokuhankan
Museum of Art, Rhode Island School of Design
Philadelphia Museum of Art
Rijksmuseum
Scholten Japanese Art
Staatliche Museen zu Berlin, Museum für Asiatische Kunst

Poem of the Pillow, Kitagawa Utamaro, p.2
The Sunrise at Futamigaura, Utagawa Kunsada, p.8, © Honolulu

Museum of Art, Gift of James A. Michener, 1959 (14446)

Yellow Rose and Frogs, Utagawa Hiroshige, p.18, © Honolulu Museum of Art (29951S)

Akashi Gidayu – One Hundred Aspects of the Moon, Tsukioka Yoshitoshi, p.24, © Scholten Japanese Art, New York

Unravelling the Threads of Desire, Kitagawa Utamaro, p.30, Metropolitan Museum of Art (JP3166)

The Actor Nakamura Shikan IV as Washi no Chokichi, Toyohara Kunichika, p.40

Chrysanthemums and Horsefly, Katsushika Hokusai, p.48, Minneapolis Institute of Arts, Bequest of Richard P. Gale (74.1.210)

The Courtesan Kasugano of the Sasaya Brothel, Chōkōsai Eishō, p.56, © Honolulu Museum of Art (29762S)

Charcoal Foot Warmer, Itō Shinsui, p.64, Minneapolis Institute of Arts, Gift of Ellen and Fred Wells (2002.161.85)

Notes on Events in the Ansei Period, Utagawa Kuniyoshi, p.72, © Museum of Civilizations – MPE 'L. Pigorini'

Ario-maru Struggling with a Giant Octopus, Utagawa Kuniyoshi, p.84

Nakamura Utaemon III as Gotobei Moritsugu, Utagawa Kunisada, p.90, Rijksmuseum, Amsterdam, Bequest of H.C. Bos (RP-P-2008-167)

Comparison of the High Renown of the Loyal Retainers and Faithful Samurai: Chiba Saburohei Mitsutada, Utagawa Kuniysohi, p.96, © Art Gallery of Greater Victoria, Purchased with Funds provided by Judith Patt (2012.031.009)

Snake, Pheasant and Canna (Kanna ni kiji to hebi), Katsushika Hokusai, mid-1830s, p.108, Gift of Mrs John D. Rockefeller, Jr.,

Photography by Erik Gould, Courtesy of the Museum of Art, Rhode Island School of Design, Providence

The Psyche of Fish (Sakana no kokoro), 1830–44, Utagawa Kuniyoshi, p.120, © Staatliche Museen zu Berlin, Museum für Asiatische Kunst, Photography courtesy of Art Research Center, Ritsumeikan University, Kyoto

Picture of the Eastern Beauties, Kitao Shigemasa, p.128, Metropolitan Museum of Art, Rogers Fund, 1914 (JP195)

Onoe Kikugoro in the Role of Samurai Hayata Hachiemon Committing Seppuku, Toyohara Kunichika, p.140, Art Gallery of Greater Victoria, Purchased with funds provided by Barry Till (2004.017.001)

Coiled Dragon Panel for Higashimachi Festival Float, Nagano Prefectural Treasure, Katsushika Hokusai, p.152, © Hokusai Museum, Obuse

Okano Kin'emon Fujiwara no Kanehide – Pictorial Biographies of the Loyal Retainers, Tsukioka Yoshitoshi, p.172, © Scholten Japanese Art, New York

Meshimoriosugi Ichikawa Monnosuke, Utagawa Toyokuni I, p.180, © The Tsubouchi Memorial Theatre Museum, Waseda University (001-0841)

Crow in the Snow, Kawanabe Kyōsai, p.196, © Honolulu Museum of Art, Gift of James A. Michener, 1991 (24730)

Hydrangeas and Swallow, Katsushika Hokusai, p.206, Minneapolis Institute of Arts, Bequest of Richard P. Gale (74.1.215)

A Beauty Looking at the First Sunrise, Eishōsai Chōki, p.214, Minneapolis Institute of Arts, Gift of Louis W. Hill, Jr. (P.70.134)

Poppies, Katsushika Hokusai, p.222, Minneapolis Institute of Arts,

Bequest of Richard P. Gale (74.1.206)

The Great Wrestling Match at Akazawa, Utagawa Kuniyoshi, p.230, © JapanesePrints-London.com

Looking in Pain, Tsukioka Yoshitoshi, p.242, © The Fitzwilliam Museum, Cambridge

Nakamura Kichiemon I as Mitsuhide, Natori Shunsen, p.252, © Honolulu Museum of Art, Gift of the Charles Alfred Castle Memorial Collection, 1999 (26556)

Poem of the Pillow, Kitagawa Utamaro, p.262

Moor at the Foot of Mount Fuji – The Soga Brothers Achieving their Avowed Wish, Utagawa Kuniyoshi, p.276, © Japanese-Prints-London.com

Kyōsai's Pictures of One Hundred Demons, Kawanabe Kyōsai, p.290, Metropolitan Museum of Art, Purchase, Mary and James G. Wallach Foundation Gift, 2013 (2013.767)

Kumonryu on a Moonlit Night in Shi Clan Village – One Hundred Aspects of the Moon, Tsukioka Yoshitoshi, p.294, Rijksmuseum, Amsterdam, Gift of J.P. Filedt Kok, Amsterdam (RP-P-2003-450)

Hibiscus and Sparrow, Katsushika Hokusai, p.306, Minneapolis Institute of Arts, Bequest of Richard P. Gale (74.1.213)

Kisen Hōshi, from the series The Six Immortal Poets, Katsushika Hokusai, p.314, © Honolulu Museum of Art, Gift of James A. Michener, 1991 (23703)

Dragon in the Clouds, Totoya Hokkei, p.322, © Mokuhankan

Asakusa Ricefields and Torinomachi Festival, Utagawa Hiroshige, p.338, Rijksmuseum, Amsterdam (RP-P-1956-745)

Peonies and Butterfly, Katsushika Hokusai, p.346, Minneapolis Institute of Arts, Bequest of Richard P. Gale (74.1.211)

Horse and Rider, Tsukioka Yoshitoshi, p.352, Metropolitan Museum
    of Art, Gift of Francis M. Weld, 1948 (JP3133)

The Ghost of Yūgao from The Tale of Genji, Tsukioka Yoshitoshi,
    p.360, © Philadelphia Museum of Art, Purchased with funds
    contributed by the E. Rhodes and Leona B. Carpenter Foundation
    (1989-47-423)

Namauo Chōjirō Running to Left with Huge Blade, from the series
    Biographies of Fine Modern Men, Tsukioka Yoshitoshi, p.366,
    © Philadelphia Museum of Art, Gift of Sidney A. Tannenbaum,
    1978 (1978-129-47)

Crow on a Tree Trunk, Kawanabe Kyōsai, p.374, Rijksmuseum,
    Amsterdam (RP-P-1956-776)

Lilies, Katsushika Hokusai, p.380, Minneapolis Institute of Arts,
    Bequest of Richard P. Gale (74.1.214)

Crow, Shibata Zeshin, p.384, © Honolulu Museum of Art, Gift of
    Drs. Edmund and Julie Lewis, 2003 (27652)

ACKNOWLEDGEMENTS

I have been left indebted to a number of people while writing this book. Most obviously all those whose funding brought it into existence. Every pledge was hugely appreciated for the step they took me closer to full funding, and I was lucky to receive some extremely generous support. But each also gave an emotional boost on the publishing journey which, for all its excitement, can have its lonely and bruising moments.

There was less obvious but equally important support from others. (Great Auntie) Hazel Keyser's parting gift funded my time in Japan writing the book and changed my life in numerous ways. My parents and sister, far from disowning me, provided support for another hare-brained scheme. The Hiratas welcomed me into their family despite my unconventional circumstances. Mio unknowingly refined the book and took my life on a new and vastly improved path. And Kimi, who despite making no conscious effort to help the book or enhance my life, has made it a far better place all the same.

Some others provided very practical support. John Howell gave me some insight into the aftermath of losing a finger. Aiko Hiratsuka provided invaluable translation support – without which I would likely have a completely different *horimono* to the one I thought I was asking for. Josh Baldock shared some great anecdotes. Chris Armstrong gave very helpful feedback. And Richard Higson was a superstar creating my fundraising video.

I'm also very grateful to Scott Pack and DeAndra Lupu at Unbound for their corrections, improvements and general support. Scott in particular for taking the project on in the first place.

Thanks also to Emiko Hirata for the beautiful calligraphy created for the special edition print and the extra efforts of Cameron Hilker and the other Mokuhankan team members.

Some belated thanks for my last book to Lucy Ashken, Lee Poh Chu, Richard Wei, Amar Malhas and the photographer Michael Gladstone.

Unrelated but far more importantly, I must say the most heartfelt of thanks to Mr Giuliani and Mr Thompson's teams at Great Ormond Street Hospital for Children, and the wonderful nurses from Chameleon Ward. Words can't express how grateful I am.

A number of wonderful writers and artists allowed me to use their work as part of the fundraising process. They are David Bull and the team at Mokuhankan, Sonia Leong, Joan Sinclair and Liza Dalby. Manami Okazaki not only provided support in this way but was pivotal to my *irezumi* education and put me in touch with Horitoku. The chance to work with such inspiring people made the hard work of crowdfunding a pleasure.

For those who like the woodblock prints and are interested in owning one, there are still a handful of artisans creating them. They use identical processes and pigments to the originals, meaning the new prints look exactly the same as the artists envisaged them. You can find them at:

Mokuhankan: mokuhankan.com

Takumi Woodblock Studio: takumihanga.com

The Adachi Institute of Woodcut Prints: adachi-hanga.com

Finally, I am in the dangerous position of knowing enough about aspects of Japanese culture to write about them, but not nearly enough to do so without error and possibly offence. I hope I have kept the latter in particular to a minimum as the book came from a love of the country that I hope will be passed on to others.

A NOTE ON THE AUTHOR

Nick Hurst spent three years training with a kung fu master in Malaysia to write his first book, *Sugong*, which was published in 2012. He has written for the *Guardian* and *Time Out*. He lives in London.

Unbound
Liberating ideas

Unbound is the world's first crowdfunding publisher, established in 2011.

We believe that wonderful things can happen when you clear a path for people who share a passion. That's why we've built a platform that brings together readers and authors to crowdfund books they believe in – and give fresh ideas that don't fit the traditional mould the chance they deserve.

This book is in your hands because readers made it possible. Everyone who pledged their support is listed below. Join them by visiting unbound.com and supporting a book today.

Chris Armstrong
Jason Ballinger
Dr Deepti Bhuwanee
Nelly Bostock-Low
Mark Bracegirdle
Adam Buchler
Rachel Butterworth
James M Calnan
Ed Carter
Nick Clifton-Welker

Laurence Collings
Craig Cooper
Jane Curtis
Jerome De Silva
Phil 'The Duke' Donert
Luke Doran
Robert Dowling
Nick Dugdale-Moore
Kevan Edinborough
Michael Fidler

Clare Franks
Mark Sparks Bruiser Bubba
  Freeman
Steve Gibbon
David Gladstone
Florence, Lola, Nadia and
  Alice Gladstone
Joel Gladstone
Michael Gladstone
Simon Glover
David Goodman
Tom, Sarah and Leo Goodman
Millie Graham-Campbell
The Great Britain Sasakawa
  Foundation
Ed Gunner
Jeremy Hill
Takashi Hirata
Philippa Holland
Janice Holve
John Howell
Aleks Hughes
Claire Hugman
Kate Humber
Brian and Rhona Hurst
Jacob Hurst
Mooki and Peter Hurst
Rebecca Hurst
Sam, Roz and Savannah Hurst
Alastair Hutchison
Matthew Irvine
Johari Ismail

Vin Jauhal
Tristan John
JoMac
Rémy Jugault
Vinnie Khairallah
Dan Kieran
Joanne Kilgour
Blanka Kolenikova
Ivan Langham
Jilly Leech
Emma Lester
Phil Lewis
Arthur McGibbon
John Mitchinson
Isabel Morgan
David Napier
Bruno Noble
Krysia Oastler
Peter Oastler
John Osmotherly
Scott Pack
Clare Pattenden
Ashim Paun
Dan Peters
Justin Pollard
Tara Pritchard
Alun Rishko
Lucy Ashken & Duncan
  Rowden
Robert Sheaf
Duncan Smith
Ben South

Karen Stenning
Nick Stickland
Paul Stirling
David Strafford
David Strafford and Dr Deepti
    Bhuwanee
CG Tan
Kim Tan
Tzvia Teller
John Gethin & Felicity Theobald
Dan Thwaites
Grahame Tinsley

Andy Todd
Rob Veling
Neville Wall
Gwen Watson
Cassy Waugh
River Hurst Wells
River, Tania & Matthew Hurst
    Wells
Paul Willett
Derek Wilson
Gareth Wilson
Benjamin Zola